# The Dark Side of the DRAGON

## L.D.Ridgley

**Oak Ridge Publishing**
**Lady Lake, Florida**

ISBN: 978-0-9814735-0-5

**Published by Oak Ridge Publishing**

www.oakridgepublishing.biz

**P.O. Box 682**

**Lady Lake, FL 32158**

Printed in the United States of America

This story is for my wife Shirley... a true computer widow. Thanks for your understanding.

## Other books by L.D.Ridgley:

*Pine Cones and Blood*

A story of greed, murder, prejudice, love and lust in the timber country of Louisiana.


**A collection of short stories available on amazon.com (Amazon shorts)**

*The fish Preferred Pantyhose*

*The Newspaper Route*

*Harold and Gerald*

*Murder by Fright*

*The Funeral*

# THE DARK SIDE OF THE DRAGON

# PROLOGUE

## July, 1945 Village of Xixin, nine kilometers from Beijing, China

The sun had not quite fulfilled its promise of a new day, but had provided enough light for one to see clearly. The scrawny brown and yellow rooster crowed for the third time as he strutted along the top of the stone wall. When he reached the mud brick hut, he hopped from the wall into the open window and disappeared inside.

Chang Siew Pang opened one eye in time to see the bird peck a single grain of rice from the old and unpainted table and then jump to the dirt floor. He had been awake awhile, struggling with the urge to pee, but not wanting to escape the warmth of the covers. He found the rooster an interesting distraction and pinched the object of his discomfort to get more time. Before strutting out the open door, the bold feathered one left a deposit of black and white in the doorway.

"*Waibu, gongji!*" (Get outside, devil rooster!) his grandfather shouted, waving his arms at the bird.

Chang's bladder was pleading for relief and would wait no more...

a phenomenon which had now caused his thirteen year old staff to become as rigid as a garden pole. He scooted from the covers, approached the open doorway, avoided the pile of poop and let go a high arcing stream which scattered the dust when it hit the ground.

"Grandson! Stop peeing out the door... the neighbor men are getting jealous!" Chong Pei yelled. "Are my words falling on deaf ears? Can you not hear?"

"Yes, grandfather," the boy said, continuing to relieve him self, proud of his erection.

"Now I have to deal with rooster dung and grandson pee!"

"You are the one that is jealous, you old skin full of bones," his grandmother added, smiling at her own joke. "His firmness reminds me of better times, heh?" She went back to picking the bugs out of the wild mushrooms they were going to have for breakfast.

The old man ignored her comment. "At least put some pants on... you are too old to run around like the smaller boys. You are getting hairy!" He shuffled to the doorway and with the help of a stick, retrieved the small lump left by the rooster and carefully put it in a pot containing his tomato plants. No need to waste good fertilizer.

Chang crept back under the covers. "Not as hairy as Chen Lim Hua," he mumbled, "and he is thirteen the same as I." The two boys were cousins and frequently went swimming together in the pond behind the house in the complex. There was no knowledge of bathing suits.

Chang's parents had left their small house an hour before daylight to go work in the rice fields. Mother, father, son, grandfather and grandmother shared the one room mud brick house.

The cooking area was outside under a lean-to. The bathroom was... well, where ever you were when the need arose. There was a small outhouse built over the pond, but only his grandmother ever bothered to use it.

There was little modesty in the family. There was little modesty in anybody's family for that matter. When it is common for five people to live in a ten by twelve foot house... there can be neither modesty... nor privacy. One learns to have their intimate moments quietly, and the others around them learn to ignore such events and let on like they don't notice. Chang did notice, however, that the grunts and squeals were coming a lot less from his grandparents these days.

"Get up and put some clothes on. Today is *thumb chop* day, remember?" his grandfather asked.

Chang was up in a second. "I forgot! Yes. We should hurry. I want to get a good spot. I'll go get Chen!" He pulled on his pants and was out the door.

The two boys ran ahead of Chong Pei, down the path between the rice paddies and along the canal that carried the precious water that would soon be flooding the fields. They met Duck Herder Sichou and scattered his seven ducks in four directions, then laughed as he cursed after them. The old man tried to apologize for their actions, but was also met with a barrage of curse words as the herder of ducks ran after his flock, trying to get them under control with his long bamboo pole. A muddy water buffalo watched all this happen with little interest, his attention more on the clump of grass he was chewing.

The village town square was half a mile away and the two boys were there in less than ten minutes. The old tree stump was already in place, its bark-peeled sides stained and streaked with the blood of previous offenders, and the top was crisscrossed with the scars of countless knife and ax wounds.

"Why are they only cutting off his thumbs? Didn't he steal like the man whose whole hand they cut off?" Chang had asked the night before at the evening meal.

"Yes, he is a thief," his grandfather explained. "But, he stole food. By removing his thumbs, he will never be able to use chop sticks again. It will be a reminder to him that he stole another's food. Also, all who see him try to eat by gripping a spoon with a thumb-less fist will know of his crime. It is much worse than an honorable death."

"The old ways are not always good," his father had added, glad he would be planting the tender shoots of rice and not be a witness to this practice. "Someday we will not be so uncivilized!"

There were stalls set up around the square to sell drinks and food, and several of the farmers had brought wares in hopes of making a few Yuan from the huge crowd normally attending these public partial executions. There were perhaps four or five hundred people gathered to witness this crude justice. The two boys got permission to climb on top of one of the stalls and scurried up top and lay on the thatch with their heads pointing toward the stump. They had a perfect view.

"Who does the chopping?" Chen asked, rolling over and watching the clouds blend together.

"I don't know. No one knows. He wears a mask."

"I would not want that job!"

"Nor I! You would have to take a bath to get the blood off!"

"Oh, no! Not a bath!" The two boys laughed. *Kepade!*

"Where are you going to find work next year?" Chen asked. It was customary for young men to start working after their fourteenth birthday... unless they worked in the fields with their parents, or unless they were in the top five percent of their school. Neither boy wanted to work the rice fields, and neither was in the top five percent.

"I am going to go to the city. I want an office job. I plan to be a Party member," Chang replied.

"I'm going to the city also... but I want to be a bus driver."

They were interrupted by a small group of men approaching the center of the square. One had his hands tied to a wooden pole and another wore a black mask which covered his entire head. Two others held the prisoner pole securely.

When they reached the stump, the prisoner's left hand was untied from the pole and the fingers were lashed together with thin bamboo strips and held on top of the log. His thumb was separated as far from the rest of his hand as possible and two nails were driven in place to keep it in position.

The man in the hood drew a large knife from his belt, said a few words to the gods of justice, and placed the blade along side the man's index finger. The huge crowd became silent as all eyes were riveted on the stump. With careful deliberation, the masked man slowly raised the huge knife upward. The morning sun reflected off the blade, sending a bright glint into the eyes of the two boys.

"Hieeeeee!" The masked man shouted and brought the knife down with all his strength. Blood spurted at least three feet onto the dirt and all over the guard's feet. The man screamed and fell to his knees as the crowd roared their approval. The masked man yelled again, raising the bloody knife toward the sky, and the process was quickly repeated with the other hand. The people were now in frenzy, yelling and screaming and waving their arms in the air. Many began chanting, "Thief...thief...thief." The man in the mask raised the bloody knife to the crowd and slowly bowed. The ceremony was over.

The severed thumbs were thrown into a nearby crate of pigs, quickly disappearing among the squeals and shoving as the animals fought to get at the tasty morsels. After a minute, the small group of men walked away, leaving the prisoner crumpled on the ground, writhing in pain and bleeding profusely. His family broke free of the crowd and rushed to his aid.

"Remind me never to steal food," Chen muttered.

"Remind me never to steal anything!" Chang replied.

The two boys climbed down from their perch and went looking for their grandfather, but he was nowhere to be seen. So, they spent some time looking at the pigs that had enjoyed munching on the thumbs only a few minutes before. Then Chong Pei appeared on the other side of the crate.

"Come, grandsons... it is time to go home."

"Can we have some money? We are hungry!" Chang whined.

The old man dug in his pockets and came out with a few coins. "Here... spend these wisely."

They each bought a dried lizard on a stick to munch on during the walk home. They had walked only a few feet on the well worn path when Chen slowed and held his cousin back until their grandfather was several feet ahead of them. When he was out of range, Chen asked excitedly, "Did you see?"

"See what?"

"Grandfather... he has blood on his feet!"

Chang's mouth dropped open. "Really? Could he be...?"

"Bless the gods... he must be! I saw the blood with my own eyes!"

"We must never tell... no one!" Chang ordered.

"Agreed!"

"I wonder where he keeps the mask."

"I wonder where he keeps the knife!"

The two boys walked along in silence, having a new perspective of this old man, previously thought of only as *Grandfather*.

"Next year, we should go to the city together," Chang blurted, suddenly feeling the need for support.

"Yes. It will be safer if we are together."

## 5 Years Later, 1950

It was mid afternoon and the two cousins were enjoying the comforts of the small restaurant only a block from Tiananmen Square.

"Congratulations on your appointment! Compei! (bottoms up)" Chen raised his glass with Chang and they drank the small shot of Mao Tai in one gulp.

"Thank you, Cousin Chen. I am told that I am the youngest member of the Party to be assigned as an aide in the Great Hall of the People. I am very proud!"

"You should be! We have come a long way, cousin. Next week, I start as the personal driver of the Assistant Director of the Beijing Police force. Let's have another drink."

"I can't stay long. I have an appointment... with a lady."

Chen smiled. "Whose wife are you stabbing tonight... with that overgrown weapon of yours?"

"That, my dear cousin, I cannot tell." Chang returned the smile. "We must keep some secrets, heh?"

"Oh, yes. And we have many secrets to keep, don't you agree?"

"Yes, I agree. More every day."

The two young men were silent for moment, each remembering past experiences. They had never discussed the thumb chop incident of five years ago.

Their attention was drawn to the front door of the restaurant. A colorfully dressed woman of some age was attempting to enter the establishment. She was wearing a large straw hat and her face was covered with a veil. She was obviously one of the many different minorities coming into the city in search of work these days. They were not looked on favorably by the locals and, periodically, they were driven back to the countryside by the Beijing police. Her kind was not allowed in this establishment.

The woman was confronted by the owner of the restaurant who was wielding a large knife. Words were shouted and the woman became surrounded by the waiters and cooks and quickly she was hidden from view. When the small group dispersed in a few minutes, the woman was nowhere to be seen. She had disappeared.

"Another secret to keep, heh, cousin?"

"You must be mistaken. I saw nothing."

"Of course." Chen smiled." I must be going. Don't forget to tell me about your conquest tonight. Oh, by the way, I am using the name of P. K. Chen from now on for my professional name. I think it is more sophisticated than Chen Lim Hua, don't you think? "

He stood and walked away without waiting for an answer, stepping over the few drops of blood in the doorway.

Chang watched his cousin disappear. "You have been a loyal companion, dear cousin. When I reach a certain level of power, I will reward you." The words were wasted. No one to hear.

# Chapter One

## February, 1989 Chicago, Illinois

"Maguire, Brickhauer wants to see ya as soon as you can. Drop these production reports off on Halleron's desk while you're over there." Martin's boss threw a stack of print-outs on his desk and walked on out the door into the shop area, the ever present cigarette dangling from his nicotine stained lips. 'Over there' meant the main office building which housed the administration offices and other support departments for WCI, a global company which manufactured all types of construction equipment. WCI stood for World Construction Industries.

"John Brickhauer? Wants to see me?" Martin asked out loud, to an empty office. "Must need a favor." He downed the last few drops of coffee from the paper cup, threw it in the waste basket, retrieved his winter coat from the rack and headed across the outside storage lot for the main building.

It was a typical February day in Chicago; gray skies, snow flurries whistling in the stinging wind and a cold that managed to get in under whatever one had on, no matter how many layers of clothing it had to go through.

Martin Maguire... thirty-six years old, ruggedly handsome out door face, six one, one hundred eighty pounds, smart, ambitious... and bitter. Bitter at being stuck in a go-no-where type job, working for a manager who was so caught up in his own alcohol dependency that he simply didn't care anymore, and had long forgotten that part of his job was to develop people for possible advancement within the company.

In spite of his bitterness, Martin continued to work hard in his assignment as manufacturing foreman, desperately hoping someone would recognize his efforts and reward him with a better job; one that offered potential growth, both professionally and financially. Some days, he thought it was only a dream, sure that no one was looking and that no one cared. He was wrong.

John Brickhauer, known around the company as 'The Brick', was the Project Manager for Foreign Investments. He had been watching Martin's results for some time now, knowing that soon he would need to put together a team of talented individuals to carry out the company's plan to market products in mainland China. It was a complex plan, involving a technology exchange agreement with the Chinese prior to building manufacturing facilities and establishing dealerships for WCI in China. A few months ago, Brick had noticed that Martin's production results were way above those of his peers. This was a little surprising, because on the surface, Martin appeared to put forth a fraction of the effort displayed by his less successful counterparts. It didn't take long for the answer to become clear. Martin was a good trainer and delegated responsibility to his subordinates for tasks most supervisors did themselves. It was easier for his employees to get things done by dealing with people on their own level than it was for a supervisor trying to get a lower level individual to do them favors. Martin was fair, consistent in his daily activities and had very few problems with the union brothers. The combination of manufacturing experience and the ability to train people was exactly what Brick was looking for.

Martin knocked on John Brickhauer's office door at 9:20 A.M. deciding on the way over that whatever it was this man wanted made on the sly, he would refuse. *If nothing else, I still have my integrity,* he thought.

Brick looked up from his papers. "Martin! Good. Come on in." He rose and walked around the desk. "Take a seat... let me get that door."

Martin settled into a chair, his interests heightened by the action of closing the door. That could be significant. Perhaps he was wrong about the purpose of this meeting.

Brick returned to his chair and leaned back, smiling. "Well, wondering why you are here?" he asked, coyly.

"Yes." Martin smiled back. "I certainly am, sir."

Brick waved a hand. "Oh, forget the sir stuff. Brick will do just fine." He paused, gathering his thoughts. "I won't keep you in suspense, Martin. I need a guy for a project I've got going. I need to find out if you are that guy, and if you are, I'll make you a job offer... today. I suspect it wouldn't break your heart to get out of the factory and live like a human for awhile, would it?"

Now, he had captured Martin's full attention. He took a deep breath. "No, it wouldn't break my heart." His heart was pounding. A job offer. Out of the factory. Finally, maybe it was going to happen.

"Good, let's get started. Any reason it would be difficult for you to do some extended travel, say for a month at a time?"

"No, none that I can think of."

"Your wife able to manage with you gone for a month?"

"Well, I think so. She's pretty independent. Has her own career. Where am I going?"

Brick held up his hand, a gesture which said 'in due time'. "What about kids? You have kids?"

"No, not that I know of," Martin replied, barely able to contain his excitement.

"Any prejudices against the Chinese or Communist China?" Brick waited.

That caught Martin by surprise. "Well, I guess we've all been brainwashed against Communists. Frankly, I normally think of Communist in conjunction with Russia, not China. Seems like all our confrontations have been with the Russians. China just seems to be there." Martin paused, thinking. "I won't say I don't have prejudices, but nothing radical. I don't have any problem doing business with the Chinese, if that's what you mean."

Brick nodded and, for a second, was obviously deep in thought. "Brace yourself, Martin. World Construction Industries has signed a technology exchange agreement with the Peoples Republic of China. The agreement is sixty-five pages long, but I'll simplify it for you. We have sold the technology to make some non-current construction equipment. This includes all the engineering drawings and specifications, heat treat instructions, manufacturing documents, weld procedures, machining methods, assembly techniques... the whole ball of wax. There will be tons of paper going to China. Also, we have agreed to train their people, here in our facility, and then go to their factories in China to help them implement what they've learned. The agreement will be fulfilled when each factory is able to build our product, with forty percent content built locally in China, and pass a performance test. I need someone with a manufacturing background to fill the job of Manufacturing Engineer for the duration of the project. Want to go to work for me and spend the next couple of years going back and forth to China?"

Martin was overwhelmed with the enormous possibilities of such a project. What an opportunity! He answered quickly. "I must be dreaming," he said, shaking his head in wonder. "Yes... hell yes! Damned right, hell yes! When do you want me to start?"

"As soon as I can notify the factory to get your replacement in place and make the transition. I'm really glad you said yes. I think you will be perfect for the job." Brick held out his hand and Martin eagerly accepted it.

"Thank you, Brick. I won't let you down."

"I know. I know more about you than you think. You didn't ask about a promotion... or money. Aren't you curious?"

"It doesn't matter. I'll take the job. How much do I have to pay you?" Martin asked.

Brick laughed. "Well, in that case... how about a two grade promotion and a fifteen percent salary increase, and... you go on an expense account the day you start."

Martin was sure his mouth had dropped open. All he could manage was a one word answer. "Wow," he said softly.

## Beijing, Peoples Republic of China

"Your bicycle tube is old and fragile, young sir. I must be careful not to make the hole worse," the old man spoke softly, hoping his words would not make this man angrier than he already was... this man whose face resembled that of a mule.

"See that you are careful, you illiterate ass gas!" He spat on the ground at the old man's feet, then turned and faced the crowds of people making their way to work in the early morning hour... thousands on foot, more by bicycle, and buses so crowded people were hanging out the doors. He took a pack of Marlboros from his pocket, careful to make sure the people passing could see he was a man of some means, able to afford imported cigarettes from America. A street dentist had set up his chair next to the bicycle stand and was tending to a man with a swollen jaw.

The old repairman returned to his task of fixing the flat tire, keeping a watchful eye on this mule-faced man who wore a uniform. Uniforms meant trouble. He knew uniforms... still had terrible dreams about uniforms, even after twenty years.

"I will be done soon, kind sir," he muttered.

Xin Luk Lin lit the cigarette and inhaled deeply, letting the smoke escape from his nostrils. He smiled to himself, thinking of his recent good fortune. The gods certainly had blessed him. Only two months before, he was working as a gardener at the Ministry of Agriculture building two blocks off of Tiananmen Square. In the rear of the complex was a huge, overgrown, ill-kept garden. He had been assigned to trim the hedges in a remote part of the garden, which suited him just fine because he would be by himself and could go at his own pace. His superior rarely left his tiny dark office except to relieve himself, so he was in little danger of a surprise visit.

One warm sunny afternoon, after taking lunch in the shade of a very dense thicket, Xin made a crude bed from leaves and lay down for a nap. A short time later he was awakened by the unmistakable sound of two people engaged in the age-old act of sex. At first he was afraid to move a muscle for fear of being discovered. Then, as the moans and groans become more intense, curiosity overcame his fear and he rose up to peer over the low shrubs to see. At precisely the same time as his head appeared over the bush, the gentleman partner in the sexual exchange reached a climax. He grunted loudly, reared back on his knees, and lifted his upper body to an upright position as he buried his shaft into his partner. At this very instant, his head came level with that of the gardener and only two feet separated them. For a second, they stared at each other in shock, and then both screamed at the top of their lungs. Xin bolted through the underbrush and didn't stop running until he was safely hidden away in another part of the garden as far away as he could get. He was more frightened than he had ever been in his young life. He would surely be be-headed, or sliced in two like a pig in the market. He pulled himself into a ball and began praying to all of the gods he had ever heard of. He knew he was in deep trouble; a face that resembled that of a mule was not easily forgotten, and to make matters worse, the person he had been face to face with just a few moments before was none other than the esteemed First Minister of Agriculture, the highest ranking official in the building! Xin never got a look at the First Minister's partner, but it was safe to assume it would not be his wife he was lying with in the weeds.

Actually, the female partner in question was the Deputy Minister's wife, her husband conveniently sent away to Sichuan Province on a business trip, solely so his superior could take advantage of his absence. She was young, beautiful, and only too happy to receive the attentions of another, since her husband was quite old and only able to perform once a month or so. Unaware of the presence of the gardener, her assumption at the reaction of the First Minister was that he had reached that glorious pinnacle that all the men she had ever laid with had eventually come to, but never so loudly and never with such a feverishly jerking of the body, which resulted in them becoming disconnected. His seed splattered clear to her chest, covering her heaving breasts with his juices.

The First Minister had intended to keep his stalk fully buried into the warmth of his partner when he sowed the seeds of life, but was unable to stop his withdrawal and his manhood, flopping wildly in the air, from making a mess out of things. Quickly, he lost all thoughts related to his sexual encounter, realizing he had a lot to lose in this matter unless he acted prudently. He wiped himself off with his lover's undergarments, pulled his own clothes back into proper alignment and ushered wife of number two out into the street through a back gate and then headed off to find his security chief.

The process of finding Xin Luk Lin took only a few minutes when the security guards combed the gardens. He was ushered into the security room and tied to a straight- back chair in front of a worn, bare, wooden desk. He was so frightened that he was visibly shaking and the sweat poured down his unsightly face.

The First Minister entered and dismissed the security chief and his guards. The security chief, not happy about being excluded from the proceedings, left gracefully, but not before he had activated the secret tape recorder hidden in the old desk.

When they were alone, the First Minister sat behind the desk and stared off into space for a minute then faced the terrified gardener. He spoke slowly.

"What did you see?"

"Nothing, Your Excellency." He wasn't sure he was using the proper address, but thought 'Your Excellency' might help his cause.

"Who did you see?"

"No one, Your Excellency. I saw no one!"

"Why were you in the garden?"

"I am a gardener. I work in the garden."

"Did you see me in the garden?"

"No, I have never seen you in the garden, Your Excellency."

"Never?"

"Never!"

"I can have your head for a door stop."

"Yes, you're Excellency."

"I can have your guts spread over the street."

"Yes, you're Excellency."

"Why should I believe that you have never seen me in the garden?"

There was a glimmer of hope. "If I am allowed... by the Goddess Kwun Yum and your compassion... to live to be an old man, on my dying breath, I will swear that I have never seen you in the garden. Never!"

The First Minister paused, thinking about his next move. Xin Luk Lin sat motionless, eyes on the floor, barely able to take small breaths. He was praying as hard as he could to Kwun Yum, the Goddess of Mercy.

"Perhaps, I could think of a use for your worthless self... to be my servant... in some way that would benefit me." He nodded, agreeing with this latest thought.

Xin did not waste the opportunity. "Oh, yes, Your Excellency! For every minute of my worthless life, I will serve you. You are a very wise person!"

"Humm. Yes, perhaps that is the answer. I will find a use for you."

"Oh, thank you, Your Excellency! I will repay you this kindness one thousand times one thousand!"

"Yes, you mule-face gardener, you most assuredly will!"

One week later, Xin Luk Lin received a letter from the Ministry of Agriculture. He was very frightened, having received only one other letter in his entire life. All his neighbors were excited as well. The news had traveled fast that one on their block had received a letter... from an official Ministry, no less!

In the privacy of the shared and smelly necessary room, the only room in his housing complex with a lock on the door, he opened the envelope with shaking hands. For several minutes, he stared at the document, so official looking with the government chop. Then, slowly, he folded the paper and replaced it in the envelope. He must go find teacher Wu. Having only two years of schooling, he had not mastered the art of reading to a level that he trusted to understand such an important document. He unlocked the door and walked out into the street.

Teacher Wu was playing mahjong next to the tea house on Fishback Street. At first he was disturbed at being interrupted. He was leading in the game in which he had wagered a bottle of MaoTai, but quickly conceded to his opponent when he saw the seal of the Ministry on Xin's envelope. He knew of no one who had ever received an envelope from a Ministry of the People's Republic of China. He was very impressed. They retreated to the shade of a mulberry tree where a small group of children were playing. A wave of his hand along with a warning and the children scattered, leaving them alone. Wu opened the envelope and read slowly and carefully:

> *Xin Luk Lin,*
> *You are hereby officially notified that you will report to the People's Customs Bureau Office at the Beijing International Airport at 0900 Monday next to begin training for an assignment as a Customs Agent for the People's Republic of China, so ordered.*
> *Rung Fulong, Customs Official*

"You have been chosen, Xin. I know not why, but you have been chosen."

Xin nodded. He knew why, but he wasn't about to let Teacher Wu know. He thanked the esteemed elder and quickly disappeared into the crowd on the street. *I must remember to send a bottle of Mao Tai to Wu,* he thought, and then promptly forgot all about it.

Early the next morning, Xin slipped into the garden through a back gate, preparing to spend another day pulling the insistent weeds that made up most of the vegetation in the garden. He had walked only a few steps when he was met face to face by a security officer. "You will come with me," he stated.

"To where?"

"Shut up and follow, stupid gardener."

Soon he was in the same straight-back chair in the security chief's room as before. The guard indicated he should sit still and left him alone. Xin sat and waited. For three hours, he waited. Finally, the door opened and the security chief entered, approached the desk and, unseen by Xin, flipped the switch that activated the hidden tape recorder.

"The Minister is on his way," he announced, and left the room.

A few minutes later the Minister entered and sat at the desk. Xin sat up straight, giving his complete attention.

"I have found a use for your otherwise worthless body."

"Thank you, Your Excellency. I am most honored."

"You will thank me by following my wishes exactly, mule-face!"

"Yes, Your Excellency." Xin tried to look humble.

"I have people in certain key positions that do important work for me with the knowledge of no one but me. You are about to become one of those persons. You will be paid the same as any other Customs Agent, but the main benefit you will receive is to go on living. If anyone finds out about our arrangement, it will result in the immediate death of all your family members, witnessed by you. Then I will personally chop your worthless body into little pieces, starting with your little shriveled piss stalk and your pea sized juice balls. Understand?"

"Most assuredly, Your Excellency. I understand."

"Good. After your formal training, I will arrange for another meeting where I will tell what you are going to do for me, and how you are going to do it. Then, you and I will never meet again... unless I come to kill you."

Later, the security chief played back the recording, elated at this information. This would surely lead to his good fortune as well.

Xin found the training easy, including the English lessons, and the job was extremely exciting. He surprised himself at how quickly he picked up the language, never having had any formal schooling in that area. He loved the feeling of power, dressed up in his official uniform, even though it was several sizes too large for his small frame. And power he had; power over people, important people, from all over the world. There was a steady stream of businessmen in fancy suits and their smelly ladies with lots of jewelry and slippery underwear. He never could have even dreamed of such things before. He didn't know such things even existed. He had long ago accepted his fate to live out his life as a gardener.

The scam was simple and the profits were enormous. The agents worked in pairs, choosing tourists as their targets, assuming most tourists had little experience in traveling in foreign countries, especially a Communist country. They were easily distracted, nervous and intimidated by thoughts of being detained by a government they did not trust. Thus it was rather easy to remove items of medium value, such as cameras, jewelry, watches and similar things from their luggage. These items, along with those items confiscated legitimately, such as too many cigarettes, liquor, any type of adult magazines or samples of certain goods, brought a steady stream of valuables. Most of these items were not missed by the owner until they opened their bags in the hotel room, and even if they made a report to the authorities, the bureaucracy of the system took over and the complaints were, to say the least, ineffective.

Xin was supplying his 'boss' with an abundance of these valuables, and was quick to realize there was plenty to go around. He, too, was getting his fair share. One more good week, and he would be able to buy a new bicycle... one with new tires and a loud bell.

"Your tire is ready, young sir." The old man was holding the bike up, offering Xin the handlebars. He snapped out of his trance back to the present.

"Finally! What is the cost?" Xin asked bitterly.

"For an officer such as your self, sir, there is no charge. It is an honor to serve one who is so important," the old man spoke softly. Although his words were kind, his thoughts were quite different. *Get your ugly mule-face and your smelly foreign cigarettes out of my sight. May the gods allow a bus to run over you and crush your worthless juice sac...lou lian sishengzi (mule-face bastard).*

"You are wise to recognize a superior person, old man. I deserve no less." Xin Luk Lin jumped on the bicycle and peddled off towards the airport.

The First Minister of Agriculture was very pleased with this latest venture. Although corruption was common place among his peers, none of the scams he had been involved with in the past had produced such lucrative bounty. He had the Minister of Forestry to thank for that, having shared his latest scheme during a dinner where they both had too much to drink. His unexpected encounter with Xin Luk Lin in the garden had provided him with the opportunity to get his own man into the Customs Department. *How wise*, he thought, *to take advantage of this young man's unfortunate situation. All gods, small and large, have smiled on me for sure.* He soon would be rich beyond his wildest dreams... able to buy the best for his sexual desires, no longer forced to rely on the wives of his subordinates, a very dangerous game to say the least.

Three times each week, in the cover of darkness, a rusty, dilapidated pedal cart would appear at the back gate to unload the basket of goods sent by *his* customs agent. The contents were always good; sometimes there was foreign cash, usually a watch or two, or a nice ring to be converted into cash on the black market. His amah of many years would meet the cart and bring the basket to his private office. The baskets were sealed and never opened by anyone but himself, and his amah knew better than to have questions. He was particularly pleased when the basket contained magazines with pictures of busty, western ladies. It never occurred to him that he was receiving only a portion of the goods confiscated by *his* custom agent.

Xin Luk Lin, on the other hand, was also pleased beyond words with this 'punishment' bestowed on him by the Minister of Agriculture. Like his superior, he too acknowledged that he had surely been blessed by all the gods. For a peasant such as he to be removed from poverty that was so widespread and accepted by the multitudes of Chinese was indeed a miracle of some magnitude. He was very careful to make sure the baskets were generously filled with valuables, content to take only a small portion for himself, realizing he could jeopardize everything if he became too greedy.

Xin quickly learned the names of the popular soft porn magazines such as Playboy, Gent, Hustler, etc., and would pass a few of these on to his boss. He was never challenged when he stated these were not allowed in his country in order to avoid the moral corruption of his people.

# Chapter Two

## Chicago

Three months had passed since Martin's first meeting in Brick's office. The China Project group was now fully formed. In addition to Martin, who was handling the manufacturing issues, a quality engineer by the name of Jack Donnelly and an assembly engineer, Bill Strickner, had been assigned to the team. Martin and Donnelly had worked together before and had always gotten along. Strickner, on the other hand, was a stranger, and not immediately accepted as a colleague. Small in stature, he was a quiet man, rarely participating in discussions, and when questioned, he rarely seemed to give a straight answer. He preferred to be alone, not going to lunch with the group, and never initiated any social conversations. Although he refrained from saying anything to Brick or to Donnelly, Martin was convinced that Strickner would be a problem somewhere down the road.

Around the office, the team had been labeled as the 'China Connection Sponge' because of their activity of gathering up countless documents from the various departments. To date, they had shipped over four tons of paper overseas. And now, it was time. The group was preparing for their first trip to the mysterious People's Republic of China. Brick had already left for a meeting at the Hong Kong office and was to meet the rest of the team in Beijing on Tuesday. He was also making reservations for the team to spend a few days in Hong Kong on their way back to the States.

"What time is our plane Monday?" Donnelly asked, for the third time.

"10.22 A.M., arriving Beijing 5:40 P.M. the next day. Going to be a hell of a long flight," Martin responded, trying to hide his own excitement.

"Got your rubbers packed?" Donnelly smiled.

"You talking about the ones you wear on your feet?" Martin grinned back.

"That's the only kind I've used in years. That way I get to use the extra-large size."

Martin laughed. The reference to condoms had to do with Brick's warning a few days earlier about not getting involved with the Chinese ladies. "You can look, but don't touch," he had said. "They'll throw your ass in prison, so I'm told."

"How about Hong Kong?" Donnelly had inquired.

"Hong Kong is a different matter. Just don't do anything that will embarrass the Company, or yourselves, for that matter."

*Good advice,* Martin thought, remembering the conversation.

Strickner was taking no part in this exchange, even though he was sitting only a few feet away. He completely ignored the conversation.

"How about you, Bill? You taking any condoms?" Donnelly asked, winking at Martin.

Strickner looked up from the drawing he had been studying. "Condoms? No, I don't expect to need anything like that. I'm married, you know," he said without humor.

"Aren't we all!" Donnelly stated.

Three hours into the flight, Martin was wakened by the sound of the flight attendants preparing to serve their first meal. He was seated next to Donnelly and they had chatted some about the training schedule for the Chinese, and then both had dozed off. Strickner was seated across the aisle, but had left his seat early in the flight. Martin glanced to his right to find the seat still empty. He nudged Donnelly.

"You seen anything of Bill?"

"Nope. Fuckin' weirdo might be flying the plane!"

"I'm worried about him," Martin confessed.

"Yeah, me too. Strange one, he is." Their food trays had arrived.

As soon as the seat belt sign had been turned off, Bill Strickner was up and moving... looking. He left the comfort of the Business Class section and walked to the rear of the plane. There were only a couple of passengers in the last section and they had covered up with blankets and settled in for the long flight. He found the last row empty and sat next to the window, covering his lap and the small back pack he carried with a blanket. There were no flight attendants in sight. He slipped the flask from the pack and took a long drink, breathing a sigh of relief. It had been nearly three hours. That was close to his maximum tolerance. He took another swig, propped up the flask carefully in the next seat, pulled the blanket up around his neck and prepared for the alcohol to take over. William Emerick Strickner was a very sick man.

After the meal, Martin took a walk to the head and half heart-edly tried to locate Strickner. *Oh well,* he thought when he didn't see him. *He's a big boy.* He returned to his seat, took a mild sleeping pill, pushed the seat in the reclined position and dozed off again.

The next time he was fully awake came hours later when the First Officer announced that the 747 had began its initial descent into the Beijing airport. "We should be on the ground in about forty-five minutes. If you need to stretch your legs or go to the bathroom, this would be the time to do it. Seat belt signs go on in fifteen minutes."

Martin sat up straight, fully aware that Strickner's seat was still empty. Donnelly was stirring as well. "He's never been back," he said, nodding his head in the direction across the aisle.

"Where in the hell..." Martin was interrupted. Bill Strickner had returned...pale faced and eyes glassy.

"You okay, Bill?" Martin asked.

"Yes. Just sick at my stomach. Motion sickness. I was in the bathroom throwing up."

"The whole trip?"

"Well, yes, most of it." He fastened his seatbelt and closed his eyes, terminating the conversation. Martin and Donnelly ex-changed looks of disbelief.

"Yeah, right," Donnelly breathed.

The big plane touched down with a thump, throwing every-body forward against the restraints of the belts, slowing quickly as the crew applied the brakes, then taxied for several minutes. It was dark outside, as dusk was creeping into the city; the lighting on the tarmac was sparse and dim. They could see little through the windows.

The plane lurched to a stop and a portable ramp was pushed up to the door. The passengers were anxious to deplane after the long trip and niceties were non-evident as they retrieved their carry-on bags and prepared to exit, shoving and pushing.

When Martin stepped out into the air, he was greeted with a cold blast, bitter and acrid. He took a deep breath and his lungs burned, causing him to cough. Later he would find out that what he was breathing was coal smoke, the number one heat source for cooking and other things in China. As he looked around at the surroundings, his vision was blurred by the thick haze. The poor lighting added to the dismal reaction to his first look at mainland China. Dark and dirty. It was a feeling that never really left him while he was in country. He was very disappointed.

He followed the string of passengers as they proceeded into a large building through a set of dust-streaked glass doors that had not been cleaned in a long time. Inside, the corridor was damp and dim with patches of standing water on the bare concrete floor. The walls were cinder block and paint-less. There was no artwork, no signs and no advertisements... nothing to welcome a first-time visitor or a returning countryman.

Martin turned to see if Donnelly and Strickner were following and ran into the person in front of him. The line had stopped. A new smell was working its way through the crowd. Martin squinted in the semi-darkness and could make out the universal sign for a rest room a few yards up ahead. They really didn't need the sign. The smell said it all.

"Quite fancy, huh?" Donnelly asked, over Martin's shoulder. "Looks like they spared no expense... none at all."

Martin half smiled. "Isn't this something? You think this is the main way into the terminal?"

"Surely not. This is more like a cattle chute."

The line began to move again and everyone picked up the pace to get past the awful smell. They entered a large room where the lighting was a tad better and Martin noticed the reason for the delay. Two armed soldiers were standing on each side of doors which had been chained and locked a few moments before. They were allowing the passengers through one at a time. A yellow sign with large red Chinese characters hung overhead. If one looked closely, they could read the small black letters underneath which announced in English, *Immigration Hall.*

Donnelly got ahead of Martin in one of the queues and was chopped in with no problem. *Well, at least our visas are in order*, Martin thought. Donnelly stepped through an exit gate and stopped to wait for Martin. A uniformed officer approached and pointed toward the baggage claim area.

"I'm waiting on my friend," Donnelly explained.

If the officer understood English, he didn't let on. He pointed again and gestured dramatically for Donnelly to move.

"I'll just be a moment, sir. My friend is coming!" The soldier took hold of his shoulder and pulled, muttering something in Chinese, his patience wearing thin.

"Wait a minute, dammit!" Donnelly said with anger, jerking away.

"It's okay... I'm here," Martin said, arriving at Donnelly's side. "Let's go before we piss him off. He's got a gun and we don't!"

"What about Strickner?"

"He'll find us. Let's go." Martin took off in the direction of the baggage claim. *We sure as hell don't want any confrontations here,* he thought, noticing several uniformed men, apparently military, many with automatic weapons. The uniforms were ill-fitting and the men were very young and unprofessional appearing. If the surroundings hadn't already given him an uneasy feeling, the soldiers certainly would have.

Strickner joined them just as the luggage started to arrive on the worn conveyor belt. Relieved, Martin said, "Let's try to stay together till we get out of here."

"Yeah, if they'll let us!" Donnelly replied.

When all the bags had arrived, the three of them headed towards the Customs tables. Here, two Chinese men waited at each table, going through every piece of luggage. No one was being passed over. On the other side of the tables was a line of open doors and a roped off area where a thousand Chinese waited for arriving passengers. There were armed soldiers guarding the rope, stationed every twenty feet or so. The noise from all the people shouting at their loved ones as they came to the tables reminded Martin of a turkey farm he had visited once.

On the other side of that rope was The People's Republic of China; a mysterious culture, communistic… dangerous in some ways, hard to understand for sure… and, perhaps for some, the edge of freedom.

Donnelly was first in line and hefted his heavy suitcases up on the table and unlocked them. The two customs agents begin going through them with slow, meticulous care. One of the agents, whose face looked similar to that of a mule, held up an aerosol can and asked, "What it is?"

"Bug spray. Raid. To kill insects…bugs," Donnelly responded.

"Bugs? Chouchong! No bugs allowed in China. Not allowed," mule-face said, the can disappearing below the table.

"No, not bugs! Bug spray!" Donnelly said, frustrated. "I need that!"

"You are done. Please go," Mule-face replied, and pointed towards the large room with all the people.

"Shit!" he exclaimed, giving up. "What's next?" He removed his bags from the table and proceeded all the way through the rope before he stopped to wait. He had learned quickly.

Martin was next and had no problems. He silently breathed a sigh of relief as he closed his bags, passed through the doors and joined Donnelly on the other side of the rope.

"What the hell's wrong with bug spray," Donnelly asked.

"Beats me! I had a can as well, but he didn't even look at mine." Martin looked around. "Ain't this something?" he asked Donnelly for the second time. There were at least a thousand Chinese... going here and there... families dressed in near rags, business men in ill-fitting suits, all chattering loudly, waving their arms... excited. The smell of mothballs and stale food was strong. Several of the men were still wearing the old blue Mao jackets that had to be at least twenty years old.

"Sure not what I expected," Donnelly agreed.

"Mister Maguire?" The inquiry came from behind Martin, perfect English, but with an Asian accent.

"Yes," Martin turned. "I'm Maguire."

The young man was neatly dressed in a blue, pin stripped suit, light blue silk shirt and matching tie. "Good. I'm David Choi from the Hong Kong WCI office. I've been assigned as the interpreter for your trip. Mr. Brickhauer sent me to meet you. He's waiting at the Holiday Inn Lido. I have a car waiting." He held out his hand.

"And you, sir? Donnelly or Strickner?" they both shook his hand.

"I'm Donnelly... Strickner is right behind us at Customs."

"Please call me David."

They turned to look for Strickner, but he wasn't right behind them. He was nowhere in sight.

"Now what?" Martin exclaimed. He noticed that Mule-face was not at the Customs table either. "Shit! David, he was there a minute ago. Now, he and the Customs guys are not there. Something's wrong."

"I'll see what's going on. Just stay here and I'll return in a minute." David Choi was out of sight in a second.

"Are we going to have problems with this guy the whole trip?" Donnelly asked.

"I don't know." Martin shook his head in dismay. "I think Brick was forced to take him. Something he said."

"Probably the only guy engineering would give him. If you're short on people, you don't let your good ones go."

"Thanks a lot. You think that's how I got here?" Martin asked, jokingly.

"No, Martin, not you. I know Brick had to fight to get the shop to let you go."

David Choi had returned. "Guys, we have a small wait. Mr. Strickner is being detained for having material in his luggage which is not allowed in China. He should be along in a few minutes."

"You're kidding," Martin said disgustedly. "What kind of material?"

David was embarrassed. "Perhaps, sex photos... magazines."

Donnelly was furious. "That dumb sonofabitch! Didn't we go over that stuff? What the fuck is wrong with that guy?"

Martin was equally perplexed, but was briefly troubled by another thought. How did David Choi, a Hong Kong resident, an employee of WCI, obtain this information so easily?

"Who did you talk to, David?"

"The Customs agent in the interview room," David Choi responded. Instantly he realized his mistake. Perhaps, he hoped, Martin hadn't noticed.

Martin, however, had noticed. David Choi was more than a simple interpreter. A mere interpreter from Hong Kong would not have been allowed into the Customs interview room. Now, what does that mean? Who is this guy?

"What will happen to him?" Martin asked, careful not to let his suspicion show.

"I'm not sure." Choi tried to repair the damage. "Perhaps just a fine... and they will surely confiscate the materials in question. With a U.S. passport, he should be okay. Why don't we move out of the traffic a bit where we can be more comfortable?" A family had just vacated a bench a few feet away and the group quickly took it over.

"How's Brick doing?" Martin asked.

"Mr. Brickhauer is good. He wants you to call him as soon as you get checked in the hotel. His room number is 2455."

"Here comes the wonder boy," Donnelly announced. "I'll go get him."

The Customs officer who looked like a mule was escorting Bill through the door into the main terminal. Donnelly met them and helped Bill with his bags over to the bench.

"Sorry, Martin, I had some technical documents they were concerned with. Turned out they were no problem after all," Strickner said.

"Okay, Bill... good. David is our guide and interpreter for the trip. He went to check on you for us... to find out why you were detained. We were concerned."

So they know, Strickner thought, analyzing Martin's face.

"I'm David Choi, Mr. Strickner." They shook hands. "We should get going. I have a car waiting."

"David, do you come to Beijing often?" Martin inquired, as they walked toward the exit.

"Yes, every couple of months. WCI has a small business office here."

"Is the airport always like this? The utter chaos... and the place is so dark and dirty?"

"Yes, unfortunately. It never changes. You will find standards here are not what you are used to in America, and certainly not what I'm used to in Hong Kong."

Just at that moment, as if to emphasize what David Choi had just said, a middle- aged lady in a colorful silk dress leaned over in front of them and blew a wad of mucus onto the floor from her left nostril while holding a finger to side of her nose. Martin smiled, in mild shock. Donnelly was a little more vocal.

"Jesus Christ, did you see that Martin? Now that's class!"

David Choi laughed. "You fellas are in for a good time."

As they walked out into the night air, the smoke from a hundred thousand sources hung heavily over the poorly lit parking lot. It was just as busy as inside; people shoving and pushing, going in every direction... taxi drivers shouting for attention. David led them to a small, unidentifiable van, nearly void of all paint.

After some confusion, they were all able to get inside, although each had to hold part of the luggage on their laps.

"Nothing but the best for WCI, huh, boys?" Donnelly asked sarcastically as the driver slowly pulled the aged vehicle out of the congested parking lot.

"Nothing but the best!" Martin agreed, smiling.

# Chapter Three

Xin Luk Lin was extremely happy. It had been a very good day. Earlier he had confiscated two bottles of French perfume from an older lady traveling with a tour group, managed to slip a pair of red silk panties out of a suitcase, and then the smelly American had come along. He told the man that he was being fined 100 Yuan for bringing pornographic material into China. The poor barbarian was so nervous he had given him a U.S. $100 bill, more than eight times the value of 100 Yuan! Plus, he now had four very good quality sex magazines! A very good day indeed!

The van left the dimly lit airport complex onto an even more poorly lit street as they made their way toward the city. The headlights on the van were inadequate as well, making it difficult to see more than a few feet down the road. Martin glanced at his watch, noting the time was 7:10 P.M. It had taken them nearly an hour and a half to get out of the airport.

Suddenly, the van lurched to the left, swerving to avoid a mule-drawn cart loaded with hay.

"Whoa! That was close!" Donnelly exclaimed. "What in the hell is a mule pulling a cart doing on the main road to the airport... especially at night?"

David Choi smiled. "Remember, guys, I told you, you're not in America. Things here are a little more, how shall I say, rustic perhaps. Most of the people are very poor, trying to make a living any way they can... even hauling a load of hay on a busy highway at night... with no lights."

Martin was quiet, lost in thought. What little countryside he could see was not pleasant. Piles of dirty snow lined the street and hoards of people were everywhere... almost as busy as the airport. What buildings he could see appeared to be in shambles. Nothing was well lit. He was definitely in culture shock. And this thing with David Choi. What is going on there? Was he really just an interpreter as he claimed? Was there a reason for him to be anything else? He shook his head as if to rid himself of all the questions.

"You all right, Martin?"

"Yes, Jack. I'm fine. Just a little tired from the trip." No use to alarm Donnelly. Not yet, anyway. "I could sure use a drink."

"The Lido has a fine lounge, Martin. They will have anything you want," David Choi responded.

When the van pulled onto the grounds of the hotel, it was like going into another world. The parking lot was well lit and the hotel lobby bright and inviting. A uniformed doorman greeted them and the bell hops were quick after the luggage. David led them to the reception desk and spoke to the clerk in Mandarin.

"Ah, yes, our Americans. Welcome to China and to the Lido." The young Chinese gentleman was neat as a pin, wearing a black suit and a black tie. "I hope your stay is comfortable. All I need is to see your passports. You have already been registered by a Mr. Brickhauer. Which of you is Mr. Maguire?"

"That's me," Martin replied, handing over his passport.

"Very well, sir. I have a message for you." The clerk gave him an envelope which he quickly ripped open. The note was from Brick. 'Call me when you get here. Room 2257.'

"Anything important?" Donnelly asked.

"No, just a note to call Brick."

"Gentlemen, here are your room keys. Your bags will be delivered shortly. Your rooms are through the double doors to the left. Enjoy your stay."

As soon as he was in the room, Martin called Brick.

"Yes?" The familiar voice inquired.

"Good evening, General. Your troops have arrived."

"Martin! 'Bout fucking time! Was your plane late?"

"Not exactly, boss. We were delayed in Customs. Seems as if your assembly engineer didn't get the message about bringing dirty magazines."

"You got to be shittin' me!"

"Unfortunately, no. I'm not shittin' you. He lied about it, but David Choi had already found out why he was detained."

"Christ! Did you say anything to him?"

"No. but I thought you would want to know."

"Yes, of course. Listen, why don't you meet me in the bar for a drink. Just the two of us. There are some things... well, I need to bring you up to date. Call the gang and have them join us in an hour and we'll all go to dinner."

"Okay. See you in a few minutes." Martin called Donnelly and then dialed Strickner's room. There was no answer. "Where in the hell could he be already?" he muttered, disgustedly. He called the reception desk and had them deliver a message for Strickner to join them in an hour and headed for the lounge. He really needed that drink.

Bill Strickner threw his backpack on the bed and headed back out into the hall. They had passed a small market located inside the hotel and he noticed they had a liquor department. No more Customs to go through until they were to leave the country, so he could stock up. He had purposely packed one suitcase light in case the opportunity arose. Ten minutes later he was back in the room, so intent on the four bottles of vodka he had just purchased, he didn't notice the blinking message light on the phone. Quickly he uncapped one of the bottles and let the smooth, clear liquid burn its path downward.

*Okay,* he thought. *Now I'm okay. But I did fuck up. Forgot the magazines were in the backpack. Meant to put them in the back of my pants when we came through Customs. Damn! Now, they know about them. Alicia will be mad.* He took another drink from the bottle. *Sweet Alicia.*

He closed his eyes and let her image materialize in his mind. She was naked, so beautiful, so desirable. Eyes still closed, he took another drink and lay back on the bed.

Martin walked slowly through the well-lit lobby, enjoying the lavish Oriental decorations of mock terracotta warriors and ancient chariots full of armed soldiers. He stopped a bellman and asked for directions to the lounge. The young man pointed up to the second floor and then to the escalator. Two very attractive and very young Chinese girls, wearing long red dresses of the finest silk, slit to the hip, were guarding the moving stairs.

"Good evening, sir. Welcome to Peacock Lounge." The one on the right spoke first. Her smile was genuine and beautiful.

"Ladies." Martin nodded, the temptation to flirt overwhelming. "Do they have any vodka up there?"

"Oh, yes, sir. We have wery much *wadka*. Wery good! You see?" The one on the left responded, holding a hand out toward the escalator.

"Yes, wery much *wadka*," the other one chimed in.

"Great! I want very much *wadka*," Martin laughed. At the top, he was greeted by a third hostess just as attractive as the two below. This one was in white.

"Good evening, sir. Would you have seat at bar or table?"

"I'm to meet a gentleman... a fellow American."

"Oh, yes. This way please." She swished off with Martin following the sensuous movement of her buttocks under the thin silk. No underwear and she smelled of gardenias. Brickhauer was seated at a low table with a glass of wine in front of him. Seeing Martin, he arose.

"Hey, guy! Welcome to China!" His welcome was warm as he held out a hand and motioned to a seat. "Sit down... what are you having?"

"Vodka on the rocks, please... with an olive," he informed the girl.

"Wery vell, sir, *wadka* on ice with olive. Right quickly, sir." She was gone.

"Nice legs," Martin said.

"Yeah, too bad we can only look, huh, Martin?" Not waiting for an answer, he continued, "Tell me about Strickner."

Martin related in detail the situation in the plane and the incident in the airport. Brick was not amused.

"Sonofabitch! Martin, Bill is an alcoholic. He promised us that he would stay off the stuff while on this assignment, a condition of employment, I might add. This job is his last chance. Sounds like he's drinking already, isn't he?"

"That's my guess. I don't understand about the magazines, though. I thought he was smarter than that."

"Maybe he's addicted to those as well. Who knows?" Brick was silent for a minute. "Listen, Martin, you've had a lot more experience supervising people than I have... what do you think I should do?"

Martin's drink arrived. He sipped at it, trying to hide his surprise. His boss, asking him what to do... wasn't he supposed to have all the answers?

"You have to confront him head on, Brick. Let him know of your suspicions. If he thinks you know of his drinking and aren't doing anything about it, he will take that as approving of it. Tell him I know about his problem as well and will also be watching."

"Okay, you're right. I'll talk to him tonight. Thanks." He took a drink of his wine. "New subject, Martin. This thing with China, it's... it's much bigger than we originally planned. It's going to be big... really big. The Chinese no longer only want the technology improvements they've paid for, they want us to build manufacturing facilities in China. They want us to erect the buildings, install the latest tooling and equipment, and manage a work force of their laborers to make several of our products. It's a hell of an opportunity. If we can carry off this technology thing, we have an exclusive deal that will mean billions of dollars to the company. They've agreed that we'll be the only foreign manufacturer of construction equipment in country. I've been told that we must not fail with this project. Our CEO is worried about having the right people in place to make this happen. He is quite willing to replace our gang with more experienced people, if there are any. I assured him, through Peterlie, that we probably already had the best crew available. So, I guess I've put our careers on the line. Does that bother you?"

Martin was in mild shock, trying to grasp the brevity of this news. "So what you're saying is, if we fuck this up... we're dead?" He watched Brick's face.

"If we fuck this up, we will surely wish we were dead, that's for sure. Anyway, I thought you ought to know. We're no longer just trying to teach a bunch of unsophisticated, uneducated, non-English speaking people how to build a ditch digger; we are out to convince the People's Republic of China that we are the best in the world... the best company for them to do business with. We can not fail!"

Martin nodded his head in understanding. "Okay, boss. Then we won't fail. I didn't plan to fail anyway. Nothing's changed for me. I know we can do it." He wasn't even sure he knew what *it* was.

Brickhauer raised his glass. "Okay, Martin Maguire... let's drink to success!" They clicked glasses and sipped. "Oh, by the way, no need to say anything about this to the others. This is still not for publication." Brick looked up. "I see some of our gang coming now."

Martin turned to see Donnelly and Choi approaching. Strickner was not with them.

"Welcome to China, Jack." Brick offered his hand.

"Thanks boss. Where's the weirdo?" he asked, looking around. Tact and diplomacy was just not part of his daily plan.

"Probably tired from the trip. Most likely just went to bed early," Brick offered.

"Yeah, right!" Donnelly replied, sarcastically, "And I'm the tooth fairy! Man, I'm starved. Are we going to eat?"

## Chicago

Alicia Strickner was just waking up in her luxurious king-size bed. She was thirty-eight years old, twenty years younger than her husband of three years, and in the prime of her sexual life. She sat up in bed to survey her breasts in the mirror on the wall. They were full and erect. *Breasts of an eighteen year old,* she bragged to herself.

"Sam... wake up! You got to get going. It's almost seven." She poked the still sleeping figure next to her.

"Uhhhh, in a minute," came the muffled reply.

Alicia threw back the cover to reveal his nakedness. "Come on, baby. I've got to get going. That thing is worn out anyway." She jumped out of bed, threw a robe over her charms and headed for the bathroom.

The man in the bed sat up and put his feet on the floor. "Your husband going to be gone a whole month, you say?" he yelled after her.

"Yep! Ain't it great? We can do this every night for a month!" she answered, from the bathroom. He heard the shower start.

"Fuck," he muttered to himself. "I'd be dead in a week. No wonder that poor bastard drinks, trying to satisfy this one."

They had met in Graucho's Bar the night before. A couple of dances, a couple of drinks, and she had her hand down the front of his pants checking him out.

"Ooh, I like the size of that. You want to come home with me? My husband just left for China and he'll be gone for a month. I want to see this one... this one right here." Enough said. Twenty minutes later they were doing it on the kitchen table.

Sometime during the night, in between rounds when they were resting, she told him about having sex with her husband nearly every night; however, he was getting old and couldn't satisfy her any more.

At that point he decided this would be a one night stand... if he survived.

"Why did you marry such an older man?" he had asked.

"Because, he's the only man that I've ever had an orgasm with. I don't know for sure why. Sometimes he just gets me really excited... although it has been quite a while now."

Now, he was pulling on his shoes and making tracks for the door. With any luck, he would be blocks away before she got out of the shower.

## Beijing

Somewhere, buried in the bowels of the Great Hall of the People, a single, naked light bulb hung over the plain wooden desk on which was one of only eight computers in the entire building. The phone rang.

"Wei?" (Hello?)

"They are here, your Americans. I have delivered them to the hotel."

"Good. Keep me informed." The line went dead.

The three Americans, along with their Hong Kong guide, had

dinner at the German restaurant, one of four located inside the hotel complex. The meal was good, the wine perfect, and the conversation was full of excitement about the next few weeks to come. Martin and Jack filled in David Choi on their ideas for training at the Chinese factories. Brick mostly listened, impressed at how proficient the plan was, knowing that most of it had been developed by Martin. He had tried calling Strickner's room again, but there was still no answer. Strange.

"Martin, Jack... since we have a day's layover tomorrow, I've taken the liberty to hire a car for us all. We are going to go see the Great Wall, the Ming Tomb and the Forbidden City. How does that sound?" Brick asked.

All agreed that sounded great.

"Good. Let's meet for breakfast at seven. They have a great buffet here!"

Martin returned to his room, turned on CNN for a few minutes, then headed for the shower. Under the warm spray, he relaxed, letting the events of the day play through his mind like a video tape; the grueling flight, Strickner's strange disappearance, the Customs episode, the airport, the dismal van ride to the hotel. *Oh, shit! I forgot to say anything to Brick about my suspicions of David Choi. Oh well, Maybe I should just wait. See what happens. Probably nothing to worry about. Just a feeling.*

Martin, Donnelly and Choi were all seated in the coffee shop when Brick appeared the next morning. He was visibly upset.

"Talked to Bill. He's not coming with us. He's sick. Says he going to stay in bed all day and try to get over it. Has a severe headache and has got a case of the runs."

"Does he drink?" Donnelly asked, bluntly.

"Well, he used to. Says he doesn't anymore. Why?" Brick asked.

Donnelly shrugged. "Sounds to me like he has a hangover. I thought he was drinking on the plane and then nobody could find him last night. Just curious."

Brick was silent. Martin spoke up. "Well, Jack, maybe he is really sick. We should let Brick handle it."

"I'll talk to him when we get back," Brick took the lead. "You could be right, Jack. If you are, I'll handle it."

Donnelly nodded his head and attacked his omelet. Wasn't any sweat off his brow, anyway.

Bill Strickner waited until he was sure the group had left for the Great Wall. There was a time in his life when he would have given anything to see such a wonder, but not today. He had only one thing on his confused mind at the moment. Get more vodka. He had consumed two of the precious bottles during the night before passing out, collapsing on the bathroom tile, urinating all over himself and the floor. Now, all he could think of was replacing the bottles. He slipped into his dirty clothes and headed back to the liquor store. He looked and smelled like hell; unshaven and un-bathed, bloodshot eyes, and his breath smelled like that of a camel.

He found the store, got two more bottles of vodka, shoved the strange foreign bills at the clerk, depositing the change in his pocket without looking, not bothering to count it. That would have been a futile attempt at best, his mind barely functioning. Holding his precious cargo in his arms, he retreated back to his room, hanging the 'Do Not Disturb' sign on the door. Inside, he began to drink quickly, wanting to get drunk before the thoughts of Alicia returned. *I'm losing my mind*, he thought. *I can't stop... not the drinking...not the thinking about her...she's driving me crazy!* That was the last cognizant thought he would have for several hours. The vodka had kicked in.

The car was new and nice... a Mercedes, in fact. As they worked their way through the streets of Beijing, the two Americans were in absolute awe. Never had they expected anything like the sights they were seeing.

"Next trip, I'll bring a video camera," Jack said. "No way can I describe this!"

Martin was thoroughly enjoying himself. He shook his head in wonder. "It's like a giant ant hill... hoards of people going here and there. You said it was busy, Brick, but I had no idea!"

"I know how you feel, Martin. I remember my first trip. In many ways it's like going back a hundred years in time."

"Look at that, Martin!" Jack shouted, pointing at a bicycle loaded with a couch, two chairs and a small table lashed to a man-made platform over the rear fender. "It's a moving van!"

They all had a good laugh. They all had several good laughs that day.

The car left the city and continued north toward the Great Wall. They had to stop for a very long train pulled by four diesel locomotives.

The driver spoke in broken English, "Train to Moscow. Take this many days!" He held up five fingers. They watched as the dirt-streaked cars went past, one by one. Many of the passenger cars appeared to be empty. *Perhaps there are not too many Chinese vacationing in Russia these days*, Martin thought.

"Very hard to get ticket," the driver said, as if reading Martin's mind. "Mainly government and Party members."

The day went by quickly, the Americans lost in their own thoughts of the wonders of it all... the wall, the meaningless tombs, the ancient Forbidden City. It was actually too much for them to absorb in one day. *I will return*, Martin thought. *I will come back and spend some time with you, to try and understand your ways, mysterious China.*

The car returned to the hotel around five P.M. and Martin, Jack and David headed for the lounge to have a drink. There was a string quartet playing classical music in the hotel lobby. Very pleasant, sophisticated... nice. It was obvious that this event was designed to be enjoyed by foreigners... not the local people with whom they had spent the day.

"I'll catch up with you guys in few minutes," Brick announced. "I'm going to go check on Strickner." Then he headed off toward Bill's room.

Brick took the sign off the door knob and knocked loudly.

"Bill, its Brick. You okay?" There was no response. He knocked again even louder. A door opened across the hall and a pair of curious eyes peeked out. Brick stared at the person and the door quickly shut. He tried the knob and found the door unlocked. Opening it slowly, the stench hit him in the face like a blast of hot air. It was a wretched smell of stale alcohol, vomit and urine.

"Jesus Christ! Bill?" He opened the door and went in, covering his mouth and nose with a handkerchief. Bill was sitting on the bed staring at the floor. He was naked and made no move to cover up. In fact, he made no move at all, oblivious to the presence of anyone else in the room. Brick shut the door quickly. No one else needed to see this.

The bed was torn apart, the top sheet and blanket on the floor, the bottom sheet stained with urine and other things. Two empty bottles of vodka lay on the floor at the end of the bed. A third, half empty, was on the night stand. The bathroom door was open and the light was on. Brick could see human waste all over the floor. Obviously, Bill had not been able to make it to the toilet.

Brick had never been so disgusted in his life. "You filthy mother fucker," he muttered. "You filthy, drunk, mother fucker." He flipped on the ceiling light, lending a harsh realism to the scene. Bill made no move. His eyes were open, but he was not conscious.

"What in the hell have you done to yourself?" he whispered. "Bill? Can you talk to me?" There was no response.

Brick was in shock. He had absolutely no idea what to do. He just stood and stared. The phone rang, startling him, bringing him out of his trance. He picked up the receiver.

"Hello."

"Brick, its Martin. Is Bill okay?"

"No, he's not. He's a fucking mess! Drunk out of his mind and that's not all. The place is covered with puke and shit. I've never seen anything like it. I don't know what to do!" he said, desperately.

"Hang tight. I'll be right there." Martin nearly ran as he made his way to Bill's room. He opened the door and entered, equally shocked at the scene that had shocked Brick a few moments before.

"Wow! Bill, you poor sonofabitch." He shut and locked the door. "We had better call security and get a doctor in here, don't you think, Brick?"

"Yes... good idea. I'm in so much shock, I can't think. Yes, of course, let's get a doctor." Brick headed toward the phone.

"He looks like he's been scrubbing the floor with his dick," Martin remarked. Walking carefully, he retrieved a clean towel from the bathroom and wiped the puke off Bill's face. Then, he laid him back on the bed and covered his abused body with the blanket from the floor. When Bill's head touched the pillow, he moaned.

"Bill? Can you hear me?" Martin asked. He could hear Brick talking to someone on the phone.

"Alicia... she wants..." he trailed off, slipping back into a stupor.

Brick had finished talking on the phone. "What did he say?" he asked Martin.

"He said, Alicia wants something. Isn't that his wife's name?"

"Yes. He must be hallucinating. Poor bastard's lost it. We're going to have to get him home somehow," Brick mused.

"If I had drunk two fifths of vodka in one day, they'd be sending me home in a box!"

"No shit!" Brick agreed. There was a knock on the door. Martin opened it up to a young man in a black suite, holding a security I.D. for him to see.

"Please, come in," Martin offered, shutting the door behind him. "One of our colleagues has a drinking problem. He's had quite a lot, and we are not sure how he is... physically. Could you get an English speaking doctor for us?"

The man carefully surveyed the room, missing nothing. He had been well trained. "Yes, I will summon a doctor right away." His English was perfect, with very little accent. "You must understand, there will be extra charges... for the cleanup, and of course, you will want this knowledge to remain in the hotel." He made no move to call.

Brick exploded, "Blackmail? You talking about blackmail?"

"Sir, I don't know this word, blackmail. But, I don't think you understand. If this event gets reported to the local authorities, it will mean days of paper work and bureaucracy. Then your friend will certainly be deported and your company will have great difficulty in getting visas for future visits. So, everyone who is made aware of this situation will require a small payment to assure that mouths are sealed. This will include the maids, the doctor, the front desk, and of course... me."

"How much are we talking about?" Martin asked, forcing himself to remain calm. Brick was furious.

"I would think 500 Yuan RMB each for the hotel staff, 1,000 Yuan for the doctor, plus his examination fee. As for myself, I will have to make sure that everyone will fear my reprisal if they do not keep quiet, so I will require a little more, say 10,000 Yuan."

Martin was quickly calculating. 15,000 Yuan would be close to $1,800 dollars. Brick was still extremely mad, his face red and his hands were shaking. "You fucker, you ain't getting..."

"Wait a minute, Brick!" Martin held up his hand. "Just listen. If we don't do it this way, it will cost us a lot more. Think of what you told me last night. It's only $1,800 U.S."

"You are a wise man," the security officer stated. Brick was thinking about what Martin had said. $1,800 U.S. was not a lot of money, under the circumstances. He remained silent.

"Shall I assume we have an agreement? If so, I will call the doctor."

"Brick?" Martin waited for approval.

"Yeah, all right, do it." He was still very angry. Mostly at Bill Strickner.

Soon after the security officer left the room, there was a soft knock and the door opened letting a small Chinese man of some advanced age enter, caring a bucket and a mop. He began cleaning up the mess as if it happened every day. Just as he was finishing up, the doctor came. Although his nationality was not readily recognizable, he was definitely not Chinese.

He stood at the end of the bed and looked at Bill for a few minutes, then nodded his head as if to agree with himself and faced the two Americans. He said a few words which sounded like Spanish.

"We don't understand. You speak English?" Brick asked.

"A little. I am Portuguese… from Macao. You pay first."

"Fucker! I thought capitalism was not alive in China!" Brick muttered.

Martin reached into his pocket and pulled out his cash. "I got it covered, Brick," he said, softly. He started counting out 100 Yuan notes into the doctors open palm. When he got to ten, he stopped. The doctor motioned with his other hand for him to keep counting. Reluctantly, Martin counted out five more bills. Again, the doctor motioned. Martin responded. "No. That's all." He folded the remaining bills and returned them to his pocket, in a motion of finality. The doctor smiled, accepting the end of the bargaining. Martin's face had said it all. He was through paying.

He approached the bed and opened his satchel. He took Bill's vital signs and examined him thoroughly. He washed and applied a salve to his genitals. Twenty minutes later, he turned and handed Martin a small bottle of pills. "Give him two of these, every four hours. Keep him away from alcohol."

"You sonofabitch! You speak English!" Brick yelled.

"If I must, I do. It's a ghastly language."

"I think it's time for you to go," Martin said. "Before I let my friend beat the shit out of you."

"I am not afraid of your friend. He is like a gust of hot air. This one," he paused, tilting his head toward the bed, "this one nearly died from alcohol poisoning. You should take him home now. No one can help him here." He turned and went quickly out the door.

"Jesus! I'd better call the boss. Peterlie is going to be pissed. What a fucking mess! Stay here till I get back," Brick muttered, leaving Martin alone with Bill.

Martin made himself a cup of coffee from the dresser and sat down to wait. For what, he wasn't sure.

An hour later, Brick returned.

"How is he?" he asked in a quiet voice.

"He hasn't moved," Martin replied. "What did Peterlie say?"

Brick shook his head and sighed. "Martin, I'm sorry to leave you in this situation, but you are going to have to take over. The boss wants me personally to bring Bill back to the States." He handed Martin a manila folder. "Here's a copy of the Chinese agreement just in case any disputes come up. David will take care of you, and don't hesitate to ask him his opinion on Chinese culture or protocol and such. Go ahead and do everything you had planned to do, except for the assembly part. Tell the Chinese that Bill got sick and had to return to the U.S. for treatment. Cover for him best that you can." Brick paused, looking closely into Martin's face. "You okay with this?"

"Sure, we'll be fine. Don't worry about us." He hoped his words reflected more confidence than he really had.

"I'm not. You've showed me a lot about yourself the last few hours. You handled things much better than I could have. You kept your head about you when I was going off the deep end. I won't forget it. Call me every three days, ten o'clock P.M. China time. The number is in the folder. Bill and I are leaving in two hours. I paid the security guy the rest of the money. The boss thought we got off pretty cheap in view of the circumstances, so you were right about that as well."

"What are you going to do about Bill?"

"Company policy... Personnel has arranged for him to be admitted to Marion Joy's Drug and Alcohol Rehab Center. I guess we can't fire him as long as he's getting treatment. I'm to take him there as soon as we get home. Then, I have the pleasure of telling his wife. That ought to be fun, huh?"

"No, that won't be fun," Martin said.

"Well, I'll take it from here. Good luck with the training." Brick offered his hand.

"Thanks, boss. We'll do fine."

The phone in the dimly lit office rang once again. "Wei?"

"Two Americans are going back to the U.S. One is possessed by the demon of drink, the other is his "laoban" (boss). The others will proceed as planned."

"Xie xie." (thank you)

# Chapter Four

## Chicago

The flight back to Chicago was pretty much uneventful. The drugs the doctor had given Bill kept him asleep most of the time. Once when he was awake, he tried to apologize to Brick.

"I messed up, didn't I? Let you down. I'm sorry for that."

"Let's not worry about that just now. We're going to get you some help," Brick answered, unconvincingly.

"What kind of help?"

"I'm taking you to Marion Joy's rehab center. They can help you there."

Strickner was silent for a few minutes. "They can't make the visions go away."

"What visions?" Brick asked.

"Alicia... always wanting me to... to do things. Sex things. I can't make them go away unless I get drunk. They won't be able to make them go away either."

Brick didn't know what to say to that. "I don't know, Bill. We'll have to ask the doctors." His answer fell on deaf ears. Bill had slipped into a deep sleep again.

He was still in a zombie state when they checked through O'Hare Customs. Brick loaded their luggage on a cart and they took the shuttle to the parking area. Forty-five minutes later they were at the hospital. Since they were expecting him, all Bill had to do was sign the admission papers.

"Good luck, Bill," Brick said softly, and then offered his hand.

Bill made no effort to move, staring straight ahead down the long hall. It was an awkward moment. Then the nurse came around the corner.

"Come with me, please," she ordered, and they were gone. Brick stood a few minutes, gathering his wits. *Nothing more for me to do here*, he thought. He noticed the clock on the way out. 7:10 P.M. Plenty of time to go see Mrs. Strickner. Someone in Personnel was supposed to have called her today to inform her that Bill was coming home. Peterlie wanted him to see her in person. It would take a forty-five minute drive across town.

He found the house with minimum problems and was soon ringing the doorbell. He could hear faint noises from within so he rang the bell again. After a short time, the hall light came on, and the door opened.

"Yes?" The woman was clad in a bright red robe which she clutched tightly closed with her left hand. "Can I help you?"

"Mrs. Strickner?"

"Yes, what do you want?"

"I'm John Brickhauer. I'm your husband's supervisor at WCI. Did the company call you today?"

"Maybe. I didn't check my messages. Why? Is Bill all right?"

"Not exactly. May I come in? I need to discuss his condition with you."

"Of course. How unthoughtful of me. Please." She opened the door wider and, for a moment, she lost control of the robe which fell open to expose large bare breasts.

Brick was embarrassed, but couldn't help a response. "Wow!" he said under his breath.

"Sorry, Mr. Brickhauer. Please have a seat while I see to my guest. I'll be right back." She waved at the living room and disappeared down the hall.

Guest? Dressed only in a robe? That's a nice way to entertain! He found a seat on the couch, but was unable to relax. He could smell incense, similar to the smell in the Chinese temples he had just visited in Beijing. *Strange people,* he thought... *an alcoholic and a nearly naked woman. Maybe I should leave, call her tomorrow.*

She was back, the robe securely belted. "Sorry, now what were you saying? Is Bill okay?"

"No, I'm afraid not." He decided to be blunt. "I just left him at Marion Joy's drug and rehab center. He had a drinking binge in Beijing. Nearly killed himself. I brought him back this afternoon."

She shook her head in dismay. "From China? Oh, my. Where is he?"

"Marion Joy Hospital," he repeated.

She was silent for a brief moment. "I was afraid of something like this. He thinks he has mental problems, Mr. Brickhauer. Things going on in his mind. He drinks to forget them, so he says."

"Yes, he told me." No sense in going into more detail.

That got her attention. "Just what did he tell you?" she asked. "That he fantasizes about having sex with me?"

"Yes. I think the staff at the hospital are more worried about how to fix the mental thing than the drinking."

"I don't think there is anything wrong with him mentally. I think he just likes to drink." She sat on the chair opposite him and crossed her shapely legs. "Isn't it normal for most men to fantasize about having sex?"

Brick was extremely uncomfortable. "Perhaps, Mrs. Strickner. But Bill does more than just fantasize. He has to drink in order to deal with it. Anyway, he's in the hospital. You can visit him there. Here is the number if you want to see how he's doing." Brick handed her a slip of paper. "I should be going." He stood to leave, confused and shocked about her lack of concern.

Sensing his discomfort, she felt the need to explain. "Mr. Brickhauer, Bill and I are not close. We have a convenient relationship. He drinks, I play around. Forgive me if I seem a little crass. He has done this dozens of times... even been to Marion Joy before. Anyhow, thank you for coming. Don't be too concerned for Bill. He will be just fine in a few days." She uncrossed her legs, giving him a clear view. He couldn't help but stare. "Sit down, stay for awhile. Can I get you a drink?"

He sat, in a mild shock at what had just happened. "No... I think not. I... really have to be going."

"Are you a Christian, Mr. Brickhauer?"

"Of course. Aren't you?"

"No, I'm not," she said bluntly. "Are you married, Mr. Brickhauer?"

"Yes, I am. Happily married!" he felt the need to add.

Alicia Strickner smiled. "Of course you are. Do you ever get tempted to... to stray a bit?"

"Mrs. Strickner, I'm not sure this conversation is appropriate. I came here to tell you about your husband and I've done that. I really need to be going." He stood and headed for the door.

She quickly followed. "Here, let me get that for you. The door sticks sometimes." She pulled the door open. "If you must go, well, again, thank you for coming. Perhaps we will meet again under more amiable circumstances." He stepped out and she closed the door behind him.

*Wow! That's one different kind of woman*, he thought, walking quickly to the car.

Visiting hours were over. The patients had returned to their rooms and were preparing for bed. The late night staff was now on duty. Bill Strickner lay on the bed fully dressed... thinking... his mind finally clear for the first time in days. He knew the routine from before. Ten o'clock bed check, then another at 2:00 A.M. Plenty of time in between.

"I'm not going through this any more," he muttered, softly. "No more. This will put an end to it all." He felt under the pillow to make sure the scissors he had taken from the desk at the nurses station was still there. Brick had not noticed why he didn't return the offer to shake hands. His right hand held the scissors. The clock on the wall showed 9:33. A few minutes more.

Brick made the drive to his home in a daze. What a trip it would be to be married to someone like Alicia Strickner. His Peggy, so warm and soft, had been so happy when he had called to tell her he would be home tonight, instead of thirty days later. Now, as he was pulling into the drive, his thoughts were not on his lovely wife where they should have been, but of the view Alicia Strickner had given him of her most private of parts. He was sure it was a purposeful move on her part, obviously coming on to him, with a guest in another part of the house doing... what? Were they having sex? Probably. He realized he was getting physically excited thinking about the situation. He got out of the car and rubbed the bulge in his trousers. "Hope you're in the mood, Peggy girl," he muttered, softly.

## Peoples Republic of China

Martin, Jack and David were at the contract factory in Harbin, a large industrial city in the northern part of the country, only a few miles from the Soviet border. The mixing of Chinese and Russian blood was evident... the local people here were much taller and the ladies were much more filled out than in the south. The hotel was a large, six-story, brick monstrosity...not heated, dirty, dimly lit and basically uncomfortable. It was here that Martin received his first lesson about how strictly the Chinese follow rules.

He put his suitcases down and headed for the toilet as soon as he was in his room. He'd had to pee for over an hour. He flipped the wall switch and nothing happened. Damn! Bulb burnt out. There was enough light, however, coming in through the open door that he could complete the task. Once he was finished, he went down the hall to the desk where the floor manager was seated and tried to explain that he needed a new bulb in the bathroom. No luck. The young girl had no idea what he was trying to say. Frustrated, he knocked on David's door and asked him to interpret.

"Tell her the light bulb in the bathroom needs replacing."

He did.

"She says they are out of light bulbs. They have been ordered from Beijing for three months now. From the light bulb factory."

"Can you believe that? Two hundred rooms in this hotel and they got no light bulbs?"

"That's what she said." David was smiling.

"Okay... we are the only people on this floor. There are at least twenty empty rooms here. Tell her to take a bulb out of one of the empty rooms and put it in my bathroom."

He did.

"She says she can't do that. That would make the room... faulty."

"You're shittin' me. Tell her my room is faulty!"

He did.

"She says, perhaps that is true, but she didn't cause it. It she took a bulb from another room, it would be her fault that it was not complete."

"So what the hell am I supposed to do?"

David asked her.

"She says for you to take the bulb out of the bedroom and put it in the bathroom when you need to see in there. It is okay for you to take the bulb back and forth. Do not break it."

"You got to be shittin' me," he said again.

"Welcome to China," David replied. "I'm going to bed."

The training, however, was going good. The Chinese were appropriately impressed with the broad knowledge of manufacturing the two Americans displayed. After a day at the factory, they were on their way back to the hotel to rest for a few hours before attending a banquet sponsored by the mayor of Harbin and his Communist Party counterpart. All but forgotten were the problems encountered in Beijing. David Choi was performing wonderfully and the suspicions Martin had felt earlier were disappearing. He and Donnelly were having the time of their life. He was getting used to moving the bulb back and forth.

## Chicago

The night nurse, Rosie, was on her early morning rounds, making sure her patients were resting comfortably. She looked through the glass in the door and saw that Bill Strickner was not in his bed. In fact, the bed was still made, a realization that greatly disturbed her. She knocked on the door, then opened it and went in the room. The pajamas issued to all the inmates were lying on the chair next to the bed, undisturbed.

"Mr. Strickner? Are you in the bathroom?" she inquired, loudly. There was no answer. She approached the bathroom door and knocked. "Mr. Strickner? Are you in there?" Still no answer. "I'm going to open the door, okay?" Slowly, she turned the knob and pushed the door open. The first thing to get her attention was lying in a pool of blood next to the sink on the small vanity. "Jesus Holy Christ! What is that?" she muttered, and opened the door wide. Then she screamed.

Bill Strickner's lifeless body, bluish gray in color, was seated on the toilet, his legs spread wide. The scissors were lying on the floor at his side. There was a bloody clot between his legs where his penis should have been. The water in the stool was dark red with blood. Now Rosie knew for sure what the item was that was laying on the vanity top. She screamed again.

## Peoples Republic of China

Martin was ready to leave the hotel room to meet the others for dinner when the phone rang. A female voice in unpracticed English informed him that he needed to stop by the reception desk for a telex. He left the room and knocked on Donnelly's door.

"Jack? You ready to go?"

The door opened. "Been waiting on you. I hope the food is good. I think I could eat one of their dogs tonight!"

"I got a telex to pick up at the desk," Martin said.

"From who?"

"Don't know. Probably Brick." The two men got on the elevator and pushed the button for the lobby. The rickety car lurched into action and descended slowly.

At the desk, Martin was handed a piece of yellow paper. He read the words in disbelief.

*Martin, Strickner is dead. Committed suicide in the hospital. That's all the details I have at the moment. Hope things are going good there. Good luck, see you in a few weeks. Regards, Brick*

"Jesus!" Martin's hands were shaking.

"What is it?" Donnelly asked. Martin handed him the fax.

"Good Mother of God! Like the guy or not, this is terrible!"

Martin was lost in thought. *What kind of demons could drive a man to take his own life?* He had no idea. All of a sudden, the trip didn't seem nearly as glamorous as it had when Brick was offering him the job.

# Chapter Five

## Beijing

Xin Luk Lin had expanded his business. The amount of goods confiscated at his customs table had grown considerably in the past few months. Tourism was up nearly fifty percent, allowing him to satisfy his original sponsor, the first Minister of Agriculture, as well as solicit an additional recipient, a Chen Lim Hua, rumored to be a high ranking member of the Secret Police. It was a brilliant strategic move on his part and he was very careful to make sure these two influential parties were well taken care of.

Of course, his own personal wealth was skyrocketing as well. On his days away from work, he would hire a car and driver to take him dancing or to the Karaoke halls where he was becoming quite well known with the prostitutes who frequented these places. Getting a date without paying for it was out of the question, with his mule-face features, but the local whores didn't care about his looks. Once in awhile, he would treat himself to one of the Western ladies who hung around the Beijing Hotel that was preferred by the rich businessmen. He loved the white skin and large soft breasts, but the girls were quite expensive, so he wasn't able to enjoy them as much as he would have liked. Most of his friends were intimidated by them, calling them white cows, convinced their *gullies of joy* were much too large for the small equipment of the average Chinese man. Xin summoned up all his courage and actually asked one of the white cows if this was true. "I'm afraid so, Muley." she answered. "Americans are twice as big, actually, but I don't care how small your weenie is, just how much money you have." It made him very angry and he vowed never to have the pleasure of her company again.

A popular practice with the young people these days was to adopt a Western first name. He had chosen the name of Charles, pleased at the way it sounded. Charles Xin. Yes, Charles Xin was becoming a sophisticated, but ugly, person of means.

During one of his nights out, he was sitting in a booth at a new American restaurant called The Hard Rock Cafe with one of the white cows, a redheaded girl from Vancouver, Canada. They were sipping American beer and she was teaching him English. Earlier they had settled on a price of 500 Yuan, around $35 for the evening, as long as he included drinks and dinner. The English lesson alone was worth the fee, although he was anxious to see if her *gully of joy* was surrounded by the same red hair as on her head.

"No, you don't say *vater*! It is 'water'! Not v, w! You guys are always getting your *vees* and *double-u's* mixed up! You say vater for water, and wadka for vodka. Why, I don't know!" she exclaimed, frustrated.

Charles laughed. "We study English in school, but only how to read... not to say the words. Now, I listen every day. Chinese man who can speak English can make much more greater money." He said in broken English.

"Well, your English is not very good, but it is better than my Chinese!" She laughed. Under the table, she caressed his leg with a practiced move. "I heard the other girls talking about you," she lied.

"Really? What do they say?"

"That you are a good lover; that you get very hard, not so small like most, and a very generous tipper."

"Yes," he beamed.

They were abruptly interrupted by an unsmiling man of some size who forced his way into the booth next to Xin. He smelled of shrimp paste and rotting teeth.

"Take the hand of this white cow off your worthless stalk and listen to every word I am saying." He spoke in Mandarin, his words harsh and biting. "I am a member of the Supreme Secret Police. You will leave this disgusting American place immediately and go to Tsing Ming Tea Palace on Leung Mung Street at once. You will not be bedding this fat cow with the jelly tits and stinking gulley tonight. When you arrive, a man will be seated at the first table on your right. He has a proposition for you. If you choose not to go, I will find you and see that you breathe no more." As quickly as he had arrived, the mysterious man was gone. Xin was in a state of shock.

"What did he say?" white cow asked.

"I must leave. I have been summoned."

"What about my money?" she whined.

Suddenly Xin became very angry. Who did she think she was? "Shut up, you fat whore. You get nothing from me. I think your hair is red only on your head. You are fake!" He didn't look back as he left the restaurant and woke up his driver.

It took twenty minutes to drive to the Tsing Ming Tea Palace. The building was run down and dirty, with mold and disrepair the most predominant features. It was a place for old men to grow older, a place of comfort to those who have never known true comfort, a place for old men to forget the bad times. Oil lamps illuminated the entrance and a curtain, void of all original color, covered the otherwise open door.

Xin stepped inside and had to stop for a moment for his eyes to adjust to the dimness. The place smelled of tea, incense, unwashed bodies and smoked opium. After a moment, the table came into view with the man he was supposed to meet. Xin approached and sat in the only other chair.

"You are prompt. That is good," the man spoke quietly, but with an air of authority. Xin said nothing... anxious, waiting, and frightened of this person draped in shadows. He was of medium build with a hard face that sported a deep scar across his nose and down the side until it disappeared into a thick black mustache. There was no way one could determine his age from his appearance. But it was his eyes that drew the attention... like a strong magnet from which you couldn't pull away. They were emerald green, the color of sea foam... full of evil. Xin had never seen a fellow Chinese with any color of eyes except black.

"Yes. So, I am prompt. What do you want from me?" he asked, faking a confidence he really didn't have.

The man smiled, exposing very white and even teeth, also unusual for a Chinese. "A mutual acquaintance has suggested you could be a candidate for a certain secret organization of which I am a member. Do you know who that might have been?"

Xin smelled the trap immediately. It had to be Chen Lim Hua. "No, I know of no one who would say this. No one. You must be mistaken."

"I am not mistaken. You are wise not to reveal your sponsor." The man paused and lit a cigarette. "I am looking for someone who is not afraid to take a few risks for the good of our mother country. I'm not sure you fit the criteria."

"I have no idea why you are talking to me, but the fact that I'm here should be proof that I am willing to take risks. I have no assurance that you do not plan to kill me. Perhaps you have a knife under the table as we speak. It is possible. However, it also occurred to me you would not be here if you didn't already know everything of me."

"Yes. I know everything about you. I even know how many times you have emptied your bowels last week." The man brought his hands in view. He was holding a long slender knife. "I did have a knife. How did you know?"

"I didn't know, but if I were you, I would have had one."

"Do you know how to use this?"

"No. Only to clean fish, not as a weapon."

"How is your English?"

"Poor... I get by."

"What do you think of Americans?"

"I love Americans. Their stupidity has made me rich."

"Could you kill Americans?"

"Why would I want to do that?"

"Because I might order you to."

"If I were a member of the... the organization you represent, I would do anything asked of me. Anything."

"Humm. We will see. I have some arrangements to make. I will contact you when we are ready for your training to begin. Speak to no one about this matter."

"Of course. What kind of training?"

"You will learn many things. How to kill, how to interrogate, how to die... many things. Please leave now."

Charles Xin nodded his head and stood. He wanted to ask more questions, but thought better of it, and slowly walked out the door and into the night.

## Hong Kong

"You want me to show you guys around?" David asked. The group had completed the itinerary for their first visit to China and was on their way from Beijing to Hong Kong. It had been a long thirty days. Jack was seated a couple of rows ahead of David and Martin in the Boeing 727.

"Oh, I don't know, David. I think we can find our way around. The two of us are tourists now you know. We'll get a map and check things out. We're going to take the tram up to Victoria Peak the first thing," Martin replied.

"That is always a nice thing for a new visitor. You will enjoy that. I'll just have the car drop you two off at the Sheraton and then take me on home. I think I'll take a four hour shower."

Martin laughed. "Yeah, I know what you mean. So we won't have any problem buying a copy watch?"

"Are you kidding? Just start walking any direction from the hotel and the guys will find you. Don't pay any more than twenty dollars for a Rolex, though. They'll try and get fifty. Don't bite."

"Okay. Twenty it is."

"Oh, since you're just staying across the street, walk into the Peninsula and have a drink in the bar. It's unbelievable! Then count the Rolls-Royces parked out front. That's how the rich and famous live!"

"Yeah, I've heard a lot about it. We'll do that. I think we want to get a suit made also."

"Go up Nathan Road to Moody, then turn right. Find Wellfit Tailors. Tell Ronnie I sent you."

"Flight attendants prepare for landing." The announcement actually brought a feeling of relief to Martin. *Civilization. We did it,* he thought. *And, we did it good!*

The Sheraton Hotel was located next to the harbor in the heart of the Kowloon District shopping area. The rooms were large, well decorated and comfortable... something the two Americans had not experienced since leaving the Holiday Inn Lido four weeks ago. Martin was in heaven. He called Donnelly's room.

"I'm staying here forever! Call Bernice and tell her to get another jerk. I'm not leaving. Man what a view!"

Martin laughed. "Yeah, pretty nice, huh? Not near as nice as The Peninsula, so says David. Want to have lunch there?"

"Sure. Give me a while. I'm going to sit on that pot till my butt falls asleep!"

"I'll see you in the lobby in an hour."

"Okay, bye."


After a fifty-six dollar lunch that consisted of two ham and watercress sandwiches and two beers, the two friends took the Star Ferry across the harbor and then a taxi to the tram terminal. The ride up to Victoria Peak was breathtaking. The higher the cable car went, the more one could see the vast stretch of glorious skyscrapers that made up the Hong Kong skyline.

"Wow. This is fantastic! Some day, I'm going to live here," Martin muttered.

"Yeah, and some day I'm going to the moon," Jack answered.

## Chicago, Six Months Later

Martin was excited. One week to go. The first group of mainland Chinese were finally due to arrive on Monday; twenty-four trainees, three interpreters, and David Choi. It had not been an easy task to get everything in place for this trip. The list of trainees kept changing, as the Chinese government denied passports for various reasons, causing second choices to be made. Also, the factories were fighting amongst themselves on how many each could bring. Finally, a completed list was obtained, tickets were bought and the show was on. Of the twenty-seven Chinese, only two had ever flown before, and twenty-two had never even traveled outside of their own city. Now, everything was in place, including accommodations at a local motel. They had gotten lucky there; the owners were actually ex-Hong Kong Chinese who could speak some Mandarin.

Bill Strickner had been replaced by a young man named Reif Jackman. Unlike his predecessor, Reif had proven to be a team player and had contributed enormously to the training criteria.

David Choi was equally excited. This would be his first time to the land-ofplenty and, although this was not the top priority of his assignment, he was really looking forward to the trip. He had worked hard to earn the respect and trust of the group when they had visited China, even more so after the mistake he had made at the airport. No one had noticed but Martin Maguire. One sharp cookie, that one. Hopefully, he had proven his loyalty to Martin and wiped out the suspicion. Hopefully.

John Brickhauer was the mystery these days. As the time for the Chinese to come to America grew near, he seemed to become less and less interested, giving Martin more and more latitude in the preparations. He was distant, noncommittal, and obviously preoccupied with something other than his work. Donnelly had offered an opinion on several occasions that Brick must be having marital problems.

Martin had met Peggy Brickhauer a couple of times. He found her to be a very attractive, warm and friendly person, and completely supportive of her husband. If there were problems, they would surely be initiated by Brick.

Martin finished typing the last memo of the day, turned off the PC, locked his desk and headed for the door, excited about the coming evening. He and his wife were planning to have dinner with another couple in a new restaurant they had recently read about. As he passed Brick's office, he could see he was on the phone so he just waved his goodbye and went on.

Brick waved back, speaking into the phone, "Hi, honey, it's me. I'm going to be late again tonight..... No, something just came up.... Martin just handed me more changes in the Chinese schedule." The lies were coming easier these days. "I have to get a report ready for Peterlie by 7:00 A.M. tomorrow, so I'll just have to stay and get it done.... No, don't wait up. I'll get a bite on the way home. Okay, love you. Bye." He pushed the disconnect button down and then dialed another number. "Alicia! Hi. I'll be over in about thirty minutes."

Martin pulled into the drive at five-thirty. Carole was waiting on the patio, a cold beer in hand. He dropped his briefcase, took her in his arms and gave her a long kiss.

"Wow! That was nice. Too bad the Jennings are coming in twenty minutes. You kind of got me going there."

"Call them," Martin mumbled, against her neck. "Tell 'em we're going to get naked and play feely-touchy and hide the weenie for a bit. They can come another day."

Carole laughed. "Later, dear husband, later. Walt offered to drive. I was sure you wouldn't mind."

"No, of course not. We can mess around in the back seat."

Gently, she pushed him away. "Go change. They'll be here soon."

"If you insist." He took a long drink. "Thanks for the beer!"

Carole Maguire was a beautiful woman; tall, tan, hair like black satin, a trim figure and the sexiest eyes Martin had ever seen. They had gone to high school together in Cincinnati, started dating in their senior year, went to college in different States and married six months after graduating. Soon after that, they moved to the Chicago area where Martin went to work for WCI. Carole started her own real estate business, and after five years, had become quite successful.

Walt and Karen Green had been their best friends for several years. Karen worked for Carole as her top agent. Walt was a superintendent for a materials management company. Their combined salaries were similar which made being friends easier. They did a lot of social things together and loved trying new restaurants. Tonight, they were traveling to a northern suburb to try a recently opened Mexican place.

Martin changed into casual clothes and the two of them went to the front steps to wait for their friends. Soon they were in the car, relaxed and prepared to have a fun evening.

The drive was unhurried, the conversation lively, and soon they were enjoying margaritas at an out of the way table. Halfway through the enchiladas, Martin was interrupted by Walt.

"Martin... isn't that your boss over there with the two girls?"

"Where?"

"There, at the bar!"

Martin leaned around a pica plant to get a better view. He nearly choked. It was indeed John Brickhauer, with a blond... a blond dressed like a hooker... mini skirt, tight sweater with no bra, and a younger one, black hair and strikingly good looking... dressed just as provocatively. Both were hanging onto Brick for dear life. They were drinking wine, laughing at some unknown joke, touching, kissing...

"Who are they?" Carole asked.

"I don't know," Martin replied, completely shocked. "Neither of them...sure as hell ain't his wife! Wait a minute...maybe I do know who... Jesus Christ, that one on the left is Bill Strickner's wife... the blond!"

Carole was surprised. "You're kidding me! What should we do?"

"Just finish our dinner and slip out quietly. There is no reason to make a scene here. If he sees us, let him make the move." Martin went back to eating. Inside, he was shaking like a leaf. *Well, at least I know what has been in Bricks thoughts as of late!*

Brick had left the office shortly after Martin and quickly drove to Westport. It was thirty miles from his home so he was not too worried about someone recognizing his car. He picked up the two girls and drove on to the Mexican restaurant, where they decided to have a few drinks before having dinner.

He had been making the trip to Alicia's house regularly since Bill's funeral. The memory of that event was still fresh in his mind. It had been a small service with only a handful of people attending. He was the only one there from WCI, a fact which didn't surprise him much. After the short service, Alicia Strickner approached him.

"Mr. Brickhauer, how nice of you to come. Bill did not have a lot of friends at work. He would be pleased." She had been dressed in black, but no way looked like the grieving widow. The dress was tight and cut low, exposing the top half of her chest.

Brick could not help notice the whiteness of her skin, the blue veins clearly visible, so enticing as they disappeared into the blackness of the fabric.

"Mrs. Strickner... I don't know quite what to say. I'm so sorry for your loss." As soon as the words were out of his mouth, he realized how empty that phrase really was. *So sorry for your loss.* How inadequate.

"Thank you. You did everything you could... and probably more than most would have. I should have taken you more seriously that night. If I had gone straight to the hospital, perhaps Bill would still be alive."

"You can't blame yourself," he heard himself say. "Bill was sick, mentally and physically." *It could be your fault, though,* he thought.

"Of course. Frankly, he's probably better off. The psychologist said he would have been institutionalized for a long time... because of the hallucinations. We don't have a lot of money. I don't know how I would have paid for that kind of care. I want to say how grateful we are for WCI to honor his life insurance. We weren't sure what would happen since it was a suicide. The doctors said he was insane and not responsible. So we got the entire amount."

"Good. It's comforting to know you will be taken care of. You keep saying we. Aren't you alone?" He was not aware of any other family.

"Oh, no, I have a daughter. She has been living with her father, but she's moving back home with me. She's twenty-three."

He nodded. "Good, then you won't be alone. Listen, I have Bill's personal things in a box at the office. When would be a good time to bring them by?"

"How kind of you to offer. Most anytime would be okay, but please call first. I wouldn't want you to make a trip just to find no one home."

"Sure." He was about to say goodbye when they were joined by a young lady, similarly dressed.

"Hi, are you a friend of daddy Bill's?" Her voice was raspy and sensuous… exciting.

"Trudi, this is Mr. Brickhauer, Bill's boss at work," Alicia announced.

Brick was speechless, in awe of her captivating beauty.

"How do you do?" She offered a gloved hand. "Thanks for coming." Her skin was flawless except for the tattoo. At the junction of her cleavage, was a small image of a devil, complete with horns and a pitchfork, done in red ink. Brick couldn't take his eyes off it.

"That's LSD," she said softly, smiling. "The little guy you're looking at."

"LSD?" he managed to squeak, embarrassed.

"Lucifer, Satan, the Devil... LSD. He's my buddy!" she said, still smiling.

Brick didn't know what to say, so he said nothing, continuing to stare. She took a large breath, causing LSD to grow somewhat. "We're having people over for coffee and such. Would you care to come?"

He forced himself to tear his eyes away from her chest and looked into her face. "Thanks, ah... Trudi, but I have to get back to work. I will be bringing some of Bill's belongings over one of these days, though. I'll take a rain-check on the coffee," he blurted, thinking he sounded like an infatuated teenager.

"Good, I'll look forward to seeing you then." She turned and looked at a group of others standing near by. "Mother, we must go. They're waiting." And then they were gone. Gone, but certainly not forgotten.

For the next week, he had been frequently tormented with the images of Alicia and Trudi, not really knowing what to make of it all, enthralled by their obvious sensualities. On Friday, he summoned up enough nerve to make the call.

"Alicia, hi. This is Brick. How are you doing today?"

"Mr. Brickhauer, how nice of you to call. We're doing okay... trying to get on with our lives."

"Yes, I'm sure it's not been easy. Listen, is this evening a good time to bring Bill's personal things by? If not, we can make it later." He held his breath, hoping it would not be later.

"Oh, yes, this evening would be fine. What time did you have in mind?"

"Well, if I leave here around five, I should be able to be at your place by five-thirty."

"All right, Mr. Brickhauer. We'll expect you then. Good bye."

He had pulled up in front of the house and retrieved the box with Bill's things from the back seat. A couple of photographs, a name plate, a calculator... not much of a man's life...nothing of value. The door opened before he could knock and Alicia was there.

"Hi, Mr. Brickhauer, it's so sweet of you to do this."

"Oh, the least I could do, Alicia. I'm afraid there's not much here."

"Thank you, I'll go through it later." She took the box from his hands and set it in the hallway. "Please, come in... Trudi went to put some coffee on. Remember?"

"Oh, you don't have to go to any trouble," Brick said, pleased they had remembered.

"No trouble at all. Please, have a seat." She indicated the couch. "We can use the company. We don't get many handsome men coming to our house." Her smile was warm and friendly, and he could hear no chanting nor any smell of incense. He took the opportunity to look her over. She was tastefully dressed in a tight fitting business suit which accented her shapely figure... a very attractive woman indeed. She sat opposite of him and asked, "How have you been, Mr. Brickhauer?"

"I've been fine... but I must insist that you call me Brick. Every one I know calls me Brick."

"Well, then, I guess I should as well. Brick it is." She paused for a minute. "Are you married, Brick?" She had asked that before.

"Yes. Nearly eight years now."

"Happily?"

"Well, yes, I think so."

"You don't know?" She was toying with him, a smirk on her face.

"Well, yes… happily," he affirmed.

"Yeah, right." She laughed. "Well, we'll see about that." She stood. "I'm going to change. I just returned from an appointment. I don't normally dress this formal. I'll be right back."

"Of course," he replied, awkwardly.

A moment after she had left the room, Trudi entered carrying a tray of cups and a coffee pot. "Hi, Mr. Brickhauer. Nice to see you again!"

He couldn't respond. He could only stare. She was wearing cut-off jean shorts so short the cheeks of her buttocks were nearly completely in view, and a white t-shirt so thin one could have read a newspaper through the fabric. She was bare under the shirt, nipples hard and commanding attention.

"Oh, hi… Trudi." He swallowed, eyes glued to her chest.

"Shall I pour?" she asked, smiling at the look on his face. "Would you like cream?" She shook her upper body, her huge breasts bouncing from side to side.

"I don't use… cream," he managed, confused and disoriented.

"Okie dokie!" She bent and poured a cup partially full and offered it to his shaking hands. Then she stood and proudly stuck out her chest. "You like my little devil? What do you think?" She pulled the shirt down to expose the red Satan.

He couldn't answer. He had never been in a situation such as this and was totally not in control. "Trudi… I don't know what to say…" He was interrupted by the re-appearance of Alicia. She was dressed in the same red robe as when they had first met.

"Brick, sit back and relax. We are going to entertain you." She untied the robe and let it slip to the floor. She was naked.

"You got to be kidding me," was all he could muster.

# CHAPTER SIX

It was three o'clock on Saturday afternoon and the four WCI team members of the China Connection were waiting in the United Airlines terminal at O'Hare International Airport for the arrival of flight #134 from San Francisco.

"I hope this fricken flight is on time! I got things to do tonight!" Brick offered.

*I'm sure you do*, Martin thought, remembering the scene at the Mexican restaurant. Out loud, he said, "Yeah, it would be nice to get them all tucked in at the hotel and get home at a decent time."

"I'd vote for that," Donnelly chimed in.

"Can you imagine how excited they must be... their first trip anywhere, not to mention the United States?" Martin commented.

"Yeah, I remember how I felt when we went to China, and I was used to traveling!" Donnelly added.

"Is their flight on time?" Brick's focus was not on the Chinese. He glanced at his watch, obviously worried about what time he would get to leave.

"Yes, so says the monitor. They should be on the ground in fifteen minutes," Donnelly stated.

"Good... good deal! Let's get this show on the road!"

"What have you got going tonight?" Martin asked innocently.

"Oh, I... I promised to meet some people... later. Some old friends."

"I suppose Peggy is joining you?"

"Well, no. Actually, she is visiting her mother in St. Louis. She doesn't know these people anyway. Why do you ask?" Brick was suspicious.

"Carole wanted to meet the Chinese. I just thought she could pick up Peggy and meet us at the hotel." It was not a complete lie. Carole had said she wanted to meet the Chinese.

"Well, we'll have to do it later," Brick answered.

"Why don't we bring the wives to the welcome banquet on Tuesday night? I'm sure my wife would enjoy meeting the Chinese as well," Donnelly offered.

"Include me in," Jackman responded.

"Good idea. Let's do it!" Martin said.

"Yes, of course," Brick answered hesitantly.

*This ought to be interesting*, Martin thought. A few minutes later the monitor announced that United flight 134 had landed. Through the not so clean window, the four men watched in silence as the huge 747 pulled up to the gate.

With David Choi in the lead, the Chinese were the last to appear in the jet way door. Obviously, they all had been seated in the rear of the aircraft. David looked tired and a little wrinkled but was smiling from ear to ear. The Chinese looked much worse, as if they had been wearing the same clothes for days. Later, Martin discovered this to be true... four days to be exact.

Some of the faces were recognizable from their earlier trip to

China. Many were not. They exchanged handshakes and a few hugs.

David approached Martin, hand outstretched. "Martin... so good to see you! You look well!"

"David. Good to see you too. How was the trip?"

"Damned mainlanders," he smiled "Driving me nuts! Questions, questions, questions. They've never see anything like this before. They don't understand... I had to show them how to piss in the airplane toilet! One got lost in San Francisco for over an hour!"

Martin laughed. "Okay, friend. We're here to help. Let's go get the luggage."

The walk from the United terminal to baggage claim must have been like visiting Disney Land to the Chinese. The snack shops, the bars, the newsstands, the moving walkways, the ever-changing neon lights on the ceiling... how strange all this must seem to them. A far cry from the dismal Beijing airport.

When the luggage started arriving on the belt, the Americans discovered there were twenty-eight identical large suitcases belonging to the group... same color, same size.

"Can you believe this?" Donnelly asked. "All alike, all new. Must not have any luggage of their own."

"Of course not. These people have never traveled anywhere in their whole life. Why would they have luggage?" Martin responded.

"You're right. I just never thought about it."

Martin had rented four vans, three for passengers and one for the luggage. He, Jack and Reif were to drive the Chinese. Brick had insisted on driving the luggage van, and took off for the hotel as soon as it was loaded. Martin knew that would be the last he saw of him for the night.

David jumped into the front passenger seat of the van Martin was driving.

"You ready?" Martin asked.

"Does our hotel have a bar?" David asked.

"Yeah, sure."

"Great! I sure could use a drink!"

"Okay, I'll even buy!"

The traffic was light as they pulled out on I-294 and headed south to I-5. One of the Chinese asked a question in Mandarin. "What did he say?" Martin asked David.

"He wants to know, where are all your people?"

Martin grinned, remembering his amazement at seeing the hoards of Chinese everywhere at all hours of the day when they were in China. "Tell him it is Saturday. Most people are home resting or having fun."

David relayed the information. Another had a question. "Where are all the bicycles? Do they have special streets to ride on?"

Martin laughed out loud. "In America we use bicycles only for fun. Here, everyone has a car." There was a buzz of talking. Martin wished he understood more Mandarin. A young man spoke in broken English.

"I am interpreter from Xiamen. My people have many questions. Can I talk for them?"

"Of course," Martin responded. Then the dam broke.

"Why is there no farm animals eating the grass along the highway?

"How many families live in that house?"

"Why is there no farm animals around the houses?"

"How many cars do you have?"

"How much they cost?"

"Do all Americans have guns?"

"How much they cost?"

"How many square meters in house?"

"Where are all your markets?"

"Do you drive car every day?"

"Where are your soldiers?"

"Where is government house?"

"Where is White House?"

"Can we see it?"

"Is this your car?"

"Do you need permission from government to rent car?"

"How many children you have?"

"How many children does government let you have?"

"How do you keep roads so clean?"

"Where can we buy rice?"

"Where are your farms?"

By the time they arrived at the motel, it was obvious that the Chinese were in just as much culture shock as the Americans were a few months earlier in their country. All three vans experienced the same questions.

The Best Western motel was a moderate facility... nothing exceptionally fancy, but it was well lit, clean, and had a nice restaurant as well as cocktail lounge. The Chinese were very excited, yelling and pointing as they were getting out of the vans. "What's going on?" I asked David.

"They think this is some kind of a palace, like a picture in a magazine." David replied.

The lobby was nicely decorated with a large circular sofa surrounding a ten-foot high bouquet of silk flowers. The group fell into an eerie silence, obviously waiting for something of importance to happen. Some sat on the sofa, some sat on the steps leading to a second story. After a few minutes, a door marked 'Private' opened and a very well dressed Asian lady emerged. She confronted the group and spoke the Mandarin equivalent for hello, "Nee how, mah!"

The silence ended abruptly...the group surprised to hear one of their own. "I am Mrs. Liu," she continued in Mandarin. "I can speak Cantonese very well, but I am not so good in Mandarin. However, I will do the best I can."

The four Americans had no idea what she was saying. David whispered that he would fill them in later. She continued.

"I am from Hong Kong... but many years ago. These gentlemen who have brought you here are from one of the most prestigious companies in America. I am honored they have chosen my hotel for you to stay in. At your request, to save you some money, we have assigned three persons to a room. I hope you will find the accommodations comfortable. All the rooms are in the second building behind this one. This way, you will all be together. All rooms have cable TV with CNN and HBO. The restaurant is in this building, to my left. The cocktail lounge is to my right. You will see that we have an indoor pool that is open until nine each night. Once you have your keys, collect your bags and go ahead to your room and relax. I would like to meet with your leaders in my office in one hour to discuss room rates and food arrangements. Welcome to America and to my hotel. Any questions?"

Mr. Liu was not prepared for what came next.

"What are keys for?" A small fellow near the front asked.

"The keys are to open the door to your room. You should always keep them locked."

"We are allowed to keep our own keys?"

"Yes, of course. Try not to lose them. There is a charge to replace them."

"How much is the charge?"

"Five U.S. dollars."

"Ieeee! You keep keys!" The room was abuzz with thirty Chinese all talking at once. David interrupted. "Gentlemen! Ladies! This is a usual custom in the United States. The keys are your responsibility! Just take care of them. This way, you can come and go as you like. I know you are not allowed to have keys at a Chinese hotel, but remember, you are not in China!"

One of the older members addressed the group. "Don't act as if you are a water buffalo. We are in a strange country. We will do as we are told unless I say different. Understand?" This silenced the group.

"May we ask more questions, Laoban?"

"Yes."

"Mrs. Liu, what is cable TV?"

She began to get frustrated. "Cable TV means you can get many different programs."

"Are any of the programs in Chinese?"

"No, I'm afraid not."

"What is CNN and aich-b-o?"

"CNN is a program which reports news from all over the world?"

"News from China?"

"No, not so much. Your government controls what news comes

out of China." This caused a disapproving look from the obvious leader. "HBO is a channel which shows movies all the time. American movies."

One of the ladies asked, "Where do we get water after nine o'clock?"

"What?"

"You say pool is open until nine only. Where do we get water after pool closes?"

Mrs. Liu shook her head. "Oh, no, you don't use the pool for water... it's to swim in... for fun. There is water in your room for drinking and for bathing." At this point, Mrs. Liu was beginning to wonder what planet these people were from.

"How often do you bring hot water bottle?"

"Hot water bottle...?"

David interrupted. "People, listen. Again... this is America. You can drink the water that comes from the faucets in your room. There are two faucets... one for cold water and one for hot water. You can make tea with the hot water, and you can get a cold drink from the other. You will see when you get to your room." Heads were starting to nod in understanding. "Now, when your name is called, please come forward and get your key and take your suitcase to your room."

The rest of the procedure went fairly smooth and, finally, the Chinese were on their way to their rooms. David repeated the questions to the Americans and the four had a good laugh.

"Martin, where is that drink?" David asked.

"You do look absolutely exhausted, David. How about you guys... want a drink?"

"No, not for me. I've got to be getting home." Reif responded.

"Thanks, Martin, but Bernice is waiting on me. I best be going. I'll see you guys here Monday morning. 7:15?"

"Yes, 7:15. Have a good Sunday," Martin said.

Brick had arrived at the hotel a good fifteen minutes before the other three vans. Quickly, he unloaded the luggage by the entry door and headed the van back toward the rental company. Here he dropped the keys in a night slot, retrieved his personal car and headed north. He dialed a number on his mobile phone.

"Trudi, honey. Brick. I'm on the way. Be there in half an hour."

"Oh, goodie. We've got some videos."

"Videos? That ought to be interesting." He grinned. Adult movies. This ought to be fun! "See you in a bit." The thoughts of the two women and the videos... wow! He increased his speed.

Martin and David were sipping their drinks, enjoying the dim lights and the soft music in the lounge. It was still early and the bar was nearly deserted.

"Man, I needed this," David said, sipping his Jack Daniels. "I'm beat! Where is Brick?"

"He had more important plans for tonight, I guess."

"Really? What would be more important than this?"

Martin shrugged, "I don't know." He decided to change the subject. "How have you been, David?"

"Good. Things are going good. The Chinese were very impressed with your training in China. I think we have a very good relationship going."

"That's good news," Martin replied.

Brick pulled up in front of the Strickner house at 7:15. He quickly ran up the stairs and rang the door bell. The door opened almost immediately.

"Hi, Brickie!" Trudi said. "Get yourself in here!" She threw open the door and stepped back so he could enter. She was dressed in a bright red robe. "Please, sit." She motioned toward the couch. "Drink?"

"Sure. Great!"

"Mom will be back in a minute. She had to run an errand." She fixed a scotch on the rocks and handed it to Brick. "Did your Chinese get here?"

The question surprised him. He didn't remember telling them that the Chinese were coming this weekend. He must have, though.

"Yeah, they're here."

Alicia picked that time to come through the door. "Hi, Brick! Good to see you again!" She walked over to him and gave him a sensuous kiss on the lips. "Are you ready for tonight? Are you rested up?"

He smiled. "Yes, I'm ready. I'm more than ready!"

"Okay… let me go get undressed. I'm getting excited! Trudi, go ahead and start without me."

Trudi stood and removed the robe. She wore a transparent red bra and thong panties. "Okay, Brickie, get out of them clothes."

A few minutes later, they were fondling each other on the couch when Alicia entered. "Okay, Brick… time to watch a movie!"

"I'm for that," he said, excitedly.

She put a tape in the VCR and pushed play. The first images on the TV were of Alicia and Trudi, nude, rubbing their private parts, and blowing kisses.

"Oh, I didn't know these would be home movies. This is great!"

"You think? You ain't seen nothin', yet!"

Suddenly, the screen was full of a man receiving oral sex, close up. The female partner was Trudi. The camera pulled back for a wider picture and Brick nearly fainted. The man receiving the attention was himself.

"What the hell...? When...?" His erection quickly faded. Trudi laughed. He tried to stand and reach for his clothes.

"Sit down, Brick. Don't you want to see the rest?" Alicia smiled.

"No, I don't. I think I'd better leave!" He was sick. Literally sick, barely able to control the urge to vomit.

"Why... why would you record this?" he squeaked.

"We have our reasons. You see, we want you to participate with our group," Alicia spoke. "In our worship services."

"Worship service? What kind of worship service?" His naked body was becoming cold, and he shivered.

"Satan," Trudi offered. "Remember... LSD?" she pointed between her breasts.

"No way! No way!"

"Sure you will... if you don't want your wife to see this tape. Or, maybe your boss... you think he would like it?" Alicia was smiling.

Suddenly, the nausea was gone... replaced by a strong desire to sleep.

"Did you drug me?" he managed, barely able to hold his head up.

"Yes. We're going to make more movies."

"More movies?" he muttered.

"Of course! You know, if you would like to commit suicide… sacrifice your self for Satan… we would help! That would be wonderful!"

He was barely conscious, but his confused mind understood her words. *What can I do*, was his last thought before blacking out.

When he awoke, he was fully dressed, sitting in his car, the keys in the ignition. He glanced at the darkened house where he had been a few hours before and shuddered. Filled with disgust and fear, he still felt a little groggy as he started the car and quickly headed for home.

*They set me up. I should have known they were too good to be true.* One thing was very clear. He had made a monumental mistake by getting involved with them. A life- changing mistake.

By the time he arrived home he was fully recovered from the drugs. He pulled the car into the garage and went directly to the closet and retrieved his luggage. *My life here is ruined*, he thought. *Eventually, they'll show the tape, no matter what I do. I have two choices… leave or kill myself, and they would like that! That only leaves one choice really. I've got to go where nobody can ever find me. That won't be easy either.*

He packed as much as could into three large bags and loaded them in the car. *Should I leave a note? No, I'll call her later. I'll need money… enough to start over somewhere. Okay, you can call Greg Mathews and have him wire you some money on Monday. In the meantime, you've got four or five credit cards you can get cash advances on. Where to go? West… go west. Get on I-80 and go west. Take a shower... you stink. Okay, passport. In the briefcase at the office. You can get it on the way.*

Forty-five minutes later, he was on I-80 heading west. By the time Peggy returned home on Sunday night, he was in Rapid City, South Dakota.

# CHAPTER SEVEN

Martin pulled the van into the lot at the hotel at ten till seven on Monday morning. Donnelly's van was already in the lot. He walked into the entrance of the restaurant and saw him sitting in a large booth with a cup of coffee in his hand.

"Morning, Jack. How's the coffee?"

"Good, Martin, very good. We may be a little late getting to the plant. The Chinese haven't come in for breakfast yet."

Mrs. Liu approached and sat down. "Good morning, fellows."

"Good morning. How are things going?" Martin asked.

"So, so," she shrugged. "Not so good, really."

"What's wrong?"

"Your Chinese don't want to eat my breakfast. They say it's too expensive."

"Really? I'll have a talk with them," Martin replied. David Choi entered the restaurant and sat down next to Jack.

"David... have a good rest?" Jack asked.

"Hell no! There was somebody pounding on my door every ten minutes with another stupid question! Have I got time to eat?"

"Sure... go ahead and order," Martin replied.

He ordered eggs benedict and orange juice. "Any chance of moving me to another hotel?"

"Sure, if you want. You're on your own expense account," Martin answered. "There's a Holiday Inn down the street."

"No Hilton or Marriott or anything like that?"

"None close by, I'm afraid."

"Okay... Holiday Inn it is."

Mr. Chung, the interpreter from Xiamen, approached. "Good morning. My leaders ask me to tell you we are ready to leave."

"Okay, Mr. Chung. Did you have a good breakfast?" Martin inquired.

"Oh, yes. We fix in room," he beamed.

"Very well. We shall meet you all in the lobby in a few minutes. Thank you."

As the young man walked away, Martin turned to Mrs. Liu. "Do you have cooking facilities in the room?"

"No, we don't. Interesting, isn't it?"

"Yes. Wonder what they are doing?"

"I'll find out later. Martin, why don't all you guys call me Susan. We don't have to be so proper, do we?"

"Susan it is." David's food arrived.


The drive to the plant took about twenty minutes. Again, the Chinese were full of questions about the strange sights they were seeing. Martin was thoroughly enjoying himself. It was like taking a group of school children to their first zoo visit. As they approached the entrance to the plant, they were greeted by the facility manager and all of the department heads... arranged by Brick weeks ago. It was appropriate to place the proper importance on their visit. Martin was quick to notice that Brick was not among them.

In the classroom, the plant manager was giving a welcome speech, interpreted by David Choi. There were two additional speakers scheduled, so Martin had a little time. He headed to Brick's office to see what was going on.

It was obvious that he had not come to work. He checked with the department secretary and she had not seen him, nor had he called. Martin was perplexed... and pissed off. He went to his own office to retrieve the schedule for the Chinese. As he was unlocking his desk, the phone rang.

"Martin Maquire. How may I help you?"

"Martin... Peggy. Have you... have you seen Brick?" She was crying.

"No, Peggy, not since Saturday night. What's going on?"

"I'm not sure... he's gone. I came home yesterday afternoon and he was gone. Most of his clothes are gone... and his car." She sniffed. "I... I think he's left me!" she sobbed.

Martin was in shock. He didn't know what to say.

"I waited all night for him to come home... or at least call."

"Peggy, I have no idea where he could have gone. No one here at work has seen him either. What do you want me to do?"

"I don't know. I guess call me if you hear anything." The line went dead. Martin slowly hung up the phone, thinking. Then he called Brick's boss at the corporate office in the city.

Mr. Peterlie's office," his secretary answered.

"Hi, Doris, Martin Maguire here. Is Richard available?"

"Just a moment, Martin." There were a couple of clicks.

"Martin! Your Chinese get here alright?" Peterlie asked excitedly. "I'll be there in an hour to do my talk."

"The Chinese are fine, Richard, but we do have a problem. Brick has disappeared. Peggy said he's packed up and left. She doesn't know where."

"He's not at work?"

"No, sir. Nobody here has seen anything of him."

"That doesn't sound like Brick. Can you handle everything?"

*I have been for quite some time*, Martin thought. "Yes, sir, that won't be a problem. Don't worry about the program."

"Good, Martin, good. I'll see you in a little while. Thanks for calling."

The morning went off as planned. Richard Peterlie arrived and did his thing, and then Martin introduced the day's instructors and the training began. Richard called Peggy from Brick's office and offered his support. There wasn't much anyone could do until they heard from Brick. They agreed to keep in touch. Then Peterlie called Martin into the office and closed the door.

"I don't know what the hell is going on with Brick, but he better have a damn good explanation. This Chinese thing is very important. If we do this right, it will open the door to the largest potential new market in the world. Martin, can you pull this off without him?"

"Richard, yes I can. There is something I need to tell you. Brick has not been himself lately. I think he is having an affair... I know he's having an affair. He's lost all interest in what's going on here. I have planned most of the program with Donnelly and Jackman. Brick didn't have much to do with it."

Peterlie nodded. "I see. Okay, then, is there anything you need?"

"Yes, I need some additional sign line authority... to spend some company money. Brick usually took care of the expenses, but with him gone..."

"Of course. I'll stop by accounting on my way out. Do what you need to do and keep me informed. If you hear from Brick, tell him to call me, and then you call me. Good luck. We'll talk soon." With that, he stood, shook hands and left.

Martin looked around Brick's office. His briefcase was missing, along with the cardex phone file and a picture of Peggy. He's been here, that's for sure, but he didn't leave in a panic... nobody was chasing him.

He heard the phone ring in his office. Quickly, he walked the thirty feet and picked up the receiver.

"Martin Maguire."

"Martin, Susan Liu. I've got some news... not good, though. Your Chinese are tearing up my hotel!" He couldn't help notice that she referred to them as "his Chinese."

"What's going on?"

"Well, I knew they had gone to a convenience mart Sunday, but I didn't know what they bought. Brace yourself. They bought big foot tubs to take baths in because they don't know how to use the showers. Also, they bought Sterno fuel and cooking pots for rice. Those things have burned holes in the bathroom vanities of nearly every room. There is water everywhere, as a result of taking baths in the tubs, and it's leaking through to the rooms below. The ceiling tiles are falling down. The maids are refusing to clean the rooms because there is soiled toilet paper in the wastebaskets. Apparently, they don't know to flush it down with the rest of the ... stuff. If that's not enough, I got more!"

Martin smiled. "Susan… it's okay. We'll take care of any repairs the Chinese won't pay for. Don't worry. But, we have to do something… they can't keep doing these things."

"I know. I'm working on a how and how not to list. I'll go over it with them tonight. I had no idea…"

"Hang in there, Susan. I'll talk to the interpreters as well."

"Thank you, Martin. Thank you very much."

As Martin was hanging up the phone, David Choi walked in.

"How's things going in the classroom?" Martin asked.

"Good! Your guys know their stuff. The Chinese are very pleased. By the way, I know who the *Party* guy is."

"What do you mean?"

"We were told in Hong Kong to expect one of the delegates to be a member of the Party, sent to spy on his colleagues and report back to Beijing any funny business. He's the one really in charge. Anyway, I know which one it is."

"How do you know?"

"He is the only one sleeping during the presentations. All the rest are taking notes and being very attentive. He sleeps." David wrote down a name.

"Okay, thanks. He was the one in charge at the hotel. Have Donnelly and Jackman come to the office, will you?"

"Sure. See you later. This is interesting." David was gone. A few minutes later Reif and Jack appeared.

"You called, old exalted substitute leader?" Donnelly started.

"Yeah, guys. Sit down. I got news."

"You mean like, where in the hell our irresponsible main leader has been hiding?" Donnelly asked bitterly. Reif remained silent.

Sometimes, Donnelly's sarcasm was a little too much for Martin. "Don't hold back, Jack. Let it all out, why don't you?" he said with a frown. "Brick's wife called. I guess he's packed his bags and left. She has no idea where he is. Peterlie is aware of the situation and he's put me in charge for the time being. If the Chinese ask about Brick, tell them he has been reassigned to another project. I'm going to need your help, since I'll have to spend more time making arrangements and less time doing actual training. You two will have to cover my part."

"I'm sorry, Martin," Donnelly said. "Don't worry, Reif and I will take care of it. We got you covered. Didn't mean to be an ass... well, yes I did, but I won't do it any more... well, maybe I will, but... oh hell, you know."

Martin smiled. "Yes, Jack, I know. Thanks." He told them about the damage at the hotel, and about David identifying the "Party Man", then sent them back to the classroom. Next, he called Visitor Services and arranged for a driver to replace him in the van. If he was going to take over Brick's responsibilities, he was going to take over Brick's privileges.

It was the second day of training and tonight was the night for the welcome banquet. Susan Liu had presented the Chinese with detailed written instructions on how to use the shower and the stool, also explaining it was against the fire code to cook in the rooms. She gave the group a better price for their meals and everyone was happy... for the time being. The banquet was being paid for by WCI and a lavish spread had been ordered.

Martin had showered and was getting dressed for the occasion.

Carole came into the room, wearing only a slip. "So, nobody's heard from Brick yet?" she asked.

"Nope, not yet." Martin donned a shirt and picked out a tie. He looked at his lovely wife in the mirror as she looked through the closet for the black dress... her special black dress.

"You sure are sexy tonight," he murmured.

"You think so?" She turned and looked at him in the mirror. "You're not so bad yourself, skinny butt."

"Thanks. Wanna skip this thing and go to bed? I'm getting' hard looking at you."

"No way! I want to meet your Chinese... especially the women." She slipped the black dress over her head.

"Well, you will certainly be the best looking girl there!"

"Aren't any of the Chinese ladies attractive?"

Martin smiled. "Only the one who owns the hotel. She is a very classy gal."

"She'll be there?"

"Yes, I'm sure. She's running the show." He turned and kissed her on the back of the neck.

"Good. I'll have somebody to talk to. Jack's wife is such a bore, and Reif's wife... she never got off the farm. Peggy is always pleasant, but I'm sure she won't be there."

They arrived at the hotel banquet room a half an hour early. Jack and Bernice Donnelly were already seated. The room was lavishly decorated with expensive flowers on each table. They said their hellos and Martin headed to the bar for drinks. When he returned, Mr. Chung was waiting for him.

"Meester Mag-ire, may I have word?"

"Of course, Chung. What is it?"

"Some of my colleagues... their clothes not so good... for banquet. Is okay if wear same clothes as in classroom?"

"Yes, sure! Mao wenti!" (no problem)  Martin noticed that Chung's belt was at least a foot too long. "Would you like me to cut that off for you?" he asked, pointing at the belt.

"Oh, no. Not necessary. Belt not belong to me. I must return it when we go back Beijing."

"The belt is not yours?" Martin was shocked.

Chung dropped his head. "Most of my people have not clothes suitable for western culture, so our government give us clothes for the trip. We must return them."

That explained the poor fitting and outdated wear most of the Chinese had been sporting. "Chung, tell your people that classroom clothes will be just fine."

"Thanks. I think our female members have been given party dress to wear. They much excited." He grinned. "I will return with group at proper time."

Martin proceeded back to the table. Jack joined him to help carry the drinks. "What was all that about?"

"Incredible. I'll tell you later. Did you bring the gifts for the group?"

"Yeah, they're in a box under the table."

Martin nodded his approval. He watched as Carole was pretending to pay close attention to the barrage of words flowing non-stop from Bernice's mouth. He smiled to himself. Jack totally ignored her jabber, no doubt a talent he had learned long ago.

"So what did you think of China, Jack? Did you learn anything?" Carole asked.

"Well, yes... a bit of Chinese philosophy, you might say."

"Really? Tell us!"

"Well, Confucius say... 'If son want to drive car, father should not stand in way!'"

The group broke into laughter. Jack beamed, proud of his joke, even if it was as old as dirt.

"Wow, is that one of your Chinese?" Carole interrupted.

Martin's head shot up. "No, that's Mrs. Liu. She owns the place."

She was stunning... dressed in a white silk full-length dress, slit to the hip, with a high neckline that circled her neck. Her jet black hair was striking against the white of the garment and her make-up was perfect.

Donnelly nearly fell off his chair. "Jesus..." was all he could muster. Bernice kicked him under the table.

"Good evening, ladies... and gentlemen. Welcome to my hotel. Does the room meet with your approval, Martin?"

"The room is very nice, Susan. Let me present my wife, Carole. And this is Bernice." Martin stood and made the introductions. "Would you care to join us?"

"I would be honored. So nice to meet you ladies." She lowered her head and curtseyed.

"Sit here." Carole indicated Martin's chair. "We can talk better that way." Gracefully, Martin moved over to another seat.

Susan sat and directed her attention to Carole. "How beautiful you are, my dear. I am envious. Your husband is a very lucky man."

"Thank you, Mrs. Liu," Carole responded, genuinely pleased.

"Oh, please, call me Susan. I am much too long in America to be called Mrs. Liu. Tell me what it is like to be the wife of a corporate executive. This hotel takes so much of my time, I seldom have an opportunity to talk to anyone outside the business. I am so pleased to make some new friends." There was no hint of sarcasm... only a genuine attempt to be friendly.

"Well, Susan, I don't know if we can classify my husband as an executive, but I will be glad to tell you all the bad things about him." Both women laughed.

The Chinese delegation picked that time to enter the room. Martin made introductions as best he could, unable to recall the names of the Chinese except for a few of the interpreters. Everyone was seated and dinner was served. The food was superb. Susan had arranged for a local Chinese restaurant to cater the affair with a mixture of traditional mainland food and some Americanized dishes for the *Gweilos* (Americans).

There was plenty of Tsing Tao beer and Great Wall wine. After dinner, the Chinese produced a few bottles of Mao Tai...liquor that tastes exactly like high octane jet fuel. The alcohol had a positive affect and some of the Chinese tried to experiment with the little English they knew. Martin was thoroughly enjoying himself.

Gifts were exchanged and, much to Martin's surprise, the Chinese had brought gifts for the American wives. The evening was a huge success.

On the drive home, Carole slid over next to him and laid her head on his shoulder. "That was fun. Thanks for taking me. They are such interesting people."

"Yes, they are," Martin agreed.

"And you were right about Susan. All class, that girl... and, so beautiful! I wish I looked that good. She didn't have a bra on, either. I saw you looking."

"Not much there, compared to you."

"Maybe not, but I saw you looking, none the less."

"Yes, she is attractive, but she can't hold a candle to you. You are perfect in that dress. I'm very horny!"

"What a nice thing to say... even if you are lying."

He wasn't lying. They never made it to the bedroom for their first encounter of the night, stripping off clothes as soon as they were in the house, and collapsing on the kitchen floor. Later, he carried her to their bed where they were much more gentle and loving for the second and third time.

Tuesday morning, Brick had Gregg Mathews wire him thirty thousand dollars to a bank in Rapid City, which he converted to cash and travelers checks. Then, he called Peggy.

"Yes?"

"Hi, it's me."

"Brick! Where are you? Are you okay?" She was frantic.

"Peg... just listen!" He had rehearsed this speech for two days. "Don't say anything."

"Brick..."

"Stop it! I'm fine. I'm just leaving, that's all. I've done something so utterly stupid and unforgiving that I can't face you or anyone else I know ever again. So, I'm running away. I'll start over. Get a divorce. I called our lawyer and told him to give you everything.

I'm sending him power of attorney so I don't even have to sign the papers. I took thirty thousand for me to start over. The rest is yours." He could hear her crying. "When you see the tape, you will know why I had to do this. Find someone who deserves you, I sure as hell don't."

"Tape? What tape?" she sobbed.

"I've got to go. Forget about me. I'm a total... worthless... asshole." He hung up. "Tomorrow, I'd better call Peterlie," he muttered, leaving the phone booth.

Wednesday was going along fine. The Chinese were in the classroom doing their thing and Martin was in his office making arrangements to take the group to the city on Saturday for sightseeing. In between calls, his phone rang.

"Martin, hi. It's Peggy."

"Peggy, you okay?" he asked in a gentle voice.

"Yes, I'm okay. Brick called." She paused, and Martin could tell she was on the verge of tears.

"And... is he okay?"

"He's leaving us... Martin. All of us. He said he did something very stupid and can't face anyone ever again. He told me to get a divorce."

"Jeez, Peg. I'm sorry. What can I do?"

"I don't know, Martin. Just be there if I need you, I guess. My mother is flying in from St. Louis tonight to be with me. I haven't had time to make any plans yet, but I thought I should call you."

"Sure, thanks. Can Carole do anything?"

"No, I'll be fine. I'll call you later. Bye."

"Bye, Peggy. I'm so sorry." He hung up slowly and then called Peterlie. After that, he closed his door and tried to imagine what the hell was going on. What would cause a man to do what Brick was doing... leave everything he had worked for his whole life... leave his wife. Whatever it was, it had to be bad. Very bad.

Saturday, they took the delegation to the city as planned. It was a good trip and every one enjoyed it immensely. When they returned to the hotel, Susan came out into the parking lot and asked him if he had time to talk in her office. Curiously, he followed her inside.

"You have a problem developing with one of the Chinese," she said, as soon as the door was closed.

"Oh? How so?"

"Last night, we had two single girls staying with us. Both were in their early twenties and very attractive. Your Mr. Chung joined them in the pool after dinner. The girls were wearing pretty skimpy bikinis and it was evident he had never seen anything like that in his homeland. At breakfast this morning, I overheard their leader having a rather stern conversation with him. He's been placed under house arrest, so to speak. He will be reported to his superiors when they return to China."

"Well, boys will be boys," Martin remarked.

"I think it is much more serious than that, Martin. Chung is in for a tough time. He will be seriously punished for his actions. Fraternizing with Westerners will more than likely land him in prison."

"No... you're kidding?"

"I'm not kidding! He doesn't live in America. I'm not sure there is anything you can do about it at this point. I just wanted you to be aware of it."

"Sure...thanks, Susan." Martin was lost in thought. He rose to leave. "Thank you... again."

# Chapter Eight

## Tuesday, two weeks later:

The delegation was scheduled to leave on a Thursday afternoon. On the morning trip to the factory, Mr. Chung handed a book to Donnelly and spoke in a very low voice.

"I borrow book from Mr. Maguire. Tell him thanks. Tell him to inspect page two hundred very carefully. Very important. Tell him. I can say no more or I will face music."

"Sure, Chung. No problem."

As soon as the Chinese were settled in the classroom, Donnelly took the book to Martin.

"You're supposed to look on page two hundred."

"What's on page two hundred?"

"I don't know. I wanted to look, but I didn't. I was hoping you would tell me."

Martin turned to the page. Scribbled in the top margin was the following.

*I must meet you in private. Life and death. 0945 in washroom. If I not alone, I contact you later. Chung*

"Shit!" Martin muttered.

"What?"

"I think we got big problems. Chung is in trouble with the Party and I think he is going to ask us for help."

"What did he do?"

"Screwed a couple of American girls, so I was told."

"So, what's the problem with that? Happens every day!"

"No problem for us... big problem if you are a Chinese national with a Party member watching you like a hawk. According to Susan, Chung will probably be sent to prison when he gets home."

"Jesus! What are you going to do?" Martin noticed he didn't ask what are <u>we</u> going to do.

"Well, I guess I'd better meet with him. Then I'll decide."

At nine-forty, Martin walked down the hall to the washroom. It was empty. A few minutes later, Chung entered, looking over his shoulder as he closed the door.

"Mr. Chung. What is this all about?"

"I know you not like this... but, I decide to defect... to America. I need you to help me." He was shaking like a leaf.

"Chung, this is not a good idea..."

"Please," he interrupted. "You must understand. I am in danger. You do not understand the dark side of the dragon. I will go to prison... or to death place when I return. I must defect! It is the only way!" He nervously looked at the door. "You must help. I ask you... officially."

Martin suddenly realized this was out of his league. He needed help as much as Chung. Remembering the list of dos and don'ts provided by the FBI concerning the sponsorship of foreign visitors, he knew what he had to do initially.

"Okay, Mr. Chung, follow me."

"They quickly walked down the hall to Martin's office where he retrieved a folder marked "FBI". Then they proceeded out to his personal car.

Martin returned an hour later to find his office full of people.

"There you are, boss," Donnelly spoke first. "This gentleman, Chang Siew Pang, has told David he will not go back to the classroom without Mr. Chung. Seems Chung went to the bathroom and never came back."

David spoke up. "I told him that there was nothing to be concerned about... that you had probably taken Chung back to the hotel for some reason. Perhaps he was not feeling well."

"Thanks, David. How much does this guy understand English?" Martin calmly walked over and sat behind his desk.

"He understands nothing... not a word."

"Okay... ask him why he wants to know about Chung."

"He is Party man, Martin. I told you..."

"I know he is, because you told me he is. I want to know what he is going to tell me. Ask him. Tell him I want to know what business it is of his as to where Chung is."

David spoke in mandarin. Chang Siew Pang showed no emotion. After a few seconds, he gave a lengthy answer to David.

"He says he does not have to answer your questions unless he chooses to do so, but he will answer this time. He is an official in the Communist Party. His responsibility is to bring all of his people home safe."

"Oh?" Martin slowly and deliberately opened the file in front of him. "That's funny. It says here that he is a welding engineer. Is this document falsified?"

David saw where he was going and smiled. He presented the question to Chang. This time Chang was unable to hide his feelings. His head snapped up and he stared at Martin with hatred.

He answered, his voice full of anger.

"He says he knows nothing of any documents."

"David… translate this exactly as I say it. Word for word. Tell him this document is from his government. It tells the background and reason for coming for each member of the delegation. If it is false, that could have serious consequences. My government does not like it when people lie to get admission into our country. His government said he was a weld engineer coming here to learn about weld technology. Is he a weld engineer or a Communist spy?"

David was loving it. He repeated word for word. Chang was livid. His face was beet red and his hands were shaking. He mumbled some Mandarin oaths under his breath.

"What did he say, David?" Martin never took his eyes off the Chinese man's face.

David smiled. "He said something that means you are a smart ass sonofabitch and he is wishing very bad things for you and your mother."

"Tell him my mother would spit in his eye. Then, ask him again… is he a weld engineer or a Communist spy."

David could hardly sit still as he repeated Martin's words. He couldn't remember when he'd had so much fun. Chang was sweating now, his black eyes boring holes into Martin's. Finally, he spoke, gritting his rotten teeth.

"He says…that perhaps he has made a mistake. He is not a Party guy. He is a weld engineer."

"Well, that's fine!" Martin let out his breath. "Then I think it would be a good idea for him to get back to the classroom… to learn what he came here for." He stood. "We're done here."

Mr. Chang sprang from his chair and headed out the door. David followed, nearly dancing as they went down the hallway.

Donnelly had been sitting quietly, watching the entire scene with an open mouth. As soon as the Chinese were out the door, he looked at Martin.

"That was brilliant! Simply fucking brilliant!

"Well, it ain't over... not by a long shot. I just bought us some time, that's all."

"Is Chung defecting?"

"That's what he wants."

"Where is he?"

"In a hotel, Jack. That's all I can say until after I meet with the FBI. They'll be here in an hour."

"Okay. I understand. God, I'm glad you're handling this. Brick would be a fucking basket case!"

"Yeah, well, I might be too before this is all over."

"Somehow, I don't think so, Martin." Donnelly had found a new level of respect for his friend.

When Martin and Mr. Chung had left the factory, Martin called Susan Liu from his mobile phone to bring Chung's suitcase, which he had secretly packed the night before, to the front desk. "So, he's actually defecting?" she had asked.

"I can't talk about that. Just have the suitcase at the front desk," he had answered.

Next, he called Peterlie and told him what was happening. Richard was almost frantic. Then he called the first name on the

FBI list he had been issued, a Mr. D.A.Brice. After giving Martin instructions, Brice set up a meeting at the plant at twelve noon with Peterlie and Martin.

Peterlie showed up a bit early, upset and nervous as hell. "Jesus Christ, Martin, what are we doing about this guy? This could be an international incident! We must protect WCI's interest in this matter. Why does this guy want to defect?" They were seated in Brick's office. "Man, I don't need this shit!" he panted, wiping his face with a handkerchief. "Talk to me!" he ordered.

"Richard, the guy says he's in trouble. He's terrified. He thinks he has no choice but to defect. I had no choice, either. I had to follow the FBI guidelines!"

"FBI guidelines? What guidelines? I didn't know we had such a thing!"

"Well, we do. Our chief of security got them for us months ago. At the time we all thought it a bit of overkill. Obviously, we were wrong."

"I want a copy of those guidelines! What did you do?"

"I can't discuss it with anyone until the FBI gets here. In fact, I think he's here now." A tall, well-dressed man in a dark suite was talking to the secretary. She pointed to Brick's office. Martin walked out to greet him.

"Mr. Brice?" he asked, extending his hand.

"Yes. Martin Maguire?"

"Yes, please come in. This is our Vice President of Asian Affairs, Richard Peterlie." As soon as they were all seated, Brice spoke first.

"Gentlemen, I know you must have a hundred questions, and

we'll get to them. But first... let me make sure I know what is going on. We have a Chinese interpreter from the mainland who wants to defect. I know Martin has stashed him in the hotel where we instructed and, I can tell you, he is being interviewed at this very moment. Martin, tell me how this all came down."

He filled the two of them in, being careful to not leave out any details. He was particularly detailed about the exchange with the Party snoop, Chang, describing the incident nearly word for word. Brice was impressed.

"Good job, Martin! That's thinking on your feet! Even though you thought you were bluffing, you were exactly right. If he had admitted to being here under false pretenses, we could have revoked his visa and sent his ass packing back to China." Brice looked at Peterlie. "Very bright man you have here, sir. Maybe I'll hire him to go to work for the bureau!"

"Well, Mr. Brice, I haven't worked with Martin long, but I think you're right. He is a very bright young man. We're lucky to have him. Where do we go from here?"

"Our guys, along with a CIA agent, will investigate to see if your Mr. Chung meets the criteria for political asylum. If he does, you will have no further contact with him. However, if he does not fit the template, he will be returned to his group to go back to China."

"You mean you may not let him stay?" Martin was surprised. That hadn't occurred to him. This is America! Anyone can stay here!

"Oh, yes. A very few people who try to defect are actually accepted. You must understand, this is a great risk we take. Other countries, especially communist ones, don't like it when we keep one of their own. Diplomatic relationships can become quite strained. He must have something we want... special skills or specific knowledge... something that will make the risk worthwhile. Otherwise, we will return him, or her, as fast as the proverbial hot potato."

Peterlie interrupted, "So, what you're saying is, either way, WCI is out of the picture? The decisions will be made by your people?" He had heard the magic words.

"Exactly. Frankly, I doubt this guy has anything we would want. He'll probably be sent back by the weekend."

"He's dead if you do, isn't he?" Martin asked, solemnly.

"Unfortunately, that's probably true. His government will most likely deal with him severely."

"Now, Martin, that's not our concern," Peterlie said quickly.

"I understand how you feel, Richard, but you haven't spent the last three weeks becoming this guy's friend. He's their main interpreter, our main communication link. We trust him, and he trusted me..."

"Well, we have no choice in the matter. We have to abide by whatever these guys say, morally right or not. Perhaps this Mr. Chung should have considered this before he came to you with this idea to defect. You shouldn't feel guilty... you followed the guidelines. You acted exactly as you should have."

"Yes, I agree," Brice added. "You did exactly as you were told."

Martin knew they were right, but that didn't help him to feel any better. "Okay, then what do we tell the Chinese?"

"Tell them that Chung has been taken to a hospital for treatment of an acute stomach problem. Tell them he is feeling better and should return to the group in a couple of days... in time to return to China."

"Okay, Mr. Brice, I've got to run," Peterlie said. "I'll walk you out. Martin, I'll call you later today." The two men shook hands with Martin and left.

Martin went to the classroom and made the announcement. Most of the Chinese seemed to accept the explanation. Mr. Chang, of course, knew differently.

When he returned to his office, he called Carole and told her he would be home late. He had some things he had to take care of.


As soon as the Chinese were taken back to the hotel, Party man Chang placed a call to Beijing. A sleepy voice answered the call.

"Wei..."

"I am Chang Siew Pang. I must speak to the inspector."

"But, esteemed sir, he is still sleeping. Please place your call later."

"Don't you hang up, you worthless piece of dog shit! I am calling from the land of the barbarians! The inspector will talk to me... now! Wake him up or I will see that your mother drowns in your blood!"

"Oh, yes, Your Highness! Mao wenti! I will get him quickly!"

A few minutes later, inspector Wong's groggy voice came on the line. "What is it Chang... so fornicating important that you have disturbed my sleep?"

"We have a defector. Our Mr. Chung, the interpreter from Xiamen. He has disappeared and the barbarians are hiding him."

"Curse the gods!" He was fully awake now. "What does he have that they want? What is his value?"

"Nothing... that I am aware of." Chang was caught off guard. That question surprised him. "He was caught fornicating with the foreign devil cows and I suspect he is afraid of what I will do when he returns."

"Hmm. Well, now he has good reason to be afraid. Defect? From the Middle Kingdom? From the Motherland? How stupid. The white cows have poisoned his mind! You are sure he is of no value to the barbarians?"

"Yes, he is nothing."

"So then, he is only scared. They will return him to you as soon as they find out he is worthless. Then, you will return him to me. I will get great pleasure from his death."

"Yes. Perhaps you will let me help in some way. He has caused me great embarrassment and loss of face."

"You have lost more than face... you have failed in your mission! You call me if they do not return him... but not in the middle of the night, you ass gas!" The phone went dead.

Chang was not happy. He should have known the Americans would return Chung. He didn't think it through. He was too upset at Martin for getting the best of him. "Perhaps I will cut off his stalk of life before I give him up to die!" he muttered.

Martin left the plant, made a quick stop at his bank, and then drove to the hotel where he had left young Chung. *I hope he is still there*, he thought, frightened that the FBI might have taken him back to the Best Western.

He knocked on the door and was relieved when he saw the peephole darken. Then the door opened and Chung's face appeared.

"Martin! I am scared until I see it is you. Please, come in."

Chung closed the door and faced him. He was nearly in tears. "They won't let me stay. I must go back." He was shaking with fear.

"I know. They told me earlier that they most likely would not let you stay."

"I will be executed. I have committed treason."

"Are you sure?"

"Yes. I am sure. We were all warned about our behavior with American girls. I was foolish. If I not try to defect, then maybe only prison... but now... surely death."

Martin was lost in thought for a minute. "Not if you don't go back," he said softly.

"What do you mean? They say I can't stay!"

"Run, Mr. Chung. Run like hell. You can speak English. Go to San Francisco and hide. There are people there... your people... who can help you. I have spoken with Mrs. Liu. She has some names..."

For a fleeting moment there was a glimmer of hope in his eyes before the despair returned. "There are people there... but how can I get there? I have no means..."

"Fly! You are a free man here... to do as you wish, as long as the FBI is not involved. You have a visa! Go tonight. Buy a ticket and go. Tonight. No one will tell your leaders where you are. I'll take you to the airport."

"But, I have no money!"

"Yes you do." Martin handed him an envelope. "Here is two thousand dollars. It's a loan. Pay me back when you can."

He accepted it with shaking hands. "Why do you do this? I am nothing to you." He really didn't understand.

"You are my friend. That's enough."

"I owe you my life," He said, with bowed head.

"You owe me two thousand dollars, that's all."


Three days later, the training was over and the Chinese delegation returned to Beijing... without one interpreter from Xiamen. Martin told no one what he had done, not even Carole. Mrs. Liu was the only other person who knew. Everyone assumed Chung had run away on his own and it was easy to let them think that. The FBI wasn't very interested... happy to make it a case for immigration when the visa expired.

Martin told the delegation that Chung had applied for asylum but had been denied. There was no response. They had all been warned and Chung's name was never spoken again. On the following Monday, Martin received a post card with a picture of the Golden Gate Bridge. On the back were two words:

*"Nice place."*

It was enough. He knew Chung had found help. It was a good feeling.

Brick had called Peterlie and officially resigned from WCI. A few days later, Peterlie made a visit to see Martin. They met in the hall.

"Let's go into Brick's office," he suggested. Inside, he turned and closed the door.

He pointed to the chair behind the desk. "Try that out, Martin... see if it fits your ass. I want you to take over Brick's job."

Martin was somewhat surprised. He had hoped, but didn't really think it would happen. With great satisfaction, he sat and smiled. "It feels real good."

"I thought it would. You're a good man, Martin. We have a lot of exciting things ahead of us... you and me. China things. Get ready. I'll be in touch."

# Chapter Nine

## Beijing

Upon returning home, Chang Siew Pang made a full report to Wong, the Inspector for the Secret Police. He was promptly demoted for allowing such a thing to happen under his watch. It would be a long climb back.

Inspector Ku Lon Wong was not an inspector at all, but head of the Supreme Secret Police, reporting directly to the Chairman. For security reasons, the organization kept the identity of their leaders hidden. No one, except Wong and the Chairman, knew who the top man really was. Now he was faced with a dilemma. What to do about this young fool who had caused the loss of great face to the Chinese people by defecting.

*I must make an example of this rabbit*, he thought. *There will be many opportunities for others to follow, as we become more open to the western world. I must make sure they will know the consequences!* He made a call.

"Wei."

"This is Inspector Wong. Who is our most inept student... one we could afford to be without?"

"I don't understand."

"I have an assignment for someone who will more than likely muck it up, which is exactly what I want to happen."

"Why?"

"That is of no importance to you. Who do we have? "

"Let me understand clearly. You want an agent who is likely to fail at his assignment?"

"Not fail, necessarily, just do it poorly."

"I see. I will send Xin Luk Lin to see you. He has been a disappointment to our organization. I was about to terminate him."

"Bless the gods. Send him at once." Wong hung up with glee. An agent who would most likely bring a lot of attention to this assassination... at least to the China News Media which he himself controlled. He would see to that. A perfect way to send a message to other possible defectors. An hour later, there was a knock on his open door.

"You wanted to se me, Your Highness?"

The man looked like a mule... with ugly broken teeth and pointy ears. Wong looked at his notes.

"You are Xin Luk Lin?"

"Yes, but I prefer to be called Charles."

Wong's eyes deepened and he glared at this insolent pig... preferring a barbarian name to his Chinese. He might just as well have cursed the Motherland. He spat on the floor. "I don't use western words unless absolutely necessary. You will do the same in my presence, understand?" His face was full of fury.

"Yes, Your Excellency. How stupid of me," he murmured, bowing his head. *That was certainly dumb,* he thought. *My mouth is constantly getting me into trouble.* He knew he was on the verge of being expelled from the elite group, being told that just recently by Agent Chek, one of his instructors. Perhaps that is what is happening now.

"I have an assignment for you... if you can be trusted to do something for the Motherland." Wong's words were full of venom.

"Oh, yes, Your Excellency. I would be deeply honored. Thank you, Your Excellency." He hoped his words sounded the sincerity he didn't really feel.

"Very well." Wong laid a file folder on the table. "I have a rabbit I want you to kill... in the wasteful land of the barbarians. The details are in this folder. You will leave for a place called Chicago tomorrow afternoon. Now get out of my office and take your ugly image with you." He spat on the floor again.

"Yes, Your Excellency. Right away, sir. Thank you a thousand times, Your Excellency." Xin grabbed the folder and hastily made for the door.

Charles Xin was excited. His first plane ride... and to the land of the Americans he so coveted. He moved from his assigned seat to a section of the plane that was not crowded. Here, he opened the folder and began to read. His orders were to find and kill the rabbit, a Chung Lim Hua, and any one who had helped him to defect. He would need all the skills he had been taught the past few months. Now, he wished he had paid more attention to his instructors. All the WCI China Connection men were listed as possible subjects who might have helped Chung to run away, as well as the owner of the hotel where the delegation stayed, a Mrs. Liu. Chang Siew Pang was sure she was involved. There were photos... many photos from the recent visit to America of the Chinese delegation. There were class room photos, a group picture on the steps of the Chicago Museum of Natural History and pictures of the American instructors. Then there were pictures of the Americans in China... on the Great Wall... in the Chinese factories. Suddenly, he froze. He knew this guy! This funny looking American. He remembered the day at the Customs table... yes... this guy had brought sex magazines.

He had given him a hundred US. Oh, yes, he remembered. He turned the photo over and read the name. *William Strickner.* I will start with him, he thought. He will lead me to Chung. Then he recognized Jack Donnelly and his brain exploded, remembering that day in Customs. The three Americans. This was going to be fun.

## Chicago

At 7:43 P.M., JAL flight #337 touched down at Chicago's O'Hare International Airport. The terminal was clean and bright, nothing like the Beijing airport he was used to. A poster on the wall of a pretty lady offering him a rental car smiled at him as he walked to the Immigration area. His new western style suit fit him well and gave him confidence as he approached the queue to be *chopped* in. He breezed through Customs, waved on by an uninterested uniform, and proceeded to baggage claim. How different this all was. He liked it very much. This must be what freedom is like.

He retrieved his suitcase and followed the "Taxi" signs outside. The night was warm and the air smelled clean and refreshing. There was no hint of coal smoke. He gave the driver an address in China Town and settled back into the luxury of the two-year-old Chevrolet. What a waste... such a fine car for a taxi. He was thrilled at the sights, nearly forgetting why he was here.

Forty-five minutes later, the taxi pulled up in front of the Great Wall Hotel on Wentworth Avenue. He counted out the exact fare and ignored the cursing driver as the car pulled away. "Cheap mother fucker!" the driver yelled through the window.

As soon as he was in the room, he dialed the number that had been given him in the folder.

"Yes."

"This is Charles Xin. I have come to pick up the black package." He read the code words exactly as written.

"I know of no black package here." (Code for you have called the right place.)

"Perhaps you are mistaken. It is the one with the red ribbon."

"Oh, yes. One hour. What is your room number?"

The knock on the door was two light taps followed by four more. Xin opened the door to an old man dressed in dirty shorts and a tee-shirt full of holes. He had not shaved for days and the front of his shirt was stained with grease. He carried a large canvass satchel. "I have brought the black package," he said softly.

"The one with the red ribbon?"

"Yes. May I enter?" He entered the room and approached the bed. Without a word, he opened the satchel and dumped its contents. There were three handguns, one with a silencer, two knives, a roll of duct tape, two military hand grenades and two bottles of pills.

"What is in the bottles?" Xin asked.

"The red bottle is strychnine, a quick death... the blue one is a powerful sleeping agent. Take what you will."

Xin selected the nine-millimeter with the silencer, both bottles, a folding knife with a four-inch blade, the tape and the two grenades. "These will do," he said. "Please notify Beijing the package has been delivered and the assignment has started." He put the items in a small backpack as the old man was returning the rest to his satchel.

"Here are the keys to the car... the black Ford parked across the street. There is a map on the front seat. It is a rental car. When you are finished, leave it where you want. We will report it stolen and the police will return it."

"I have names... I need address where to find them. Can you provide?"

"Yes. Give me the list and call me tomorrow. Do not forget the code."

The man took the list and, without another word left the room. He had served his Mother Country again... for which he would be paid handsomely. The gods were surely smiling on him. *Perhaps I should go to the track tomorrow*, he thought. Yes, definitely. Tomorrow would be a good day.

Xin looked at the keys with interest. He had been trained to drive American cars in Beijing. But Beijing was not Chicago. He was nervous, but at the same time excited and anxious to try out his skills. He slipped the keys in his pocket, hung the "Do Not Disturb" sign on the door and went to bed. When he awoke, it was 4:00 PM the next afternoon.

Trudy Strickner was hurrying home from the Park and Shop Grocery. She had purchased two TV dinners for a quick meal for her and her mother. They had a date with two men they had met at a local bar three days before, Jed and Rich. That night they had ended up in a hotel room and in bed... the four of them. Tonight, they had invited the two to their house for a repeat performance. Alicia wanted to swap this time. *Fine with me*, she thought. Alicia's was better endowed anyway.

These thoughts were getting her excited as she walked along quickly, trying to press her thighs together for more friction. This action caused her to stumble and she nearly dropped the groceries. Snapping out of her daydream, she put the images out of her mind and continued down the street. *I guess I can wait 'til seven o'clock.*

At 7:20, Xin parked the car across the street from the address in Westport. It was getting dark, but not yet dark enough. The trip had been much easier than he expected. The streets were marked much better than in Beijing and the map was very detailed, thus, he had arrived much earlier than he had predicted. He put the window down and waited, enjoying the finery of the car. Only the very rich or very important had cars like this in China. The street was deserted, another huge difference from his homeland, where thousands would be scurrying around at all hours of the night. When the clock on the dash read eight o'clock, he put on the small backpack and approached the house. It was dark enough now.

Silently, he climbed the steps and listened. He could hear sounds of laughter and squealing coming from the living room. There were four distinctive voices, although he could not tell if one of them was William Strickner. He jumped over the porch banister as easily as a cat and went to the back of the house. He tried the door and, finding it unlocked, he slipped into the kitchen. Once inside, he removed the gun from the backpack, put the knife in his pocket and laid the pack by the door. Slowly, he inched his way across the kitchen and up the hallway leading to the living room and the voices. Without a sound, he moved into position where he could see what was happening. The sight caused him to nearly drop the gun.

The four of them were nearly naked, caressing and fondling, much too busy to observe his presence. Neither of the two men resembled the photograph of William Strickner.

*Perhaps, I have the wrong house,* he thought. Then he noticed the family picture on the hall wall and was rewarded by William Strickner's face smiling at him. He was in the right place. "The Gods be with me," he said in Mandarin and stepped into the room.

At the sound of the voice, the one called Jeb looked up from Trudy's efforts and saw the gun.

"Jesus Christ!" he shouted. "What the fuck..."

The others were quick to turn to see what was wrong. They were petrified, unable to speak. A Chinese man with the face of a mule was holding a gun at their heads.

"Do not move or I will kill you." It was difficult for him not to be affected by the bare breasts of the women.

"What do you want?" Alicia whimpered, so frightened she could hardly speak.

"I seek William Strickner. I have business."

Trudy reached for her robe. "Do not move!" Xin ordered. The man called Jeb decided to be brave. He pushed Alicia away from his legs and started to stand. With no warning, Xin shot him in the forehead and he collapsed, dead before he hit the floor.

"You crazy mother..." Rich started, but was silenced by another shot.

The two women hugged each other, never more terrified... squealing and crying... sure that they, too, were going to die.

"Now, where is Mr. William Strickner?" Xin asked. Inside, he was shaking with the excitement of the moment. He had really enjoyed the killing.

"He... he's dead. Months ago. He died," Alicia managed.

Xin was silent, letting this information sink in. "So, he not help with the Chinese people training?"

"Not for over a year," she whimpered.

His mind was racing. What to do about this news. He must have time to think. If the man named Strickner was dead for a year, he could have nothing to do with the defection of Mr. Chung. *I must look elsewhere*, he thought. *But I cannot leave witnesses. I must kill them all.*

"You are barbarian whores," he said, as if to justify what he was going to do. "No civilized woman from the Mother Country would act as you were. You must die to please the God of Decency!"

"No, please... we will do anything!" Trudy offered.

Xin aimed the pistol and shot her through the head of the little red devil tattoo between her breasts. Alicia screamed, and he shot her in the stomach, then again in the head. "You are all barbarians. You did not deserve to live." Then he took out the knife and began cutting. A few minutes later, he left the way he had come. An hour later, he was back at the hotel in China Town.

He spoke to the desk clerk and arranged to have one of the local prostitutes come to his room. He needed relief from the stirring in his loins brought on by the sights he had witnessed earlier. *I went there to find William Strickner. Instead I find white cows with large teats. They deserved to die... the American cows... and the men with their sex shafts the size of horses.* He hoped his supervisors would agree. Oh how he hoped that.

Martin entered *his* new office for the first time. He put his briefcase down, sat behind the desk, then rose and closed the door. He smiled. "Just wanted to see what it was like to close your own office door," he said softly. He sat again, not knowing what he should do first. He could see his secretary at her desk. *His* secretary... ready to take *his* orders. This was nice...very nice.

The phone rang. He saw Sherri pick it up and heard her say into the mouthpiece, "Mr. Maguire's office." It felt strange not to answer his own phone... strange, but nice.

"Yes, of course. Just a minute." His phone buzzed.

"Yes?"

"Your wife, line one."

He punched a button. "Hi, gorgeous. How you doing?"

"Hi, big shot! Got your own private secretary, I see," she teased, very pleased for her husband, and very proud.

"Yep, I do. It's a great feeling, honey, even if I don't deserve it."

"But, you do, Martin. You really do!"

"I hope you're right. What's up?"

"What was the name of that guy... the weird one that killed himself last year?"

"Bill Strickner, why?"

"Weren't they the two girls we saw at the Mexican place?"

"Yes, they were."

"Did they live in Westport?"

"Yeah... what is going on?"

"They were murdered Saturday night. It's all over the Trib. The two women and two men. A neighbor found their bodies Sunday morning. They were all half naked, and, get this... the men had their things cut off. Anyway, you better find a paper and read all about it."

"Wow! Do they know who did it?" He was in shock.

"Paper didn't say. I gotta run. Go read about it! Bye." The line went dead. He cradled the phone slowly, trying to make sense of the news. Good God! What a terrible tragedy. I'd better go down to the commissary and get a paper. The phone interrupted him.

"I'll take it, Sherri," he called to her. It wasn't fun anymore.

"Martin Maguire. May I help you?"

"Mr. Maguire. I have come for Chung Lim Hua. Where is he, please?" The man talked in English but with a definite Chinese accent. From mainland China, for sure.

"Who?" At first, the name didn't mean anything to Martin. Then he realized the voice was asking about Mr. Chung. His Mr. Chung.

"Mr. Maguire. Please do not play games. There is no time for games. I went to visit Mr. Strickner, but he has been died. Now, his worthless family is died as well. Please be aware that I have no patience to get what I want. Now, I ask again, where is Mr. Chung Lim Hua?"

Martin could hardly breathe. Fear was building in his belly, burning a path to his chest, squeezing, torturing. His forehead was covered in sweat. This animal had obviously murdered the Strickner's... and two others.

"Who are you?" he managed.

"That is of no importance. Where is Chung Lim Hua?"

139

"I... I don't know. He disappeared. I have no knowledge of his whereabouts."

There was a pause. "Perhaps this is true. Perhaps it is not. In time, I will know. If you have not tell me the truth, I will speak with you again." There was a click.

"Wait!" Martin shouted, but the line was dead. He sat back in his chair, nearly fainting from fear. He had to fight to keep from throwing up. Quickly, he searched his card file for a number and frantically dialed.

"Federal Bureau of Investigation. How may I direct you call." The female voice was quite pleasant, but Martin didn't notice. "Mr. Brice, please." he said anxiously, having to force the words.

"Do you know his extension, sir?"

"Hell no, I don't know his extension!" he shouted.

"Just a moment, please." There was a click and John Denver was singing Rocky Mountain High.

"Jesus Christ, she put me on hold!" he yelled, causing Sherri to turn to see what was going on. He waved indicating every thing was all right.

"Brice here." John Denver was gone.

"Mr. Brice... this is Martin Maguire... from WCI. Remember?"

"Yes, of course, Martin. How are things these days?"

"Not good. I've got a serious problem. I need to see you right away!"

The tone of Martin's voice brought the agent to full alert. "What's the problem?"

"I think the Chinese have sent someone for our guy that tried to defect... Mr. Chung... and I think he's the person who killed the Strickner women and the two guys... in Westport. You know who I mean?"

"Yes, I'm aware of that crime. Where are you?"

"I'm at work. A guy just called me. A Chinese guy. Said he has come for Mr. Chung. Said he killed the others..."

"Martin, don't go anywhere. I'll be right there... ten minutes."

"Okay... thanks," Martin said with relief.

Fifteen minutes later, Brice and another man walked into the room where Martin's office was located. He met them at the door.

As soon as they were inside, he shut the door and faced the two FBI agents.

"Martin, this is Matt Halgren. He's our area field operations guy." They shook hands. "Matt's the guy to take care of things if there is a threat of... if someone is in danger."

"Good, well, I think you might be busy. Several of us could be in danger."

"You helped Chung to run, didn't you?" The question came from Brice. "I figured you had, but I didn't say anything. I felt sorry for him myself. I hope we don't live to regret it."

"Yes, I helped him. I thought that would be the end of it," Martin said, head bowed.

"Okay, let's start from the top...see what we got."

Martin told the two men everything.

# Chapter Ten

Charles Xin had been lucky. Jack Donnelly was the next one on his list, but when he had called the WCI facility, he was told that Donnelly was retired and no longer employed there. So, he asked for Martin Maguire. 'Of course, sir,' he was told, then Martin answered the phone. It felt good to scare someone, as he had been scared many times before. I will visit him tonight... at his home. He will tell me of Chung Lim Hua... if there is anything to tell.

He started going through the photographs again and stopped when he came to the group picture taken in front of a hotel. The sign said Best Western. There was a Chinese woman in the picture, but she was not one of the members of the delegation. Then he remembered seeing that the receipts for the hotel expenses had been signed by a Mrs. Liu. She must be the owner of the hotel, he decided. Quickly, he checked the list and confirmed this was true. A Chinese who had become an American. Who better to help a fellow countryman to defect? Who better to know how to do such a thing? He would visit the hotel now. Maguire later tonight.

Martin finished his account of Chung's flight to San Francisco. He had been foolish to think the Chinese would just forget about

Chung. Now he realized he had made a serious mistake.

"Well, we need to make some plans. Brice, this is my show. Thanks for helping. Go chase some foreign spies... or something. I'll let you know if there is anything else you can do," Halgren said.

"Okay... let me know what's happening. Martin, I leave you in good hands. You did right calling us immediately. Sounds like this guy means business. Matt knows how to handle these things. Follow his lead and you'll be fine. Good luck." He shook hands and left.

"I take it you two have had different training?" Martin asked.

Halgren laughed. "Well, yes. Brice is in foreign affairs... keeps tabs of foreign operatives, or spies, as you call them. He does this mostly with his computer, working with the CIA. Me... well, lets just say I've trained for more physical stuff. When his computer finds a bad guy, he calls me to take care of him."

"You mean to kill him?" Martin asked, wide eyed.

"Well, if I have to. Frankly, most of the time that's not required. There are other ways of persuading bad guys to go home. But to protect someone, or myself, I won't hesitate to... you know. Now, you feel better or worse?"

"I'm not sure," Martin said truthfully. "What do we do now?"

"I want you to go home. Right now. Stay there. Call your wife and have her go home as well. Right now. I'll have one of my agents there as soon as possible. He'll be able to monitor the phone and keep an eye out. In the meantime, I'll go talk to the Westport authorities. See what leads they have, if any, and let them know we might have an international hit man involved. If we can find him before he finds you... well, that would be better. Being Federal, I can go a lot of places where the Westport guys can't. We'll keep tabs on Donnelly and Jackman as well. He might try to get to one of them next. Anybody else you can think of?"

"No, I don't think so."

"Fine, then go home."

"I'd better call my boss first. The last guy that had this job got fired for not coming to work," Martin said, half joking.

"Well, we wouldn't want that. I'll see you real soon."

Martin called Peterlie and explained what was happening. Of course, he was frantic, which was expected. Then he called Carole.

"Hi… listen, I don't want to scare you, but I want you to go home now. I'll be there soon. There will be a FBI agent there, probably by the time you get there. We've a bit of a problem brewing."

"What's wrong?"

"The Chinese have sent someone looking for the guy that tried to defect… some kind of a hit man. He's probably the one who killed the Strickners. Now go home, now!"

"Martin, you're scaring me. You can't be serious!"

"Yes… I can't be more serious. Just go home… please."

"Okay. You want me to let the FBI guy in?"

"Only if he has identification, okay? And if he doesn't look like an Oriental."

"Okay, I'm not stupid."

*No*, he thought, *you're not stupid. You just don't realize how much danger you could be in.* He tried to call Jack Donnelly. No answer. Same with Reif Jackman.

By the time he had put things away and headed for the parking lot, it was nearly three o'clock. He hit the Interstate and headed west towards his house. As he was coming off the entrance ramp, he was greeted by a billboard with a familiar message...*Why pay more? A clean room, a soft bed... and we'll keep the light on for you!*

Susan! Damn! He had forgotten to tell Halgren and Brice about Susan. She had helped as much as anyone, except himself, of course, with her contacts in China Town. He had to warn her. The hotel was behind him and the nearest legal turnaround was four miles ahead, so he whipped into the first "Authorized Vehicles Only" access and with tires screeching, he headed back the way he had come. *I think I'd be classified as an Authorized Vehicle today*, he silently told himself.

Ten minutes later, he pulled under the canopy at the hotel and ran inside, going straight to Susan's office. The door was locked and no one answered his knock. Whirling around, he retraced his steps to the reception desk.

"Mrs. Liu... is she here?" he asked breathlessly.

"No, sir, she isn't here right now. Can I help you?"

"I have to find her. Where has she gone?"

"What's so important? I just told the other man... she's at her hairdressers."

"Other man! There was another man? What did he look like?" Martin was frantic.

"Well, he was Chinese... and, I'm sorry to say, he was ugly. He said he was an old friend."

"Did you tell him where she is?"

"Yes... he said he had to catch a plane soon... wanted to say hello..."

"Where is she? She's in a lot of danger!"

"Mister... she... the beauty shop is in the Midtown Mall... on

Orson Road. It's called Nancy's Shop... I didn't know... I told him where..."

"Call the police!" Martin shouted. "Tell them somebody is trying to kill Susan and tell them where she is. Now!" He ran out to his car and raced for the mall.

Susan was finished early and was feeling happy. As she approached her Mercedes, a young man called to her by name. A fellow Asian in need of directions was her first thought. The man, although dressed in a very nice suit, was not pleasant looking, but he was smiling and appeared friendly.

"Yes, may I help you?"

"Yes. Please get into your car, and don't make sounds."

For the first time, she saw the gun, partially hidden by his coat, pointing directly at her chest. Her heart jumped and she nearly stumbled, but recovered and did as she was ordered. When she opened the driver's side door, the strange looking man held it open as she sat down, then pushed the unlock button and got in the back seat. He held the cold steel of the gun on the back of her neck.

"Drive to the edge of the parking area... away from too many eyes."

Careful not to make any sudden moves, she started the car and slowly drove to the outer aisle of the lot, where she stopped and put the car in park. *He is going to rape me*, she thought.

"What do you want?" she managed. "I don't have much money."

"I want to know where is Chung Lim Hua."

"Who?"

"The one who you helped to defect." He decided to take a chance.

He heard her gasp for breath and knew he had been right.

"I don't know what you're talking about."

He leaned over the seat, put the pistol to her right foot and pulled the trigger. The bullet shattered her instep. She screamed. The pain was immense.

"I don't have patience. Please answer my question. Where is Chung Lim Hua?"

For minute she considered her options, and then decided she had none. "He is in San Francisco," she whimpered, holding her bloody foot.

"So you helped our rabbit to run?" He liked using the name "rabbit" from the inspector. Susan did not respond. "Do you know an address?"

"No," she moaned. "Only a name. Robert Quan. That is all I know." Blood was flowing freely onto the floor from her ruined foot. She knew she would never be able to walk again. She cried out in pain.

Xin knew she was telling the truth. There was nothing else to be gained from her. He put the gun to her head and started to pull the trigger. *Wait,* he thought. *I will use her to make headlines... for my superiors.* He removed a roll of duct tape from his pack and securely taped her head to the headrest of the seat. "Make no move or I kill you."

He got out of the car and joined her in the front seat, laid the gun on the dash and then taped her hands together and then to the steering wheel. Next, he taped her bleeding foot along with the good one to the brake pedal. She was immobilized. She could not move. Finally, he taped her mouth shut. He removed the keys from the ignition and walked around to the driver's side of the car, made sure the doors were unlocked, then took one of the hand grenades from the bag and pulled the pin. Next, he wedged the bomb between the side of the seat and the door, making sure the lever was held in the safe position. He then pushed the emergency flasher button and walked around to the passenger side and raised the window.

Susan Liu was terrified. When her door was opened, the grenade would go off. And she could do nothing.

"Thank you, Susan Liu. I will find Chung Lim Hua and he will be killed, as you will, for the Mother Country. Good bye." He walked away.

*This should make headlines*, he thought. *This should make my superiors happy*. He returned to his car and parked where he had a clear view of the Mercedes.

Martin ran out of the hotel and jumped in his car, speeding off in the direction of the mall. Traffic was heavy at this time of day and the going was slow, even though he was darting from one lane to another. *How could I have forgotten about her*, he thought, as he approached Orson Road. He turned north, ignoring the red light and nearly colliding with a truck making a left turn in front of him. Ten more minutes, he figured.

Frankie Durbin was twenty-eight years old and, just three months ago, had realized his lifetime dream of becoming a police officer. He was married and the proud father of two-month-old twin boys. It was a time in his life when everything seemed to be going his way. He was indeed a very lucky guy. Dispatch had said a lady's life was in danger. *More meaningful than stopping speeders*, he thought, excited by his first *real* emergency.

The police car, lights flashing and siren whaling, screeched to a stop in front of the beauty shop. The officer ran inside and returned in a few seconds, searching the lot for a Mercedes. Then he noticed the car with the lights flashing. Quickly, he jumped into the squad and drove next to her car. He could see a person inside, bound and gagged.

"Good God! What have they done to you?" he muttered, approaching the car.

The person inside was frantically shaking her head from side to side, making muffled sounds of terror. Her eyes were wild looking, wide and darting, trying to warn him of the danger.

"Poor girl... give me a minute, I'll get you out of there." He reached and opened the door, faintly hearing something drop, but not seeing the object. He reached to pull the tape from the mouth of the victim. One tug and it was free.

"Run!" she screamed at the top of her voice, knowing in her heart it was too late. That was the last word she would ever speak, and the last word Frankie would ever hear.

Martin pulled into the lot just as the blast occurred. He saw the puff of black smoke and heard the loud boom, then saw a car door go flying in the air. By the time he arrived at the scene, the Mercedes was a ball of flames. The force of the explosion had propelled the young officer backward, into the side of his police car, which brought his body to an abrupt halt, nearly severing his head.

Bringing the car to a stop, all Martin could do was watch what used to be a person in the seat of the Mercedes burn and bubble into a black lump. Seeing the crumpled body of the policeman lying next to his car was more than he could bear, and he became violently sick.

The unobserved black Ford slowly left the parking lot, heading back toward China Town. The driver had not recognized Martin Maguire or he would not have left the scene so soon.

A little while later, Martin was sitting in the back seat of Halgren's car. His face was red from the intense heat of the flames. Shortly after the blast, several police cars had arrived... summoned to the scene by several frantic calls to 911. At his request, one of the officers called Matt Halgren at the FBI office. He was there in fifteen minutes.

"Well, Martin, this sonofabitch certainly means business. We've given this top priority...checking all incoming flights over the past few days for known operatives. The CIA is interested as well... will most likely assign someone to look into it all."

"He has a hit list, Matt, of the guys involved. I forgot about Mrs. Liu. This is all my fault. If only I had remembered, she might still be alive."

"Now, Martin, you can't blame yourself for the actions of some friggin' animal! I saw the photos of the Strickner place. You wouldn't believe... he cut off their dicks!"

"I heard." A shudder went through his body at the thought. "Jack Donnelly... is there someone with him?"

"Well, there would be, if we knew where he was. His house is under surveillance, but the neighbors think they drove to Michigan for a few days. The Michigan State Police are looking for his car."

As the ambulance with the two bodies was pulling away, another rather plain car pulled up and a well built, middle-aged man got out and approached.

"Scott Johns... CIA." He flashed an ID so fast it could have been a cereal box top for all Martin knew. "Matt, isn't it? Long time." He held out his hand to Halgren.

"Yeah, Scott, thanks for remembering. Your people found out anything yet?"

"Not really. There's been over twelve hundred Asians enter the country in the past week. You Maguire?"

"Yes. Right now, I wish I was somebody else."

He nodded, understanding. "Yeah, I suppose so. Did either of the Strickners or the hotel owner know anything about where this Chung fellow is?"

"Not the Strickners. But Mrs. Liu gave Chung a contact in San Francisco. I'm pretty sure he's there. I got a postcard. I don't know if she told the guy... who killed her."

"Okay, let's assume she did. I'll alert our San Francisco people. Matt, you should do the same. Maybe we can catch him coming into the city. In the meantime, why don't you drive this guy home. I don't think we should leave any of the probable targets alone."

"I agree, Scott. I'll drive him and one of my guys can follow in his car."

In the back room of the Tiger Garden Dim Sum Restaurant, Kim Lee Fat was washing the last of the dishes of the evening. He was nearly ninety years old and had been in America for fifty-three years. He loved America. She had been good to him... much better than his "Mother China" as some of his people called their country.

He was nearly starving when he had lived in Shanghai, foraging for any food he could find... going through the garbage thrown off the ships docked in the harbor. Driven by desperation, he had climbed the anchor chain of an American freighter like a rat, hiding away in the bowels of the ship, eating uncooked rice and drinking water from the fire buckets. Twenty-three days later, he heard the anchor chain being lowered once again, and under cover of darkness, he swam to the shores of San Francisco. A few years later, he moved to Chicago and opened his restaurant. In 1960, he became a US citizen... the proudest day of his life. He held no love for Mother China... or for this young man with a mule-face who had been drinking and bragging since early evening.

There weren't many secrets in China Town. The triad members controlled most everything, providing "insurance" to the various shop owners, as long as they paid, to assure that nobody messed with them. Most everybody paid. Joss. A way of life. The local police had long given up trying to stop the triads, and they talked freely about their activities. The latest news... a man had been sent from Mother to find and kill a deserter. A deserter like himself. Wu Jin had taken this man weapons... orders from Beijing. Wu Jin was a good friend, spending many hours together studying the tiles of Mahjong, and was also a part time cook in the restaurant.

When Charles Xin had entered the restaurant, Wu Jin pointed him out to Kim Lee Fat. "That is the one who I take weapons to... the mule-faced one."

"Why do you do it?" Kim Lee Fat asked his friend. "Someday, they will kill you... to keep your mouth quiet!" He had had this conversation with his old friend before.

"I do it for money, you old fool! You pay me pennies to cook in your stinking kitchen. I make more delivering one black package than you pay me in one month!"

"Yes… and I will win it all from you with the tiles! Now, who is the old fool?"

"Gods be cursed, you are right. You always win!" Wu Jin blew his nose Chinese style, on the floor, and went back to his wok.

Kim Lee Fat, remembered the terrible life he had while in China, and was always ready to help out anyone who was brave enough to escape the old way of life. He had given the hotel lady the name and address of a person in San Francisco who could help the young man trying to avoid a certain death if he returned to his homeland. He had done this before, although, he never said anything about it to Wu Jin, because he still had ties to the old ways. They paid him money.

There were still a few late night patrons drinking beer with the mule-face one when Kim announced he was closing and ushered them out the front door. He returned to the kitchen to find Wu asleep on a dirty cot they kept at the rear of the store. Quietly, he returned to the dining room and to the telephone by the register. He dialed a number and waited. Eleven o'clock in Chicago was eight o'clock in San Francisco.

"Wei?" the voiced answered.

"Quan… this is Kim Lee Fat. Listen close… I say only once. There is a young lost brother from Mother who come to you three months ago. Mother has sent a dragon to kill him. This dragon has killed four already, those who helped our little brother to run. He must be warned of his danger."

"Wa ming bei! (I understand) I will take care of it. You are well?"

"Yes, I am well friend, and you?" Before he heard the answer, Kim Lee Fat dropped the phone and fell to his knees. He could speak no more. A knife blade was protruding from his throat, having been thrust from behind his neck. He turned his head to see his old friend Wu standing behind him. Blood was quickly rising in his mouth and he was choking. He felt no pain.

"The Gods defecate on you, you worthless dog... betraying Mother!" Wu Jin jerked the knife free and wiped it on his dirty apron. Kim fell backward and lay still, drowning in his own blood. Wu Jin picked up the phone and replaced it in the cradle, then bent over Kim.

"I will miss you, stupid old friend. I will lose my money to you no more."

In San Francisco, Quan hung up the phone slowly. Something bad had happened there... to his friend, Kim Lee Fat. *I will call Wu Jin*, he thought. *But first, I must go warn young Chung of the danger at hand.*


Jack Donnelly and Bernice were leisurely driving along Rte. 40 in western Michigan, heading toward Holland. They had had a nice seafood dinner in a restaurant in Filmore and were heading back to the motel.

"I told Aunt Shirley she should just sell that farm. All it does is cause her headaches, anyway. Think she'll listen to me? Oh, no, she won't listen to me. She'll still be paying taxes and arguing with her tenant farmer ten years from now... if she lives that long." Bernice's voice droned on and on and on. Jack was paying no attention, lost in thoughts about what he was going to do tomorrow when, suddenly, red lights came on behind them and a spotlight flashed in the side mirror.

"Shit!" he mumbled, pulling to the side.

"Were you speeding?" Bernice asked.

"Hell no I wasn't speeding! Maybe I ran a stop sign or something. I didn't see any, but who knows?" He lowered the window and waited for the policeman, ready to accept whatever fate had in store.

"Mr. Donnelly? Mr. Jack Donnelly?" The officer was young, barely appearing to be out of his teens.

"Yes, I'm Donnelly. What did I do?"

"Nothing, sir. Nothing at all. There is some kind of problem. The FBI wants to talk to you for some reason. I'm told you could be in some danger. I'm to stay with you and the missus until an agent arrives. Why don't you pull off into that empty lot ahead, and sit with me in the squad car."

"You're not kidding, are you? What the hell is going on?" Donnelly was confused.

"I'm not kidding, sir. I wouldn't do that."

"Jack, do as he says. I'm scared!" Bernice whined.


Martin and Carole were sitting at the kitchen table. Matt Halgren was pouring himself a cup of coffee at the counter. There were two other FBI agents in the living room, one hooking up a device to the phone, the other working on a laptop computer.

"You guys want a warm up?" Matt asked.

"No thanks, Mr. Halgren," Carole answered.

"Please call me Matt. This could take some time... we'll probably get to know each other pretty well before it's over." That would prove to be an understatement.

Martin was dejected. "All I wanted to do was help a little Chinese guy. I can't believe it's come to this."

Carole gave him a hug. "This is not your fault. You did the right thing, even if you didn't tell me anything about it."

"She's right, Martin. There are thousands of Chinese nationalists who find their way to the States every year and people are always helping them. Most of them go unnoticed. I'm not sure why the Chinese are making a big deal about this one."

The phone rang and the FBI guys went into action, pushing buttons and putting on earphones. "If it's our guy, keep him on as long as you can," Matt said. "Okay, pick it up."

"Hello. Oh, yes, of course." He handed the phone to Matt.

"Halgren…. okay, thanks." He put the phone down. "They found the Donnelley's… they're ok."

"Good!" Martin said, relieved. "So, what happens now?"

"Well, we have people at all the airports checking any Orientals heading west. Also, we are watching incoming passengers at San Francisco."

"What if he drives? He could drive!" Martin offered.

Halgren shrugged. "Well, either way, he's heading away from us!"

"Yes, but he's going toward Mr. Chung."

# Chapter Eleven

## San Francisco

Lee Quan locked the front door of the Oriental Antique Shop in Chinatown then slipped out the back door into the alley. He must go quickly to warn the young man known to him as Walter Chiu, the name Chung had chosen for his change of identity.

A few blocks away at the Lung Street night market, Walter was unloading crates of vegetables from a truck onto the dock. He was used to hard work and the pay was more for a week than he made in a year back in China. He made twelve dollars an hour, of which he paid his foreman two for allowing an illegal alien to work. It was well worth it. His room over the antique store was only twenty dollars a week, and by eating frugally, he had managed to save over three hundred dollars a week. There was now a little over two thousand stuffed behind the light switch in his room.

He slid the crate of celery onto the dock and turned to see Mr. Quan standing in the shadows beside the truck. The look on Quan's face caused his heart to skip a beat. There was trouble. He jumped to the ground.

"Mr. Quan... why are you here?"

"You must go, Walter. You are in grave danger and so are others around you."

Suddenly, Chung noticed the man was carrying a suitcase. His suitcase. "I... I don't understand..." he stammered.

"Mother has sent a dragon... from secret police to kill you for defecting. Already, four who help you in Chicago have died." Chan whispered.

"Curse the gods! Who... do you know names?" His heart was full of pain and breathing was difficult.

"No... I know nothing more... except he is coming for you. You must find another place. I am sorry."

"Of course, I will go quickly. First, I must to go back to my room."

"No... I have brought all your things."

"But I have money there!"

"No, it is here." The old man handed him the two thousand three hundred dollars.

Chung stared at the money. "You knew... where it was?"

"Of course. To protect myself, I must know everything. It is all there... I am not a thief. Now go." Quan turned and walked away, hoping he had acted in time. He wanted nothing to do with the dark side of this dragon.

Walter Chiu now had a new problem... where to go. He found his foreman and informed him he had to quit.

"Hell, Joe, what for? You wuz doin good. One of my best workers!"

"I'm in danger... I have to go. If I stay, you in danger also."

"Hell, Joe... I've been in danger all my life. What does this dude look like and I'll take care of him for you."

"No, you don't understand. This person... he will kill anyone who is in way."

"Okay, if you say so, Joe. If you ever come back, you got a job here...anytime. Here, let me get your pay." He dug in his pocket and came out with a large wad of bills and started counting. "Thirty hours times twelve is three sixty... here ya go." He offered the money.

"Don't forget...two dollar. Sixty less."

"Naw...keep it. Severance pay. Good luck to you, Joe." He offered his hand.

"Thank you... do you know where is bus station?"

At the bus station, Chung checked the schedules for all departures leaving in the next hour going east. He removed a business card from his wallet and found a phone booth. He had to find out... was it his new American friend who had paid the supreme price for helping him?

It was nearly twelve midnight when the phone rang. Carole had gone to bed and Martin and Matt were sprawled on the couch in the den watching a late night movie. The other two FBI agents were asleep in the living room. They all sprang into action at the sound, instantly wide awake and alert. Matt knocked the beer he had been drinking on the floor.

"Hello," Martin answered tentatively.

"Oh, Mr. Mac-wire! You are good?"

"Chung! Is that you?" Martin shouted.

"Yes... is good I hear your voice! I am told my country send assassin. I have put you in grave danger. Tell me...who is killed?"

"Mrs. Liu from the hotel. She is the only one you know."

"Oh, such a terrible thing. I am most sorry."

"Yes, it was not a good thing. Are you okay?"

"I am good. I must stop this dragon before he kills again. I know what I must do. They want only me. I will come back to Chicago and then you will be safe."

"No, Chung! You can't do that! You will be killed!"

"Mr. Chung, this is Matt Halgren with the FBI. I think it is a good idea for you to come back and give yourself up to the immigration authorities. You are correct. That will remove the danger from your friends."

"Chung... no! There must be a better way," Martin pleaded.

"Thanks, Mac-wire, but I know what I must do." The phone went dead.

"Chung!" Martin shouted into the dead mouthpiece, and then slowly put it in the cradle.

"Martin, this is best. It will stop the killings." Halgren said.

"Except for Chung," Martin replied. "What if you find the hit man first? Won't that stop the killings?"

"They'll just send another. For some reason, the PRC wants to make an example out of Chung. I don't think they will quit till he's dead."

Martin was silent...thinking. "You're right, Matt. They won't quit till he is dead. Have another beer. I've got an idea."


Chung bought a one-way ticket to Chicago, with stops and layovers in Reno, Omaha and Des Moines. He had an hour to wait for departure. *I must let them know I am coming,* he thought. It would do no good to return unless they knew. He returned to the phone and retrieved a document from his suitcase. It contained a list of numbers for emergencies. He dialed the number for the Chinese Embassy in Chicago.

A sleepy voice answered. "The embassy is closed. Only security is here. Call tomorrow."

"I need to speak to the Chief of Security."

"What is the nature of your call?"

"It's a matter of Chinese national security... a matter of great importance... put me through now!" Chung hoped the lie would work.

After a few minutes, another voice came on the line. "This is Inspector Rui. I am night security supervisor. What do you want?"

"My name is Chung Lim Hua. I am a defector. There is a secret police agent from the mainland sent to find me. You must get word to him that I am coming back to Chicago to give myself up."

There was a pause as the man considered his request. "I know nothing of this matter. I do not get involved with such things!"

"Yes, but you can report my call to Beijing Secret Police. They will know what to do."

"Perhaps. I will consider it. Where are you now?"

*He knows of me,* Chung realized. "I will arrive in Chicago by bus in two days. Just tell them that." He hung up the phone and returned to the wooden bench to wait for the bus.

When Charles Xin next reported to his superior in Beijing, he would be told not to bother going to San Francisco... the rabbit was coming to him.

Martin and Matt had been talking for over an hour about Martin's idea.

"You're crazy. It won't work," Matt said for the tenth time, shaking his head.

"So, you got a better idea?"

"No," Matt admitted.

"Fine...I'm going to bed. Do it," Martin ordered.

Matt sat for a long time, considering Martin's plan. When he looked at his watch, he was surprised to find it was nearly 2:00 A.M., 11:00 P.M. on the west coast. He made up his mind, picked up the phone and dialed. *Always easier to get forgiveness than approval,* he thought. No time to get official approval anyway. "Hope I still have a job after this." He said out loud, as the phone on the other end of the line began to ring.

Martin was having a terrible dream. He was standing in front of an iron cage in the center of the Beijing airport lobby. There were thousands of Chinese around him...yelling and screaming. Inside the cage, Bill Strickner was standing, arms outstretched, a pair of scissors in his hand. He was wearing a pair of white hiking shorts. The crotch area was bright red and dripping blood.

"I solved my problem, Martin!" He yelled. "I'm no longer obsessed. Isn't that great?"

"What the hell did you do, Bill?" Martin asked.

"I cut it off, Martin! Don't you see... that was the only thing I could do!"

David Choi appeared at his side, holding the severed penis between thumb and finger high in the air for all to see, a weird smile on his face. "Hi, Martin...I guess you're next. Soon as Bill bleeds to death. Take about three minutes is all. Mule-face will help you cut it off." He threw the hideous piece of flesh into the crowd and they roared...wanting more. The customs agent with the ugly face suddenly grabbed Martin by the arm.

A commotion near the gate area caught his attention. A group of workers, dressed in painter coveralls, were erecting scaffolds on each side of the gate entrance. Several five-gallon buckets of paint were brought in on a dolly, and soon there were three workers painting the ceiling. One of the scaffolds had blocked his view, so he moved to a better vantage point. Still two hours to go. Xin went back to napping.

Chung saw the sign through the dirty bus window. 'Welcome to Chicago', said the smiling face of Mayor Daley. He looked nervously at his traveling companion, who sensed his concern.

"We still have about fifteen minutes till we get to the station. You'll be fine. Just follow the instructions."

"Yes. I will do my best." Chung answered, hoping his best would be good enough.

One of the workers, an FBI agent named Waters, was high on the scaffold where he could watch Charles Xin as he napped, keeping careful attention to the time. *He must have the weapon in the bag*, he surmised. His job would be simple. Wait until the right moment... then eliminate the mule-faced one. The timing would be critical.

At 10:15, he and one other *worker* climbed down from the scaffold, sat on the paint cans and opened lunch boxes and began their morning break. Completely natural. No one paid them any attention... including Charles Xin.

At 10:45, the bus arrived. Xin went to the doorway where he could see the passengers step down. He recognized his target as he walked to the back of the bus to get his luggage. His hand was already inside the camera bag. Silently, the safety was clicked off in anticipation. Chung retrieved his suitcase and began walking toward the doorway into the terminal.

Xin took a couple of steps back from the doorway. He didn't want his prey to see him, get spooked and end up running. His hands tingled with excitement.

Suddenly, there was something wrong. Shouting and pushing near the doorway. One of the workers was standing in the doorway holding a gun pointed at his rabbit. His rabbit! Xin froze, trying to figure out what was happening.

The worker was yelling at Chung! "Stop! FBI! You are under arrest!" He held up a shield and continued to point his gun at Chung's chest! Without warning, Chung dropped his suitcase and pulled a gun from his pocket and aimed it back at the worker. The worker fired first, apparently hitting Chung in the chest. Staggering, he raised his arm and returned fire before collapsing on the floor.

Passengers and others were screaming and running, trying to escape from the danger. Charles Xin, not wanting to get caught up in this mess, turned to run, only to find his way blocked by one of the men in painting clothes. He turned to his right, only to find another worker with a gun pointed at him. He started to raise the bag, but felt the sting of the bullet at the same time he heard the gun go off. For a split second, there was no pain, only a sense of floating as he was going down. The camera bag jumped as his hand convulsed on the trigger, the bullet going harmlessly into the floor. His face hit the concrete with a splat and he moved no more. Charles Xin had just been eliminated. The bullet from the FBI agent's gun had found his heart.

As the crowd drew back, screaming and shoving, a Greyhound security guard arrived on the scene with his gun drawn and ready.

"FBI!" an agent in painter clothes shouted, holding up an ID. "It's all over. Everything is okay now!"

A Chicago policeman had joined the security officer. "What the hell is going on?" he demanded of the agent.

"We were making an arrest," he pointed at Chung lying in the doorway, "when this guy drew on us. We had to take him out. But he managed to get off a shot... hit this poor guy over here." He pointed his gun at Charles Xin's lifeless body. The camera bag had mysteriously disappeared. "I'm afraid he didn't make it either. Could one of you get us some help here?"

Just inside the gate, Roy Chow was bent over Chung's body. The chest area was covered with blood and there was blood seeping from his lips. He whispered. "Don't move, my friend. Everything went exactly as planned."

Chung made no outward sign that he had heard, but inside, his heart was pounding! *Free... maybe I'm free*! It took all of his self control not to smile.

As the police were calling for help, a pre-arranged ambulance appeared in the area where the buses were parked. Quickly, they picked up the dead fugitive and loaded him into the waiting ambulance. The innocent victim inside the terminal continued to lie in a pool of blood. A reporter had arrived on the scene and was taking video for the evening news.

In the speeding ambulance, Chung opened his eyes and then smiled with joy. He was looking into the face of his friend, Martin Maguire.

"You can sit up now, Mr. Chung. Welcome back to Chicago," Martin said.

The evening news carried the entire story... complete with pictures of Charles Xin, lying dead on the bus station floor, accidentally shot by a fellow Chinese who was trying to flee the FBI and Immigration authorities. The FBI also provided a file photo of the fugitive, a Chung Lim Hua, the man who attempted to kill the FBI agent who was there to arrest him. An unfortunate mess.

The Security Chief at the Chinese embassy taped the episode which aired on WGN and promptly sent a copy to Beijing by overnight courier. After reviewing the tape, the Director of Secret Police, opened the file folders of Chung Lim Hua and Charles Xin and laid them side by side. Next, he took out an ivory chop, pressed it on a red ink pad, and stamped a Chinese character across the face of both photos. The character looked like a red spider with one broken leg. If the Chinese character had been in English, it would have read 'DECEASED'. He threw the two files in his basket on top of a file cabinet. Cases closed.

# Chapter Twelve

## Chicago

It had been a little over four months since the incident in the bus station. All involved hoped that would be the end of that kind of excitement. The correspondence from the Chinese factories appeared to be positive. The members of the delegation had returned home and began making the parts required to build their specific products at each factory. The master schedule now called for the Americans to make their second trip to China... to help in the assembly of the perspective machines.

Martin walked into the office of the Superintendent of Planning, knocking on the open door as he entered.

"Pete! Wake up!"

Pete Wahl looked up from the report he was reading. "Hi, Martin... what's up?"

"I need a man."

"Again?" he groaned. "When are they coming?" He had provided a man to help train the Chinese in the classroom during the previous visit.

"They're not. We're going. I need a hydraulics guy to go with... for a month. Of course, I want your best."

"Why is that not a surprise to me? My best, huh? Martin... you may not want my best. He's a little, what shall I say... unpolished?"

"I'm not too concerned about him being polished. We're going to China... not to Paris."

Pete grinned. "Okay. I would tell you to go to hell, but you would just go over my head and get whatever you need anyway. My best... Bobby Mayfield. When do you leave?"

"Two weeks... but I'll need him earlier to prepare."

"I guess I should have asked when you want him."

"Tomorrow. Eight o'clock. Thanks, Pete."

The next morning at five till eight, Martin's office door became filled with a very large man... grinning from ear to ear. He was six foot six, weighed just four pounds shy of three hundred, and had a full head of red hair.

"Are y'all Mr. Martin?"

"Martin looked up and smiled. "Yes. Are you Bobby?"

"Yes, Suh. Pete said I belonged to y'all for the next six weeks. Said we're going to China?"

"Sit down, Bobby. Yes, that's the plan."

"I've never been on an airplane before, Suh. I've never been anywhere except Georgia... and here."

"I need a hydraulics tech... not a world traveler. Do you know hydraulic systems?"

"Oh, yes, Suh! I do know hydraulics. I could take the space shuttle apart and put it back together and it'd run like a Swiss watch."

Martin laughed. "I don't need a Swiss watch. How about our equipment? Can you handle that?"

"In the dark... or under water, Suh!"

"You're my man. Where in Georgia are you from, Bobby?"

"I'd rather you had not asked that. I'll tell you what... can we drink beer in China?"

"Sure, as long as you don't go to extremes."

"Okay, Suh... some night... you and me, drinking beer... I'll tell you all about my... home town, and my bringing up. But, not now, please." He shook his head. "Not now."

"All right, Bobby. You got it. I won't ask again. Anybody ever call you Red?"

"They only call me that one time, Suh. I make it clear that my name is Bobby."

"I feel the same about being called "Sir". I prefer Martin."

The huge man smiled and nodded. "Martin it is then... Suh."

"Okay, Bobby. Let me tell you what you're in for."


## Beijing

Chang Siew Pang was stomping up the damp and dark back steps which led to his superior's office. He was, as they say, a man on a mission. It was nearly time for evening meals and the Great Hall of the People was almost deserted. He hoped his boss had not already left.

He reached his destination and stepped into the room. The uniformed aide stopped him. "You have an appointment?"

"I must see the Director. Get out of my way."

"You no longer have those privileges... remember?"

"Listen, you pig gut! Someday I will be back on this level and you... your juice balls will be mine to play with! Understand?"

The young man's courage faded quickly. "Yes, of course. He has an open appointment at this very minute. Please let me announce you." He disappeared into the other room and returned quickly. "Please, the Director will see you now."

"What has gotten your intestines all snarled up now?" His boss was putting on his jacket, ready to leave for the day.

"They're coming back... the Americans... from WCI. I just read a telex with the name list."

"So... it is part of their contract."

"Yes, I know. But... he is coming... to us. Maguire will be in China. No FBI to protect him!"

"What are you thinking? You want more problems?"

"No... I only want to repay this Maguire... for costing me my job!"

"The American did not cost you your job. Your stupid actions cost you your job. All the American did was to be a lot smarter than you."

Chang's eyes squinted to mere slits. "I want his head. I want to spit on his lifeless body."

"You idiot! You would risk all that we have worked for... the joint ventures... for misplaced revenge? You will do nothing, you understand? Nothing! If you jeopardize this program... if anything happens to the Americans... I will see that it is ten times ten worse for you! Now, get out of my office. I am going home."

The trip schedule called for the team to start in the north and finish in the south. Their first stop was in Xiamen, an industrial city of six million people and part of the Chinese SEZ (Special Economic Zone). It was a city designed to attract foreign investments. Special care had been taken to provide nice joint venture hotels and restaurants representing the different countries of the world in the center of town. From the air, one could see numerous high rise apartment buildings along the outskirts of the city. It appeared as if the city was expanding at a rapid pace, putting modern housing in place. The entire area was fake... a fact discovered by the team from WCI who had to go through this area on their way to the factory. The high rise buildings were merely empty shells... no electricity, no plumbing... not even glass in the windows. Nobody lived there. Since most visitors were never allowed in this area, the farce worked.

The Xiamen Machine Works, one of the four factories selected for the program, had chosen a WCI non-current dirt loader as their product to make. The loader had a bucket capacity of six cubic yards of material. The reports said that they were ready to test their first machine.

The WCI team arrived early at the test site, armed with cameras, stop watches and anticipation. When they got out of the transportation van, they were met by the manager of the factory and several of the Chinese trainees from the delegation who had gone to America. The machine was covered with a large tarp.

"Welcome WCI experts! Welcome," the manager proclaimed, smiling broadly.

"Mr. Lee... good to see you again," Martin replied.

"How would you like for us to demonstrate our loader?" the interpreter asked. The factory manager was beaming.

"Well, why don't we start by seeing how quickly you can load a truck?"

The manager froze upon hearing Martin's suggestion.

"Load a truck? What truck?" he asked, through the interpreter.

"Mr. Lee... our loader is designed to pick up a bucket full of material... dirt or rock or whatever, and put it in a truck so it can be hauled to the work site. We want to see how quickly it can load the truck. That is how we measure productivity."

The rest of the Chinese huddled around the interpreter as he repeated Martin's words. Then, they broke out into a stream of shouting and talking, wildly waving hands and pointing, each seeming to be angry with the other.

"What's going on?" Martin asked.

"I'm not sure," David Choi replied. "Something is wrong... they were not expecting this."

The factory interpreter approached the Americans.

"Mr. Martin, my leaders are embarrassed. Our machine will not load a truck. We have no truck. Not large enough to hold the capacity of the bucket. We have only the two wheeled carts that will hold only 1/4 cubic meters."

"Can't we borrow a truck?"

"There is no truck... large enough in all China. There is no truck."

It was beginning to sink in. "They have built a machine capable of loading six yards of material in one cycle... and there is nothing to put it in," Martin said softly.

"Jesus Christ... what's next?" Donnelly said disgustedly. "This is unbelievable!"

Bobby Mayfield smiled. "You said I'd get a lot of surprises, boss. I guess this is one of them?"

"So... you plan to haul the material to the job site with the loader... one bucket full at a time?" Martin asked.

"Yes. One bucket full is much more than our bicycle truck can haul!"

Martin thought a minute. "Okay... Mr. Lee... you show us what you had in mind for the test."

That seemed to calm the group a bit. "Okay, we show!" the interpreter repeated.

The tarp was removed and the Americans nearly fainted. The machine was unpainted, rusted iron... a wooden crate for a seat... only the silhouette resembling the WCI version.

"We are waiting on paint coming from Beijing paint factory for three months... also, we have not found supplier for leather seats. We are hoping you can send us a seat from America," the interpreter explained.

"Of course... I think we can do that," Martin managed, still in shock.

"Good... we do demonstration."

An older factory worker, so proud that he had been selected as the operator, climbed up on the machine and started the engine. Since it had been made in America at the WCI facility, it started immediately and ran smoothly with a sound that promised power. Next he put the machine in gear and tried to move it forward. It screamed. It literally screamed... a sound so loud the spectators had to hold their hands over their ears.

"What the hell?" Donnelly shouted.

"Shut it down!" Bobby yelled at the operator, who shut off the machine immediately. There was no interpretation needed.

"Man... what the hell was that?" Martin asked.

"We don't know how to stop the sound," the interpreted replied. "We hope WCI experts can help."

Bobby smiled. "Get me a set of socket wrenches and y'all come back in a half hour. I know what the problem is."

"This is the only thing on the agenda today, Bobby. We'll just wait," Martin answered.

It only took twenty minutes. The machine was restarted and the operator put it in gear and it lurched forward... making no more screaming sounds. The Chinese applauded, jumped up and down and yelled... happy and excited. Bobby Mayfield was a hero!

"What was wrong, Bobby?"

"They had the spool in the wrong way in the hydraulic valve, Martin. It's happened before. That sound was the relief valve popping open. Our newer models have been idiot-proofed so we can't put the spool in wrong."

"Okay... nice going, Bobby. Can you make us a big truck?"

Two days later, the team was in a Russian-built car driving down a seldom traveled road... seldom traveled by anything except bicycles and horse pulled carts. They were on the way to the city of Yichun, located in central China.

"Martin, I need to tell you about something that happened at the factory yesterday," Bobby started. "I guess it was a lesson in understanding different cultures... at least for me."

"Oh? Tell me."

"Well, my interpreter was taking me on a tour of the factory and I asked to see their hydraulics department. We went into this small building and there were two different groups of guys working on some hydraulic cylinders. They were squatted down on the dirt floor, like they were getting ready to take a dump, trying to take these cylinders apart. When I saw this, I told the interpreter that they should get the worker some tables to work on... that it would be a lot more productive, and comfortable, if they didn't have to squat on the floor. Beside that, hydraulics need to be kept clean. He immediately went over to the supervisor and told him about my suggestion."

"That was a good idea, Bobby." Martin offered.

"Ya think? Well, let me tell you whut... after lunch, my interpreter said they wanted to see me back in the hydraulics room. So we went. The supervisor met us at the door and told me that his guys thought I was about the dumbest person they had ever met and were very upset. When we walked inside, I almost shit my pants... here was his workers, up on top of the tables, squatted down, working on the cylinders... but now, they were upset. Because of this dumb American, they had to climb up on top of the tables to work."

The entire group of Americans burst out laughing.

"These guys are so used to working in a squat position, it never occurred to them to stand up with their feet on the floor. I was so embarrassed; I didn't know what to say. I just told them to get rid of the tables and go back to working on the floor."

"For some, it will be a long, long journey," Martin said, still laughing.

"I guess so." Bobby shook his head. He decided this was the time. "The girls now... that's a different story."

"How so?"

"I should take one of these girls home with me."

"Really? Why is that?"

"Well, they're all so small... and my daddy always said to marry a girl with really small hands." Bobby set the trap.

"And... why is that?"

"It makes your pecker look bigger."

Yichun is a small city by Chinese standards. Only one million in population and the least developed cities involved with WCI. Because it was the site of a military factory that built tanks and other weaponry, it was a 'Closed City'. No one was allowed to visit without special permission from the Chinese Military, not even the local Chinese. Thus, since nobody ever came here, there were no hotels... none. Accommodations had been arranged in a government barracks. These accommodations consisted of a bed without sheets and a hole in the floor for a bathroom stool. The mattress was dirty and covered with mold. There were no pillows. A single wooden chair and a small table holding a wash basin under a dirty mirror were the only accessories. There was no shower. There was no bathtub. The walls were unpainted concrete. The floors were unpainted concrete. There were no windows. There was no lock on the door.

The Americans were in shock.

"How long do we have to be here?" Donnelly asked.

"Three days... so says the schedule," Martin replied. The three men were standing in the doorway of Martin's room... observing the finery.

"No way! No fucking way!" David Choi muttered. "God damned, uneducated, ignorant mainland Chinese! I'm ashamed to be of similar heritage! I'm not staying in this shit!"

"What choice do we have?" Martin asked. It was getting late in the afternoon.

From Donnelly, "There's got to be something we can do."

"I can make it one night," Martin claimed. "We do our thing at the factory tomorrow morning and get the hell out of Dodge. Anywhere will be better than this. David... tell them... tell them we have to cut our visit short... that we are needed more in another factory. Try not to hurt their feelings... if that's possible. Tell them we must leave by noon tomorrow."

"Okay... I'll do my best to be diplomatic... but don't expect miracles!"

"Nobody will believe this. I'm taking pictures!" Donnelly offered.

The group walked to a nearby restaurant for dinner. At least they tried to have dinner. The local people had never before seen any foreigners in their city. Never. A crowd formed around the table where the Americans were seated and soon there was no room in the restaurant for the other patrons. As the word spread, the street outside filled with curious people trying to get a glimpse of these strange looking aliens. The waiters had difficulty bringing the food to the table, shoving and pushing to get through the hundreds of Chinese packed inside the room. The experience was very unsettling, and although they were in no real danger, the Americans were not sure what was happening.

Finally, there was a siren and shouting from the street and, as if by magic, the crowd disappeared. The police had arrived.

The officer in charge wore a uniform shirt stained with the remnants of a hundred meals and a pair of equally stained baggy shorts. He had a sidearm strapped around his tiny frame, which was all of four foot eight inches tall. He approached the table, clicked his thong-clad heels together, gave a small bow and spoke. The factory leader replied.

"Interpret please, David." Martin asked.

"He has asked the factory leaders to produce our authorization papers... to be in his city. Mr. Lee told him to get lost... the papers are in his desk and they are in good order."

The two men exchanged more words.

"The policeman is not too happy, but I think Mr. Lee outranks him. He now only wants to know who we are."

"Ask Mr. Lee if he would like for me to introduce the group."

"Mr. Lee said that would be a good idea."

"Okay... stand with me, David." Martin and David stood up. "Word for word now... no deviations please."

"Of course!"

"I mean it, David! Tell him we work for a large American company and we are honored to be in his lovely, lovely city." David repeated word for word. The officer smiled and nodded. "Tell him I will now introduce our security chief from America. Bobby, stand up and offer to shake his hand."

Bobby Mayfield... all six foot six of him... stood and approached the policeman.

"This is Robert Mayfield. He is a highly trained law enforcer like yourself."

The police officer took two steps backward, a look of disbelief on his face. He ignored the outstretched hand of this giant man. He mumbled something in Mandarin and nearly ran out of the restaurant. David chuckled.

"You did it again, Martin. He said something to the effect of 'Have a nice time.'"

Mr. Lee spoke. "You scared the shit out of him and he won't bother us anymore." The group all had a good laugh.

After the meal was finished, none of the Americans were anxious to go back to their ghastly rooms. The conversation had turned technical concerning the hydraulic system on the WCI machines. Martin had little knowledge of the subject and wandered to the front of the restaurant to watch the people in the street. An old man dressed in rags came by pushing a small cart loaded with strange cocoon-looking objects that caught Martin's attention. David Choi had appeared at his side.

"What are those, David?"

"I don't know. Let me ask." He stepped out in the street and stopped the old man, inquiring about his wares. He turned and addressed Martin. "They're crickets! They make these little cages out of dried grass and insert a cricket... to keep you company at night. They sing to you, so he claims. Kind of like the Chinese version of a FM radio."

Martin smiled. "How much are they?"

"One Yuan. About 13 cents."

He reached in his pocket and took out some bills. He had no ones so he gave the man a 10 Yuan bill. "Tell him I want one and to keep the change."

David made the transaction and the old man bowed several times, thanking this strange looking man, while at the same time, convinced he was very dumb for paying ten times the value of his cricket.

Martin put the small basket in his shirt pocket and returned to the table. He could see no evidence that there was anything inside.

"You fellas ready to go?"

"Can't we just sit here and drink some Chinese beer?" Bobby asked.

"Let me ask the waiter," David offered, leaving the table to find him. He returned in a few minutes. "Yes... it's okay. In fact, he suggested that we go up on the roof. They have a small bar up there and we can look at the city lights while we drink our beer. We can stay as long as we like, as long as we're buying drinks."

The WCI team, along with a few of the factory personnel, climbed the stairs to the roof where they were pleasantly surprised. There were colored lights strung overhead, a small dance floor, and a bar stocked with a variety of strange spirits. Plastic chairs were gathered, drinks were ordered and the group settled in to watch the sun go down. For the time being, the nastiness of their rooms was forgotten.

As the darkness arrived, so did a few locals... young people for the most part. A karaoke machine appeared and the Chinese took turns singing... mostly western songs. Even though they weren't great singers, the visitors enjoyed their attempts. It was a fun time.

When the group finally returned to their rooms, David Choi found a broken chair outside and dragged it inside. He was not about to sleep in the filthy bed. He padded the wooden structure with his dirty laundry and settled in for the night.

Martin sat on the bed studying his dismal surroundings. Suddenly, he remembered his purchase and retrieved the small grass cage and sat it beside the bed on the small table. Immediately, the cricket began to chirp... a shrill cadence that he found rather soothing, and the stresses of the day began to fade. He put his carry-on satchel on the bed as a pillow and, still fully dressed, lay down to rest. "Can I make it through this, cricket?" he asked.

The cricket was answering... time after time. It seemed to be singing... 'You can... you can... you can...'

Some time later, Martin fell asleep. A little while after that, the cricket died.

The next morning, the team observed the factory's efforts in making one of their old ditch diggers. It would be kind to say their prototype was very poorly built. Actually, it was a disaster. None of the parts fit correctly and it was obvious they had been made by hand... perhaps as a blacksmith would do... by heating and beating. The machine, same as the one in Xiamen, was void of paint and rusting badly. The engine was the only item that worked properly... because it was imported from the WCI facility in Chicago.

"You fellers have a long way to go," Bobby informed the Chinese factory leaders.

"Yes, there is much work yet to be done," Martin added. "You need to send another delegation to the U.S. and visit our factory again. You have not applied any of the training we gave the previous group. You have not implemented any quality control, nor have you changed your manufacturing processes. I am very disappointed in your results."

There was absolute silence after David interpreted Martin's remarks. Several of the Chinese hung their head in shame. They knew they hadn't done the job.

"We will discuss your comments and report back our intentions in one hour," the factory leader said as the group left the room.

"Can you believe this?" Donnelly asked. "They have wasted their time!"

"And, ours!" Martin replied.

They were interrupted by a small, older lady whom Martin recognized as one of the people who had made the first visit to the U.S. She came into the room, looking over her shoulder, making sure no one was watching.

She indicated for David to translate as she spoke. "We have lost much face. Our delegation did learn from your training in America, but when we return with all these new ideas, our leaders scoffed at us. They said your technology is too difficult and too expensive... and that it was not needed to build a good machine. So, we do the best we can with great limits. We are not allowed to purchase any new machinery. We are not allowed to make dies or molds... we must still make piece parts by hand. Please do not tell my leaders that I am telling you this. Your training was very good. This is not a fault of your training." She quickly left the room.

"I suspected as much," Martin said. "Give me a few minutes to formulate a response for when they come back."

"Good. I'm taking a nap! I got no sleep at all last night. Watched a rat chew on my candy wrapper for an hour. That was the only TV channel they had," Bobby offered.

# CHAPTER THIRTEEN

The flight to Nan Chang was delayed. As far as the Americans could find out, the pilots were late. There was no explanation given as to why. When they finally arrived, it was after 8:00 P.M. and darkness had overtaken the city. Except for their fellow passengers, the airport was empty at this hour. There were only two flights a week into and out of the city, and since this flight was three hours late, everyone had gone home... including any taxies that had been waiting.

The group gathered their luggage and made their way to the curb outside the terminal. The outside lights had been turned off so it was difficult to see more than a few feet.

"Last one out turn off the lights!" Donnelly shouted, getting a laugh out of the group.

"You guys wait here... I'll go out to the main street and get us a taxi," David announced and took off on a trot.

"Can you believe this?" Martin asked. "I hope the hotel is still open." The team was to stay overnight at the Lotus Flower Hotel, a joint venture with an Australian hotel chain. The next day, they had a four-hour ride through the countryside to Liuchou, the next factory on the itinerary.

There was a blur on the left and two bicycles went by. Although the darkness was nearly complete, it was clear that the two uni-formed riders were the pilot and the co-pilot.

"Wonder where the flight attendants are," Bobby mused.

A car pulled up to the curb. It was impossible to tell what the make was, but it was no larger than a VW Beetle. The head lights were so covered with dirt, they provided minimal coverage. David emerged from the passenger seat.

"Martin, you and Jack take this one. I'll go get another for Bob-by and me. We'll have to put the luggage in the front seat. I think the two of you will fit in the back."

It was a tight fit, but they were able to get in, each holding carry-on bags in their laps. David gave the driver some money and instructed him where to take his passengers. All this done in Mandarin, of course.

"Okay, guys... he will take you to the hotel. I already paid him, so don't worry about that. We should be right behind you. When you get to the hotel, ask for Edith. She's Australian and speaks English, so you should have no problem checking in. If she isn't there, just wait for us. I doubt that any of the other hotel employ-ees can speak English. See you in a bit." David spoke to the driver again and they pulled away into the night.

It took David over a half hour to find another taxi. He had to take the back seat along with the luggage and Bobby was barely able to fit his large frame into the front seat. His knees were up under his chin and his left leg making it difficult to shift the gears. In spite of all this, they arrived at the Lotus Flower Hotel around 9:30. Inside the lobby, there was no sign of Martin and Jack. *Already in their rooms*, he thought. Edith was behind the reception desk.

"Mr. Choi... nice to see you again. Good evening, sir." She directed her attention to Bobby. "Just staying the one night?"

"Yes, just one night," David answered. "This is Mr. Mayfield. I guess you have already met the other two Americans?"

"No... they're not with you?" She had a confused look on her face.

David's heart skipped a beat. "They're not here... Maguire and Donnelly?"

"No... are they supposed to be?"

"I put them in a taxi an hour ago. I gave the driver the address and paid their fares." His face was reflecting his shock. "Could someone else have checked them in?"

"No, I'm alone tonight."

"Where in the hell could they be?" Bobby asked loudly.

"My God! They're really not here?" It was hard for him to accept. "Something very bad has happened."

The old taxi slowly left the airport complex and entered the main street into the city. The streets were crowded with people and bicycles and the driver was constantly honking the horn which, for the most part, was completely ignored.

"Smells like a dead fish in here," Jack offered, rolling the window down.

"As opposed to a live fish?" Martin responded, doing the same.

"As long as I live, I don't think I could ever get used to so many people. Look at that... they're everywhere!"

"Pretty amazing, isn't it?"

The car came to a turnabout, made a right turn and went up a steep hill, nearly colliding with a pedi-cab containing a family of four. The driver beeped his horn and shouted obscenities, waving an arm out the window as they blew past.

"Wow, that was close. Bet we scared the shit out of that family!" Jack stated.

"Yeah, I bet we did."

The scene outside the car began growing lighter as they entered an obvious marketplace. Gas or oil lights hanging from poles placed about twenty feet apart illuminated the area. Small stalls offering a variety of goods were bustling with customers. While waiting for a group to clear in front of the taxi, the two Americans enjoyed watching as a pig was hung up by its back feet and slit open, letting the entrails fall into a wide bucket.

"Want a pork chop?"

"No thanks. I'll pass." Martin smiled. "I would like to have a drink, though. It's been a long day."

They left the marketplace and the number of people thinned considerably. The old car picked up speed, bouncing and jerking along the rough road. Suddenly, without warning, the driver slammed hard on the brakes, causing the car to slide sideways and throwing the passengers hard against the doors as they came to a stop. A police car blocked the way, its tiny red lights flashing, but barely noticeable. A second police car approached from the rear and blocked any effort of reversing the taxi's position.

"What the hell is going on?" Donnelly asked.

Before Martin could answer, the driver's side door was jerked open and a uniformed man pulled the driver from the vehicle. There was a lot of shouting and gesturing, the driver obviously in a lot of trouble. Three more uniforms arrived and began beating the taxi driver with batons about the head and shoulders. He yelled and screamed, but the beating continued until he lost consciousness and fell to the ground.

His limp body was pulled into the car in front and they drove away into the darkness. A second later, the police car in back left as well.

Martin and Jack were in shock... neither able to speak for some time. It was pitch black outside. The hoards of people that had been surrounding them a few minutes before were gone. There was no movement outside the vehicle. Terror began to replace the shock.

"Now what?" Donnelly whispered.

"I don't have a clue." Martin had difficulty answering. He had never been more anxious in his entire life.

"Can you drive this thing?"

"I don't think... I wouldn't know where to go. No, I think it's best to just wait here. In the car. Somebody will come."

"This ain't funny."

"Really! David Choi is never getting out of my sight again while I'm in China. Never!"


"We must get in touch with the police and have them find Martin and Jack. They should have been here a long time ago. Edith, can you call them... the police?" David asked.

"Of course. Can you describe the taxi? Perhaps a number... or a sign?

"It was dark. The only thing I remember... it had the character for 'Rat' on the hood. There was other writing, but I don't remember what it said. The driver said he knew where the hotel was."

"Okay, I'll call the authorities."

Martin looked at his watch again. It was now 11:20. They had been sitting in the dark taxi for two hours. For him, it had been the longest two hours in his life and he was becoming more concerned as each minute went by.

"What's going to happen to us?" Donnelly managed.

"We're okay. We'll be okay. David will find us."

"By God I hope you're right!"

*So do I*, Martin thought.

There was a bump, a blur outside the window, and then the hood was raised on the car. Martin saw a man with a wrench. Twenty minutes later, they were still seated in the taxi... only now, even though they weren't aware of it, there was no battery, no carburetor, and no sparkplugs. Through all of this, no one tried to enter the car, although Martin had been ready just in case. In his briefcase was a Swiss Army knife that he carried for emergencies such as a loose screw or a bottle that needed to be opened. He had unfolded the largest blade... all of three inches long and was prepared to use it.

"What the hell you going to do with that?" Donnelly asked sarcastically.

"Maybe I'll save your sorry ass, Jack. It's more of a weapon than your mouth."

David had convinced Edith to go to the closed bar and make Bobby and him a drink as they waited in the lobby. The police finally came and, after getting descriptions of the two missing Americans and their taxi, they headed off into the night, taking

David with them. As far as David could find out, there was no report of any accidents or other incidents which would give them a clue where to look.

After an hour of wandering around possible routes from the airport, the officer in charge called his headquarters on the radio. They had a break. A taxi driver had been arrested a few hours ago for driving though a restricted area... a night market where vehicles were banned. It had been his third offense and he was dealt with severely. Unfortunately, the poor fella had slipped and fell, hitting his head, resulting in his untimely death. The police had noticed no one else in the taxi except the driver.

"They've got to be there! Hurry up, curse the gods!"

Martin noticed the flashing lights getting closer. *Please, God... let it be David*, he prayed.

"Is that the police?" Donnelly whispered.

"I don't know. Let's hope so."

The vehicle stopped alongside the taxi and a bright light was shined into the two American's eyes.

"Martin! Jack! Are you alright?" The voice belonged to David. It was the most comforting sound that Martin had ever heard.

Two days later, the Americans were on their way back to the Nan Chang airport to catch a plane to Liuchou, the final stop on the itinerary. Martin gave David explicit instructions that he was never to separate himself from the group ever again in any circumstances that could be even remotely dangerous. Jack had apologized several times for making the remark about Martin's knife. Martin knew he was as scared as he was and was just being his usual obnoxious self. He pretended to be pissed at him for awhile, hoping he would learn from it. In his heart, though, he knew that would not be the case.

As the car made its way through the busy city, Martin noticed a difference in the crowds that lined the streets. Something was up. Large groups of young people were gathering every few blocks, holding up banners with red characters, and chanting the same phrase over and over.

"What's going on, David?"

"Some kind of student demonstration. They do it all the time. Don't worry about it."

*Yeah, right,* he thought. *I'll decide whether or not to worry about it, David.*

When the group arrived at the airport in Liuchou, they were met by the factory manager just inside the terminal. He was visibly upset.

"We receive this telex early this morning. It is from your Hong Kong office." He handed the paper to Martin.

> *To Martin Maguire and David Choi.*
> *You must leave immediately and return to Hong Kong. Do not... I repeat... do not go to Beijing! Take any means you can to leave the country. Perhaps it would be safer for you to return through Shanghai. David... it is your responsibility to bring the group home safely.*
> *Arthur*

"What the hell is going on?" Martin mumbled.

"There is much trouble and violence happening in Beijing. A large student uprising. You would not be safe there... or here.

They are starting to riot here in Liuchou as well," the factory leader advised them.

"Can we start worrying about it now, David?"

"Give me your passports," David ordered, obviously very nervous. "I'll see about tickets to Shanghai and on to Hong Kong."

"Bobby, go with David. Don't let him or our passports out of your sight!" Martin ordered.


Chang Siew Pang watched the small black and white TV. A young man was reporting the news that a large crowd of students were forming on the outskirts of Beijing and other major cities. There was some type of organized activity being planned, but the officials were not sure what it was. Even the smaller cities had similar gatherings. Chang read the telex he had received the night before from the Lotus Flower hotel.

*American group leaving Nan Chang to travel to Liuchou in the morning. Delayed one day for rest.*

"Who do I know in Liuchou?" he muttered out loud. "This may be my last opportunity to get the revenge that is rightfully mine." Suddenly his face broke into a smile. "Yes... a cousin of a cousin... Rung Rue Jong. He was rumored to be a member of the feared Night Tigers, one of the new triads operating in southern China. *He will require some form of compensation. I will offer him special favors for future use!*

David and Bobby returned to the nervous group of Americans. "I have bad news. There are no flights available to Shanghai for three days. That's too long. I have booked us on the overnight train. We leave at 5:00 this afternoon."

Martin checked his watch. It was 11:15 A.M. "What do we do till then?"

"I booked us sleeping berths. They have a special VIP waiting room at the train station for people who have sleeper cars. It will be safe and the facility is nice. We can wait there. There will be food and drinks available."

"Sounds like a deal. Let's go!" Donnelly replied.

"Give us back our passports, David."

"Sure, Martin, here they are." He knew he had lost face with Martin for the taxi incident. He would have to work hard to regain his confidence... once again.

As the Americans neared the exit to the street to get a taxi, they noticed a large group of young people demonstrating outside the airport terminal. Most of the people were calm, chanting and waving banners. However, there was a smaller group near the doors which seemed to be very angry... throwing stones at the building walls and at some of the taxi's leaving the lot. There were armed soldiers guarding the line of people waiting.

"Hurry...get in the queue!" David shouted. The Americans burst through the door and ran to the line. Suddenly, without warning, Martin was confronted by a man wearing a red cloth tied around his forehead.

"You die, American pig... for my cousin of cousins!" he shouted in English, pulling a large knife from his trousers. He lunged at Martin, who managed to dodge his first attempt, stepping aside and hitting the man with his carry-on bag as he went by. The man recovered and prepared to make another lunge. Suddenly, a large hand grabbed him by the throat and another hand knocked the knife to the ground.

"Not today, piss ant. Not today!" Bobby gritted his teeth, his hand squeezing and squeezing... lifting the smaller man off his feet, holding tight until he quit struggling. Finally, he released his grip and allowed the smaller man to fall to the ground. He moved no more. Nobody in the large crowd seemed to notice this skirmish... except for the Americans... and David Choi.

"Thanks Bobby. I owe you one, now." Martin was trying to quit shaking.

"Quick... it is our turn!" David shouted, pushing a shocked Donnelly into the open door of the van. Everyone followed and, in a second, they were pulling away from the crowd and into the busy street.

"Did you kill that guy?" Donnelly asked.

"I don't know. Probably," Bobby answered. "I'll tell you whut...I don't think I had any choice."

"Of course you didn't. The sonofabitch was trying to kill me. Me. Not anyone else... just me." Martin gritted. "How in the hell did he know... me?"

"I ain't ever killed anyone before."

"It's okay, Bobby ... it's okay. He's probably just fine."

"Good God, the whole country is going nuts!"

Martin was not listening. His mind was reeling with unanswered questions. *Why? Somebody still wants me dead for helping Chung to defect? Who? Could be several people. Maybe the Party guy who came with the first delegation. How did they even know where we were? We got a spy. Somebody is reporting our activities. Who could do that? Who would do that?* It didn't take a rocket scientist to figure that one out. His initials had to be D.C.

The VIP waiting room at the train station was relatively clean and comfortable. The team, still shaken from the episode at the airport, calmed down a bit with a beer and some snacks. Bobby was as upset as Martin.

"How in the fuck did that guy know you, boss?"

"I don't know, Bobby. All I know is… that it's a good thing you were there… or I'd be cut to pieces."

"Why would anyone want to kill you?"

"Well, that's a long story. Something that happened a long time ago. I thought it was over…but I guess not." He stole a glance at David. He was either asleep or faking it. "I'll tell you about it later."


The train ride was another adventure. When the train arrived in the station, hundreds of Chinese stormed the platform, pushing and shoving to get on, making it extremely difficult for passengers to get off. The Americans stood back in shock, totally unprepared for this type of attack.

"Don't worry… we have reserved staterooms," David shouted over the clamor.

"What is the big fucking hurry?" Donnelly shouted back.

"If there is no one in a soft berth seat, or a stateroom, the unpaying people will try to stay in that seat," David replied. "The regular seats are wooden benches. Not very comfortable."

"Talk about a Chinese fire drill!" Martin commented.

When the crowd had subdued and most of the un-polite passengers were on board, the Americans handed their luggage to the porters loading the luggage car and boarded their assigned car. When they arrived at the door to their stateroom, they found it shut and locked.

"Now what?" Martin asked.

"I'll go get the porter. Just stay here," David answered. He was gone for nearly five minutes before he reappeared with the porter. "Everybody has the same problem," he reported.

"What is the problem," asked Donnelly.

"You'll see."

The porter unlocked the door and slid it open. The Americans were not prepared for came next. There were at least twelve Chinese crowded into the tiny room, holding their small sacks of belongings to their chest.

"This is what I was talking about," David said. "If there was no one assigned to this room, these guys would get to stay in here for hard berth prices."

"I don't believe this!" Donnelly offered. The porter and the group exchanged shouts and gestures, and finally, the Chinese reluctantly left, and the Americans were allowed to enter.

The room had not been cleaned in a long time. The linens were soiled and soot streaked, the floor covered with food wrappers and spills.

Martin and Donnelly shared the first stateroom. A coin toss determined that Martin got the upper berth. That would prove not to be a good thing. Donnelly found an empty plastic bag and began cleaning up the rubble.

"As long as I live, I will never understand these people," he stated.

"It must be because there are just so damned many of them," Martin answered. "If they don't push and shove and scratch, they will never get anywhere. Standing in an orderly line would just not work in this culture."

"I guess you're right. I see it… but I still don't believe it."

The train jerked into action and slowly pulled away from the station. The two Americans stared at the passing countryside through the dirt streaked window, each lost in their own thoughts. What was the eminent danger in Beijing that caused them to flee this mysterious country? Why was Martin attacked at the airport? Why...why... why?

Soon, it began to get dark and looking out the window was not an option.

"I'm going to bed," Martin announced, and swung up on the top berth. As the car lurched back and forth on the uneven tracks, the top swayed a lot more that the bottom. If his feet weren't banging into the wall, his head was. Finally, he was able to fall asleep, still fully clothed, his mind troubled and confused.

Sometime later, he was awakened by the lack of motion. The train had stopped.

"Boss? You awake?"

"Yeah... I'm awake. What's going on?"

"You gotta see this!" Donnelly whispered.

Martin jumped down and joined his friend at the window. The train had stopped in the middle of nowhere... nothing but desolate countryside could be seen in the bright moonlight. Four uniformed train employees, carrying lanterns and shovels were dragging a human body away from the train. About twenty feet from the tracks, they dropped the body, set the lanterns down and began digging. A few minutes later, the hole was ready and they rolled the body in and filled up the shallow grave. The lanterns were picked up and the four disappeared toward the back of the train.

Martin and Donnelly exchanged glances of disbelief. The train lurched and began to move forward.

"What do you make of that?"

"Fastest damn funeral I was ever at!" Donnelly offered. Neither of the two Americans got any further sleep.

The train arrived in Shanghai at 6:10 A.M. and by 8:30; the team was on a plane bound for Hong Kong.

Safely in his room at the Hotel Excelsior on Hong Kong Island a few hours later, Martin watched CNN as a brave Chinese student stood before a tank...daring it to run him over. Tiananmen Square and the Great Hall of the People could be seen in the background. Wolf Blitzer was excited. Martin switched channels and found Dan Rather standing on the balcony of the Beijing Hotel, equally excited.

"I guess I'd better call my wife," he mumbled. "She might be worried."

Carole was worried alright... but not about her husband. Tonight was to be her first encounter with a member of the opposite sex since outside her marriage. She was worried that she would chicken out... or worse...that she wouldn't please him. She jumped when the phone rang.

"Hello."

"Hi, it's me. We're back in Hong Kong. We're okay."

"What's wrong? Why are you in Hong Kong already?"

"Haven't you been watching the news for the last two days?"

"No... I guess not. I haven't been feeling well," she lied. "What's going on?"

"I don't believe this. There is some kind of student uprising all over China. The Chinese military are killing people like flies and you don't know anything about it? We had to get out of the country in a hurry."

"My God! I had no idea! Are you all okay?"

"Yes, we're fine." He paused. "I guess I'm glad you weren't worried."

"I'm sorry, Martin. I guess I should pay more attention to what's happening in the world...especially when you're gone." At least that much was the truth. "So, you're coming home early?"

"Yes, but it will still be three days. Couldn't get an earlier flight."

"Well, it will be nice to have you home." *Even though it will cut into my plans*, she thought.

"Yeah, it will be good to get home. You wouldn't believe Yic-hun. The worst night in my life!"

"Worse than Harbin?"

"Much worse. Well, I'd better go. I'll call you when I know for sure when we will get into Chicago."

"Okay, honey. Stay safe. I love you."


The trip being cut so short caused a little difficulty in getting flight reservations home. The best they could do included a nine-hour layover in Los Angeles.

After three hours sitting in United's Red Carpet Lounge at LAX, Martin decided to take a walk. The events of the past few days were weighing heavily on his mind. He needed a distraction. After half an hour of wandering around the airport terminal, he stopped into a bar and ordered a drink. The TV was on a local channel showing the best place in the area to purchase a million dollar home. Suddenly an ad for a large Cadillac dealer who was having the lowest-ever-price sale caught his eye. The sales manager touting the sale was none other than... John Brickhauer.

"Come on down to 111 West Colonial Dr. and see me... the Brick... today! You won't be sorry!"

"I'll be damned! No shit! John Brickhauer!" Martin was in mild shock. He never expected to ever see him again. "Bartender... how far is Colonial Drive from the airport?"

"About twenty minutes, sir. South of here on the expressway."

Martin checked his watch... five hours to go. He paid the check and headed for the exit. He had found his distraction.

The cab dropped him off across the street from the dealership. In the showroom, he pretended to look at the array of new cars when a small man in a plaid jacket approached.

"Yes, sir... that one is a beauty! Want to take her for a drive?"

"Well... I might. I was supposed to see the Brick. Is he here?"

"Yeah, he gets all the hot customers... last cubical down that way." The man pointed and retreated back the way he had come.

He had a bottle of coke and a package of potato chips on his desk and he was reading the newspaper. Martin stepped into the small office.

"Hello, John."

He nearly fell out of his chair. "Martin! Where the hell did you come from? What are you doing here?"

"Had a layover... saw your ad on TV. Thought I'd buy my wife a new car."

"I... I don't know what to say. I figured somebody would find me some day... I just never figured it would be you."

"Can't stay long, John. Just wanted to say hello and ask you straight out... what the fuck happened to you?"

He took a deep breath. "I fucked up, Martin. Big time. I got mixed up with the Strickner women. They took videos... of us having sex. They were going to blackmail me into participating in their devil worship sex parties. I panicked... ran like hell. I figured I'd get fired and divorced anyway."

"I know about the Strickners. Carole and I saw them with you at a restaurant."

"You did?" Hid eyes were wide. "You didn't say anything?"

"Wasn't any of my business. I just felt sorry for Peggy."

"Yeah... she deserved better, that's for sure. How is she?"

"Good... I think she's doing real well."

"Okay... well... did the Strickners send a copy of the video to her? Or to Peterlie?"

"I don't think so... they're dead. Murdered."

"You gotta be shittin' me! How... who?"

"We had a defector... from the Chinese group. The PRC sent an assassin to kill him. We think the assassin thought the Strickner girls had something to do with helping him."

"I'll be damned. So, I probably wouldn't have had to run."

"Probably not," Martin agreed. "I'm glad you did, though."

"Why?"

"I got your job."

Brick thought about that for a minute and, for whatever reason, that seemed to upset him.

"Okay... so you found me. Big deal. Now what?"

"Nothing. I'm not going to do anything. Just wanted to see for myself. Now I know. You would have failed miserably... with the Chinese, John. Miserably. A car salesman. Yes, that fits you well. Goodbye John."

Martin walked away. He would never say a word to anyone about John Brickhauer...not ever again.

L.D. Ridgley

# PART II

# Chapter Fourteen

## Three years later

Richard Peterlie leaned back in his leather chair and stared at the personnel folder lying on his desk. The name at the top was Martin Maguire.

Peterlie had just recently been promoted to President of Overseas Operations. The promotion was due to his department completing a multi-million dollar project that involved a massive technology transfer to the Peoples Republic of China... and six months ahead of schedule. That project was due almost entirely to Martin Maguire's efforts. Now it was time to reward him. Peterlie had put it off as long as he dared.

There was a soft knock at his open doorway. "Richard. You wanted to see me?"

"Ah, Meester Mac-wire!" Peterlie liked to tease Martin by pronouncing his name as the Chinese did. "Yes... please, come in."

Martin laughed. It was the proper thing to do when your boss thought he was being funny. "Yes... Meester Mac-wire at your service," he replied, as he entered and took a seat. "What's up?"

"How are things going in China? Anything new?"

"No, not really. I sent the Minister of Technology the copy of the final test results signed by the different factories. That completes the project. I've been trying to keep busy with getting all the documents copied and sent to the vault. Frankly, I'm running out of things to do."

"I thought you might be. You're not the kind to sit around on your ass and bask in past success. Would you like a drink?"

"No thanks, boss. A little early for me. Go right ahead though."

"I'll wait... you might change your mind." He paused to let the drama build. "How would you like a change?"

"A change? As in a different job?"

Peterlie decided to keep him in suspense no longer. "Our Hong Kong office is about to get a Joint Venture Project Manager for the Pacific Rim. You interested?"

Martin could not hide the smile. "Interested? Hong Kong... like... *in* Hong Kong?"

"Yes... in Hong Kong. For at least three years. Maybe more, if you like it."

"You're not kidding me?"

Peterlie smiled. "As a subsidiary department head, you would have salary grade and benefits equal to a V.P. here at home. Company car with driver, full-time maid, stock option program and an executive expense account... all that stuff. I need at least a three year commitment. What do you say?"

There was a half a minute of silence. There was no way for Peterlie to know. He had just fulfilled a dream. A dream of living in Hong Kong.

"I think... I think I'll have that drink, now."

"Hong Kong? Oh, Martin, really?" Carole was excited.

"Really. For at least three years."

She sat down on the bed, the smile fading. "Oh, my. What about my business?"

Martin studied her face. He had thought she would be ecstatic about the idea. "Well, I guess you could sell it… or let Karen run it for a few years. You could still keep control. It wouldn't be that hard to manage from Hong Kong."

"Yeah, maybe. I'll have to give it some thought." Her smile had been replaced by a troubled look.

"I have to tell Peterlie aye or nay tonight."

"Oh, tell him yes. I'll work it out. You can't turn down an opportunity like this!"

A few minutes later, he called Peterlie's home. A pleasant female voice answered.

"Yes?"

Martin was surprised. Richard Peterlie was not married so he was not expecting a woman to answer… certainly not *this* woman.

"Uh, hi. Is Richard there? This is Martin Maguire."

"Of course… just a moment please." There was a short pause.

"Yes, Martin… Richard. What's the verdict?"

"Uh… just wanted to let you know… Carole said yes."

"Great, I'll let the Board know. Thanks for calling. Goodbye."

Martin hung up slowly, a confused look on his face. Carole was watching.

"What?" she asked.

"I think Peggy Brickhauer answered the phone. Peterlie's phone."

"Oh, surely not. We haven't heard from her in years. Not since Brick left. Wouldn't somebody have said something?"

Martin shook his head. "Yeah... you're right. I must be mistaken." But he knew he wasn't mistaken. He distinctly remembered Peggy's voice. It wasn't a voice a man would soon forget. Peggy Brickhauer was at Peterlie's home... and not just as a casual visitor. A visitor would have not answered a stranger's phone.

"Did he recognize you?" Peterlie asked.

"Oh, I don't think so. He didn't let on like he did. I guess I shouldn't have answered the phone."

"Not your fault. I forgot he was going to call. If he suspects anything, I'll deal with it later. I'm still not sure why you want to keep us a secret anyway."

"I've told you, legally, I'm still married. My lawyer says not to play around until the divorce is final!"

"Why did you wait so long to file?"

"I still had hope... that Brick was coming back. But that's over. I'm ready now... to start over with you, as soon as the papers are final. I'm sorry we have to wait to go public."

"I know. I'm sorry too. You're so beautiful. Now, where were we?"

She slipped the robe off her shoulders and let it drop to the floor. "You said something about making me squeal."

Richard Peterlie's code identification was CFD. The acronym stood for Chinese Fire Drill, a name he had selected for himself, but he never shared the meaning with his superiors in the Party. They would never have understood the humor in it anyway.

Two years had passed since Richard first became an important part of the plan... a plan formulated by the corrupt government ministry responsible for advancing China's role in the world marketplace. He didn't join this group voluntarily... although he had grown to have few, if any, regrets.

He had been in Beijing attending meetings with the different government leaders about the possibility of a WCI and Chinese joint venture... a large state of the art manufacturing facility to be built just outside of Beijing. After the first day of talks, he was relaxing with a drink in his hotel room, still trying to adjust to the different time zone, when there was a knock on his door. To his surprise, his visitors were the Chinese Minister of Foreign Trade and a small evil looking man by the name of Chen, introduced as the Director of the Secret Police... China's version of the FBI and CIA.

He made drinks and after a few minutes of small talk, the Minister of Foreign Trade cleared his throat and spoke.

"Mr. Peterlie, we have a private matter to discuss...a proposition for you." He spoke softly, unsure of his English. From four feet away, Peterlie could smell his terrible breath from decaying teeth and rice wine. "Please listen carefully, and understand. If you do not readily agree to our proposal, my colleague is prepared to... persuade you." He smiled.

Peterlie was scared. The little man had an aura of evil around him. He looked like he would enjoy inflicting great pain on his victims. He became so afraid that he agreed to everything with little discussion and no resistance.

The plan was quite simple. He was to help the Chinese get as many joint ventures as possible in the next four years... not only with WCI, but he was to use his influence with other companies as well. Once the factories were established, equipped with state of the art machinery, systems in place and local management people trained... all paid for by the foreign entities, the Chinese government would simply kick the foreign devils out of the country and take over the factories.

Peterlie was appalled at first, unable to believe what he was hearing. Then the minister made his being a traitor a lot easier to accept. For his participation, he was to receive compensation. On the first of each month for the duration of the plan, there would be $50,000 dollars deposited in a Swiss bank account set up in his name only. After the plan was completed, he would be given a bonus of three million dollars. The Minister then opened up the briefcase he was carrying to show his first payment in cash... $50,000 U.S. dollars in neat bundles.

Richard summoned up enough courage to ask, "What if I say no?"

Director Chen's head snapped up, and he spoke in rapid Mandarin, his lips curled around his yellow teeth.

The Minister translated. "We know of all members of your family. You will not say no." End of conversation.

The addition of Peggy in his life came as a surprise. He had visited her several times after Brick had left so quickly, feeling a need to console her. At first, he had no interest other than helping her get through a tough time. Then he realized how much he enjoyed her company and began to cultivate the relationship. They had several dinner dates and in the middle of a romantic dance one night, desire surfaced and they ended up in bed. A few months later, he invited her to move in with him.

It was not an easy decision for her. She had loved Brick deeply and was still not able to accept the fact that he was gone forever. Finally, after another few months went by, she went to a lawyer, filed for a divorce, and moved in with Richard. Reluctantly, he agreed to keep their relationship a secret until after the divorce was final.

Richard's reason for putting Martin in Hong Kong was simple. He was the best man for the job. With Martin's guidance, Richard could be assured that the joint ventures would be up and running quickly. Hopefully, when the lid blew off, he would be able to blame the Chinese for everything and go on without being discovered as the traitor he was. That was the plan. And, he would be rich beyond his wildest dreams.

At first, the Chinese were against Martin coming to Hong Kong... then they realized that Richard was right. He would get the job done quicker than anyone else.

Chung Lim Hua had ceased to exist in a parking garage at the LaSalle Street Bus Station some three years ago. In his place was a fellow named Trevor Chan. He had a birth certificate showing he was born in Iowa to first generation-removed Chinese parents, now both deceased. He had a passport and other papers to prove he was a natural born citizen of the United States. Trevor now lived in Los Angeles and was employed by the CIA as an interpreter. For the last three years, he had made no attempt to contact his old friend, Martin Maguire, just in case Mother China was still watching. Now, after all this time, he was on his way to Chicago. This time on a plane... not on a bus.

*Won't Martin be surprised*, he thought, looking out the small oval window as the Chicago skyline came into view. *I can't wait to tell him of my new assignment.*

It was Saturday afternoon. Martin was cooking steaks on the grill next to the pool. The Greens were over and had been enjoying the warm sunshine and swimming in the warm water. Now they were all seated around the patio table enjoying a beer, talking about Martin's recent promotion.

"You must be totally excited!" Karen bubbled.

"Yeah, what a deal," Walt added. "I'd give my left testicle for a job like that."

"I'd give your left testicle if you got a job like that!" Karen offered. They all had a good laugh.

"I think I hear the doorbell, honey." Carole announced.

"Okay… I'll see who it is. Watch the steaks, Walt," Martin said over his shoulder as he went into the house. *Probably some neighborhood kid selling something*, he thought, pulling the door open.

"Hello, Meester Mac-wire. Long time you no see."

"I'll be damned!"


The five of them were sitting around the table enjoying the steaks. Karen and Carole, who never finished a whole steak anyway, graciously shared with Trevor. He was telling his story… the fake shooting, the new identity, the new job, the new home and lots of new friends. Yes, lots of new friends…but none as dear as Martin Mac-wire!

"No one must ever know about this," Martin said to his friends. "No one!"

"Don't worry about us! Let's drink to friendships and freedom!" Walter suggested.

"Oh, by way… here is IOU, Martin." Trevor counted out forty 100 hundred dollar bills and laid them on the table."

"I only loaned you two thousand."

"Old Chinese custom... pay back double for gift of trust. That's the only old Chinese custom I remember!" Trevor smiled.

Later, after the Greens had left, Trevor and Martin were finishing a beer and watching the sun go down. Carole had gone into the house to take a shower.

"I'm getting a new job, Trevor."

"You are? Is it a good one?"

"Yes. It should be."

Trevor smiled. "Me also, Martin. That's why I am here in Chicago... to train for my new job."

"Really? Great! What are you going to be doing?"

Trevor smiled again. "I'm not supposed to tell anybody... but I think you are the exception. I'm going, what they say... under cover. I'm going to be a spy."

"Get out of town! Really?"

"Yes. In Hong Kong!"

Martin could not believe his ears. "Hong Kong? You're kidding me!"

"No... I not kid you. You are surprised?"

"Trevor... my new job... it's in Hong Kong."

"Ieeee! This is surely a good sign... a blessing from the gods. Great joss! I am to be an assistant to the ambassador at the embassy, but my real purpose is to report on the acceptance... or lack of acceptance from the locals... on the upcoming handover in 1997. We want to know if there is going to be trouble."

"Oh, yes, that's right... Hong Kong goes back to China. That ought to be interesting. I'm going to be in charge of developing the joint ventures with the PRC. I started to say, with your country."

Trevor laughed. "Not my country any more. This my country now."

Martin shook his head in wonder. "Fate. Both of us in Hong Kong."

"Yes... joss. Good joss!"

Peggy Brickhauer had assumed her maiden name of Clark after the divorce was final. Richard was very helpful in making sure she received her rightful portion of Brick's company stock and retirement benefits, but came up short when it came to committing to more than living together. That was fine with Peggy. She didn't love him... but she did enjoy his company and the sex. Lately, however, Richard seemed to be occupied with other things. He was gone a lot... and when they were together, he was not the attentive lover he once was. She was becoming unhappy with the arrangement, thinking about her different options. On the same day that Trevor Chan paid a visit to his old friend, something happened to help her make a decision about a change.

Richard was playing golf and she was alone in the house. Soon after making a pot of coffee, she noticed a UPS truck pull into the drive. A young man jumped out of the truck with a package and ran to the door, ringing the bell. She signed on the line, closed the door and headed back into the kitchen, reading the label on the package. The return address was in Chinese characters, with the word 'Beijing' written in English underneath. From the weight and size, she assumed it was some type of document. It was addressed to Richard Peterlie, CFD. *CFD... what kind of title is that,* she wondered, laying the package on the counter over the sink. She picked up a dishtowel and went about washing up her breakfast dishes, when the phone startled her. As she reached to answer it, her elbow struck the package and sent it sliding right into the sink full of soapy water.

"Shit!" She grabbed the phone and at the same time attempted to rescue the floating package. "Hold on please!" she shouted, holding the phone at arm's length so she could reach the package. It was dripping wet as she laid it on a towel then returned to the phone. "Yes?"

"Hi... I'm calling for the local Community Chest...."

"Not now, dammit! Call later!" She slammed the phone down and returned her attention to the package. "Damn! I'd better open it up and dry off the stuff inside," she whispered. The water had nearly opened it anyway, needing only a little effort to finish the job. It was, as she suspected, papers... a stack approximately 1/4 thick. The water had penetrated deeply and the edges were starting to curl. "Man! Richard will be pissed if these are important." She began separating the sheets and spreading them around the kitchen, trying to dry them with a paper towel. Even though it was not her intent, one can't spread a bunch of papers around without noticing what was written on them. At first, it didn't make much sense... a report with a bunch of numbers. Then she recognized a name... *Martin Maguire*...and in the same sentence, the word *terminated*. Curious, she read the entire paragraph.

*Our man in Hong Kong will watch Martin Maguire's every move. If there is any indication that he is becoming suspicious, he will be terminated immediately.*

What the hell? She read on...*Also, if our plan is disclosed for any reason, your payments will cease.* Her hands began to shake. *What have I found?! What has Richard done?! What does all this mean? Richard... helping the Chinese... putting Martin in danger? For money?*

*What to do? What should I do?* Quickly, she ran to the bathroom and returned with the hair dryer. Carefully she dried each page, and then ran them through the fax machine, making copies. The packaging was dried and the originals replaced inside. One could tell the package had been wet, but only an expert could tell that it had been opened. She would tell Richard that she dropped the package in the water and dried it off best she could, apologizing for her clumsiness. She would not tell him that it had been opened. Next, she took the copies into the bathroom, locked the door, and carefully read each page.


"How long will you be gone?" Carole asked, setting the plate of eggs in front of Martin. She always fixed breakfast on Sunday, which they were leisurely enjoying at the kitchen table, still dressed in their robes.

"A week... all together. It takes two days to get there and a day to get back... time zone thing. That will give me four days to look things over," Martin replied, buttering his toast. Peterlie had insisted he make a trip to Hong Kong right away. 'You need to check things out... talk to the guys in the office... maybe even look at some apartments. You know, get a feel for living in Hong Kong,' he had said.

"David is picking me up at the airport."

"Oh, that will be nice... to see David again."

"Yeah, it will," Martin said, remembering the trips to China when David had been the group's interpreter and guide. He also remembered the bad things that had happened... and his suspicions of David. "It will be nice to see him again." He had never told Carole of the threat on his life in Liuchou. The team had sworn an oath of silence, mainly to protect Bobby Mayfield. No one ever knew if the man that had attacked Martin had lived or died.

"When do you leave?"

"Tuesday... early... seven something."

"Oh, so soon!"

"The earlier I leave, the earlier I return, baby cakes."

She stood and let the dressing gown fall open, revealing her nakedness. "I took my shower already... but I could take another one... with you."

Martin smiled. "Really. What's gotten to you this morning?"

"My husband is getting ready to leave on another trip to the Orient. I just want to give him a proper send off."

"That's a hell of a good idea!"

Monday afternoon, Martin was in his office packing a few items in his briefcase for the trip. He made sure he had camera and film, checked his passport and looked at his tickets once again. He picked up his trusty Swiss Army Knife and gave it a kiss. As he clicked the case shut, the phone rang.

"Martin Maguire," he answered. There was silence. "Hello... anyone there?" He started to hang up.

"Martin... hi, it's Peggy."

He knew it was Peggy as soon as she spoke. "Peggy! Hi... how are you?"

"I'm... okay. No, I'm not. That's a lie. I need to see you. Now. It's very important."

"Sure... come on over. I'll be here for a couple more hours."

"No! I can't come there. Can you meet me somewhere... private?"

"Of course. Where?" He sensed her desperation.

"Our old house. No one is living there now. It will be... safe."

"All right. Give me a half an hour. I'll be there."

"Martin, don't tell anyone. Not anyone. You are in danger." The line went dead.

*Good God... now what?* he thought.


Martin had not been there for some time, but he had no problem finding it. Peggy looked great. Nice tan, smart clothes and the same perfect figure. She was a very beautiful woman and Martin had always admired her. How Brick could have walked away from this girl, he never would understand. She gave him a peck on the cheek and retrieved a key from under a fake rock.

"Come on in, Martin...please excuse the dust. Sit here." She pulled a sheet off a chair and sat down across from him.

"You look great! How have you been?" he asked.

"Good, but that's not important." She handed him the stack of papers. "You need to read these."

"What's this?"

"Just read."

He read. At first, he was shocked and then he became sick to his stomach. It took him twenty minutes to read all the pages. Neither of them spoke a word until he was finished.

"Where did you get this?" he asked, barely able to speak.

She told him the story of the wet package. "I've been living with Richard for almost a year now. I had no idea... he was so kind to me after Brick left. I guess I let him seduce me out of gratitude. He's an animal, isn't he? He's selling out the company, selling out his country...and he's selling out you. I didn't know what to do...except to call you."

"Thanks, Peggy. You did the right thing," Martin spoke softly. "Can you hold off for a few days... without letting him know that you know about this?"

"I don't know if I can or not. I hate him."

"Can you go away...visit someone...without him becoming suspicious?"

"Maybe. I'll try. What are you going to do?"

"I'm going to go see a man ... he works for the government. He should be able to tell me what to do. Right now, I don't have a clue what that might be."

"Okay. I'll leave Richard a note telling him that my mother is sick in St. Louis and that I've gone there. I've done that before. He won't think anything of it.... I hope." She stood. "I'd better get going so I can be gone before he comes home."

Martin stood as well and reached for her hands, holding them firmly. "Thank you, Peggy. It took a lot of courage to do this."

Suddenly, without warning, she came into in his arms, clutching him close, smashing her breasts into his chest. "Martin, I'm so scared. Just hold me a minute."

His nostrils filled with the scent of her and for that brief moment, he felt a passion that he shouldn't be feeling, but was unable to stop. He was overwhelmed with undeniable desire. She felt so good...so damn good! Reluctantly, but gently, he pushed her back until he could look into her face.

"Wow! What was that?" he muttered.

"I don't know, but I liked it," she whispered.

"Yeah... me too. That's probably not good."

She nodded. "You take care of yourself. I wouldn't want anything to happen to you. This is my mother's number. Call me... let me know what is going on." Then she was gone.

Back in the car, Martin looked up a number in his organizer and dialed.

"FBI Office."

"Yes... Matt Halgren, please.

## Beijing.

Chang Siew Pang could not let it go, no matter how hard he tried. It was like a cancer...eating away at his brain... filling his mind constantly with one thought. Martin Maguire must die. And, now, Martin Maguire was on his way to Hong Kong.

*It must be seen as an accident*, he thought. *If I am suspected, my cousin will cut off my head. I must be smart about this.*

He locked the door of his meager office and dialed the number.

"Wei? Casino Royale Macau."

"Let me speak with Kim Lun."

# Chapter Fifteen

## Hong Kong

The United Air Lines 747 turned sharply to the right and the rooftops of the buildings on Kowloon appeared suddenly only a few feet from the wing tip. Coming into Hong Kong at night was a breathtaking, glorious, unforgettable sight. The huge plane straightened, and then descended rapidly the last few hundred feet to the runway. Ships and barges in the nearby Victoria Harbor went racing by as the pilot braked hard, throwing the passengers forward against the restraints of the seat belts. Just another normal landing at the Kai Tak International Airport.

The plane slowed, turned left off the runway and approached the terminal. A JAL 747 raced by where they had been just a few minutes before, lifting off on it's way to Tokyo.

The trip had been long and tiring. Martin normally was able to sleep a good portion of past trips, but not this time. He found himself going over and over the events of the last twenty four hours... Peggy, the packet, Matt Halgren... the plan. Could he pull it off? Only God knew that answer. And Peggy. He hadn't thought of her for years until he heard her voice on the phone. Now, he couldn't get her out of his mind. Not a good thing for a happily married man.

The plane came to a halt out on the tarmac. Not so lucky. No gate this trip. A portable stairway was put in place and the passengers deplaned and loaded onto the buses for the jerky ride to the terminal. Immigrations and Customs went smoothly and soon he was walking down the ramp into the reception room, pulling his suitcase. Here he was greeted by at least two thousand screaming Chinese and Filipinos straining up against the steel railings, trying to attract the attention of long-awaited friends or relatives as they appeared through the doors. About thirty feet down the row of yelling people, Martin recognized a familiar face. David Choi was waving frantically, grinning from ear to ear.

"Welcome back, Martin. You look great!" he yelled above the noise.

"David! Good to see you again." They shook hands, slapping each other on the back.

"Come... I have a car waiting."

Martin was pleased to see the new Mercedes at the curb... the type of limo service the company used for VIPs. He stopped before entering the car to smell the air. Even if he had been brought to this place blindfolded, he would have known where he was. There was no place in the world that smells like Hong Kong except Hong Kong. It wasn't a bad smell, necessarily, but it was unmistakable.

"Where you go?" the driver asked.

"Where are you staying?" David joined in.

"The Conrad, Pacific Place... Hong Kong side," Martin replied.

The driver nodded and held up his left hand, a signal that he had understood, and pulled out into the maze of stores, shopping stalls and night markets... and the millions of people that are the heart and brains of Hong Kong.

"The Conrad is very good, Martin. Near the office, as well."

"I know, David. I've stayed there before."

"I've missed you, friend. You look good... a little less hair, perhaps... but pretty good!"

"You look well too, David. You married yet?"

"Ieeeia...hell no! Never! Too many feel-good girls out there... just waiting for me to enjoy!"

"Same old David. One of these days you're going to blow your brains out through the end of your dick!"

"I hope so, Martin! That's my plan!" The two men laughed.

"What's going on at work?" Martin asked, changing the conversation. Immediately, he sensed a change in David's demeanor... as if their friendly exchange had been interrupted.

"Work is okay. Why do you ask?" The smile was gone.

"Oh, just curious. Arthur still here?" He knew that he was.

David's smile returned. "Oh, yes... he's still here. Sends his regards. He wants a meeting with you tomorrow as soon as you get to the office."

As the limo started down the ramp heading into the Cross Harbor Tunnel, Martin leaned his head back on the seat and closed his eyes, feigning tiredness. He made a mental note of David's mood change at the mention of the office. As long as they were exchanging small talk, everything was fine. But there was definitely a tension when it came to work.

"You moving to Hong Kong?" David asked, bluntly.

Martin snapped to attention. "Yeah... maybe. You know about that?" Peterlie had told him the guys in Hong Kong hadn't been told.

"Rumor talk. It could have been a lot of bullshit. I have a pretty good source."

"I'd say so. I was told that nobody here knew."

David grinned. "Most don't. Your secret is safe with me."

*I wonder what else you know*, he thought. His mind went back three years to an incident that happened in the Beijing airport. Also, when they were traveling in China, some very bad people always knew where they were going to be next. *Be careful with this guy... he's most likely not a friend in all of this mess.*

The Mercedes pulled out of the tunnel, cut across two lanes of heavy traffic, and headed towards Central District. Martin noticed they were surrounded by a Jaguar, two more Mercedes and a Rolls Royce. Yes, he was, without a doubt, in Hong Kong!

The car turned onto Queensway, made it's way up the hill to Number 88, and pulled under the hotel canopy. An Indian fellow, dressed in the white uniform of a marching band drum major, raced to open the passenger side door. The bellmen were already taking his bags from the trunk. "Welcome to the Conrad, Master."

"Thank you."

"See you tomorrow, Martin. Get a good night's rest," David offered.

Martin watched as the limo sped off and then entered through the door that drum major was holding open. Just inside, a very attractive Chinese girl in a long, white silk dress smiled sweetly.

"Good evening, sir. Mr. Maguire?"

They were good. They were damn good! He looked around at the finery... highly polished teak and mahogany paneling and marble floors reflecting the thousands of lights from the huge chandeliers. Simply the best.

"Yes, thank you."

"Welcome back, sir. It's been awhile... almost three years."

"It's good to be back."

She produced a small leather pad from behind her back. "If all your information is still the same, just sign here and I'll take you right to your room. You must be exhausted."

A second later he was following the sensuous movements of her buttocks... so visible through the thin silk, thinking that perhaps he wasn't all that tired.

The room was impeccable; covers already turned down on the king-size bed, a soft robe laying on the chair and a basket of fresh fruit along with a pot of steaming tea on the table. His suitcase was already on the luggage stand. The girl checked everything over and, once satisfied things were in order, turned to leave. "I do hope your stay with us is pleasant. If there is anything I can do... my name is Miss Ling. Please ask for me. Goodnight, sir."

*I wonder how many guys take you up on that... and how does it appear on your hotel bill?* His thoughts were interrupted by the phone.

"Hello?"

"You made it! Good. Everything all right?"

"Yes, I just got in."

"I know. I called twenty minutes ago. Nothing new here. I just wanted to make sure you got there okay. Be careful. I'll talk to you later."

"Fine. I'll be careful. Goodnight."

"You mean good morning. It's morning here, remember?" The phone went dead.

So it was... morning there. Martin stripped, lay down on the bed and was asleep in two minutes.

## Chicago

Matt Halgren hung up the phone and rolled over in the bed. The bathroom door opened and she entered the room, her naked body glowing in the morning sun.

"He is there?"

"Yes... just checked in."

"Good." She sat on the side of the bed and reached a soft hand to fondle him. "You're so different, you and Martin. He's ready to sleep after the second time. You still want more." She was getting the reaction she wanted as she increased the rhythmic strokes.

"Careful, there. You don't want that thing to go off in the air, do you?

"No way." She pointed. "I want it to go off in here."

"Great idea," he moaned.

"Like I said, you just never want to stop."

"That's because he can have you anytime he wants. I have to wait till he's out of town." He pulled her into the bed and rolled on top. "You are a prize to be had, Mrs. Maguire."

"Then go ahead and have me, Mr. Halgren!"

He did.


Richard had worked late in the office on Monday. It was nearly nine when he arrived home. Knowing he would go straight to the liquor cabinet, Peggy had taped a note on the glass door.

*Dear Richard,*

*Mother is not feeling well. She called to see if I would come down and take her to the doctor tomorrow. I knew you wouldn't mind. There's a beef roast in the fridge. Also, there's a package on your desk. It came this morning. I accidentally spilled some water on it but I don't think it got wet inside. I should be home by the end of the week. Don't go foolin' around on me! I want you all for myself!*

*Love, Peggy*

"Damn!" he said out loud. "That's why we are never getting married, sweet girl. I'm not going to St. Louis every time your momma gets sick!" He made a drink, went into his office, picked up the package and ripped off the cover. "Didn't get wet? Well, it did get wet, damn it! Not too bad, I guess," he mumbled, smoothing out the curled edges.

He sat at his desk and read the report. When he got to the part about Martin being eliminated, he paused. "Jeez, guys! Let's not get carried away. Martin will do just fine! No need to kill anyone!" He opened the bottom drawer which contained a small safe, spun the dial a few times, and opened the door. He placed the packet on top of previous reports and then removed a small note book. He made an entry and totaled up the column. He now had a little over two million in his account.

## Hong Kong

At three A.M. Hong Kong time, Martin was wide awake, his body clock registering two in the afternoon. He retrieved the number from his briefcase and dialed.

"Clark residence."

"Hi... is Peggy there? This is Martin."

"Just a moment."

"Yes?"

"Hi... it's me."

"Oh, I was hoping you would call!" Peggy's voice was full of relief. "Is everything okay?"

"Yes. How about your end?"

"I guess so. I haven't heard anything from Richard. But that's not unusual. He never has called me here."

"Good. Don't worry. I met with the FBI and the CIA. They know where you are and have assigned a man to keep an eye on you. We have a plan. They've put surveillance on Richard as well. I don't think you are in any danger. Just stay put until I get home."

"Okay. When will that be?"

"Next Saturday."

"Martin... I.... I don't know why... but... oh never mind."

"What?"

"You have enough problems right now. You don't need more."

"What are you talking about?"

"When I held you yesterday... I wanted to kiss you so bad.... "

"Yeah... I know. Me too."

"We have unfinished business... us two. You come home safe, you hear me?"

"Yes, I hear you. Bye Peggy."


The plan was simple. If it worked, it would be brilliant. It was actually mostly his idea. He was to spend a few days in Hong Kong looking things over as his boss suggested. When he returned, Richard would surely call him to his office to discuss the trip. Martin would be wearing a wire monitored by the CIA. After the expected chit chat, Martin was to tell Richard that while in Hong Kong, he was approached by a mysterious Chinese man who offered him a lot of money to expedite the joint ventures with the PRC and then to help the Chinese take over the factories. Martin would say he thought it best to tell Richard right away so the joint ventures already in progress could be halted. This news should cause Richard to react in some manner that would expose him as the corporate traitor he was. In comes the CIA... charges would be filed, and that would be the end of that. After the news of the plot was made public, any joint venture in China by any company would cease until the Chinese government made assurances that this type of takeover would not be tolerated. The Chinese were not dumb. They needed Western technology to become a major player in the World Trade organization. Their plan of taking the big shortcut would be over.

Martin called room service, ordered breakfast, then went to the window and pulled the drapes back. There are few sights more magnificent than Honk Kong at night. It is absolutely fascinating; a million lights of all colors, some moving, some still, all twinkling... some saying "Come shop here."... others saying "This where to do business." ... and several announcing "This is where I live." He became mesmerized... in a trance. *I'm going to live here. Maybe I'm going to live here.*

After he ate, it was still three hours before the office opened, so he donned a pair of shorts and a t-shirt and went for a walk.

The hotel lobby was deserted, with the exception of a lone security guard seated by the front entrance. He woke up from his nap as Martin approached and opened the door.

"Jo-san." Martin said good morning in Cantonese.

"Jo-san," the guard returned, surprised that a foreign barbarian would know of the chosen language.

Outside, the sun had not yet shown itself. There was enough light to see clearly, however. It was already hot... nearly 90 degrees... and the intense humidity greeted him like a slap in the face. Hong Kong didn't cool off much at night. Clouds were covering Victoria Peak, blotting out the familiar landmarks he was searching for. He walked aimlessly for a few blocks, getting re-familiarized with the area... taking his time, letting his body get accustomed to the heat and humidity.

A Chinese lady, old and bent, was pushing a large cart loaded with bags of garbage up Justice Drive, one of the many steep streets on the island. Martin marveled at this feat, realizing that it would be extremely difficult, if not impossible, for him to do the same, and he was one-third her age and twice her size. Fascinated, he watched her progress until she was out of sight, following her, but at a slower pace. It was much too hot to be in a hurry. He stopped to catch his breath and stretch a muscle cramp in his calf, bending over to massage the back of his leg. He heard a scraping sound that sounded like it was coming from his left. He raised his head but saw nothing. The sound was growing louder and suddenly he realized it was coming from up the hill ahead of him. Then, he saw it. The heavy cart loaded with the bags of garbage was coming straight for him at a very rapid pace, and it was only a few feet away. He jumped backward as hard as he could, managing to clear most of his body from the path of the cart, but his left foot was struck, tearing off his shoe. He fell hard on the concrete, bringing blood to both his elbows, watching in horror as the cart jumped the curb and ran into an electrical transformer, bringing a shower of sparks, one of which ignited the garbage. The fire spread to the other bags quickly. A shout was heard from a nearby building and, suddenly, the street was filled with people, yelling and running here and there. He managed to stand on shaky legs and retrieved his shoe a few feet down the hill. He was too upset to think at the moment and reacted instinctively.

Wiping the sweat that covered his brow, he limped off, turning right onto Supreme Court Road, and headed toward Hong Kong Park. He heard the sirens approach.

At this early hour, he had the park nearly to himself. Hong Kong was not known as an early riser. Most of the shops didn't open until eleven and the office workers rarely arrived before nine. He found a secluded bench and replaced his shoe, regaining control over his trembling body. He examined his stinging elbows, deciding they were only scraped and not a serious concern.

It had to be an accident... didn't it? Yes, of course, an accident. Gathering his wits about himself, he continued on through the park. As he neared the fish pond, he encountered an older man... perhaps in his late nineties, doing Tai Chi next to the water. He stopped at another park bench to retie his shoes while enjoying the old man going through his slow motion moves.. When he straightened up, he noticed a man across the park duck behind a tree. He couldn't be sure, but he thought he recognized him as the security guard from the hotel. *Accident my ass!* Martin did not believe in coincidences.

Continuing his walk, he kept a close watch behind him, but never observed the man again. Perhaps he had been mistaken. Perhaps.

By the time he returned to the hotel, it was nearly seven o'clock.

There were a few people now stirring around the lobby. The cool of the air conditioning was a drastic change, shocking his wet skin. As he reached the elevator, the sensation was gone and his body welcomed the coolness.

He punched the call button and stepped back to wait. A movement caught his attention at the end of the long hall. A blur, really, but a blur of a man… quickly disappearing through a door. David Choi? He couldn't be sure. He had only a glimpse.

*Jesus Christ, who would be next? Sherlock Holmes or Jimmy Hoffa?*

He forgot the elevator and walked down the hall to where he last saw the man. There was a door marked 'Staff Only'. He tried to open it but found it locked. *Strange,* he thought. *If it was David, what was he doing here? And why didn't he acknowledge me?* The old feeling was back. David Choi was not to be trusted and somebody was still trying to have him killed.

He walked back to the elevator troubled with that thought. Inside the room, he stripped off the soggy clothes and went to his suitcase to retrieve clean underwear and band aids from the small first aid kit, when he noticed it. His briefcase had been moved. He knew this because it had a feature which would not allow it to be opened upside down. He had opened it earlier to get Peggy's phone number, so he knew it was right side up. Now, however, it was not. Somebody had been in his case!

A quick examination found nothing missing. Somebody was looking for something, though. The question was… what? *Great security they have here*, he thought. Somebody, who looks like David Choi, probably bribed the security guard to run him over with a garbage cart and gave him a key to my room. *Might as well have some fun with this*, he thought.

After his shower, he dressed in a light summer suit and returned to the lobby, now filled with activity. Some were tourists, but most were business people like himself, getting ready to do the Hong Kong thing.

He found the manager's desk and approached. The middle aged gentleman seated behind the desk spoke softly. "May I help you, sir?" His accent identified his distinct British heritage.

"Yes, you may. I have a rather delicate matter to discuss with you. Is there somewhere we can talk in private?"

Immediately, the manager became noticeably nervous. A matter which required privacy... from a guest...certainly would be a serious matter.

"Yes, of course... come this way."

Martin was ushered into a small room containing a small desk, two chairs, and cluttered with discarded umbrellas and old computer printouts.

"What is the nature of your problem, sir?"

Martin got right to the point. "I think it is our problem... not just mine. I have reason to believe that the security guard on duty early this morning entered my room while I was out and removed $2,000 Hong Kong dollars I had lying on the dresser," he lied.

"Bloody impossible!" The manager's face had turned beet red. "Our security people are above reproach!" It was obvious that he was shocked at the very thought.

"I see," Martin said slowly. "Then I guess it will be up to the police to sort this out. I would have thought you would have preferred to handle this... internally... to avoid the publicity. Perhaps I was wrong. I will make a report to the police. Thank you for your time." Martin turned to leave.

"Wait! Please... wait." The manager recovered quickly. "Yes, of course... the publicity... you are right. This matter should be handled internally. I will personally see to it. Thank you for bringing it to my attention."

"Great! The $2,000... I want it back." Martin left quickly. One poor security guard was going to be in deep shit!

Arthur Stephens was born in London in the forties and was now the Managing Director of the WCI Hong Kong Subsidiary. He had spent nearly twenty years in Asia, starting out in Singapore developing customers for WCI before moving on to Malaysia and then Indonesia, and finally accepting the job in Hong Kong. That was eight years ago. He was a single man, but had a reputation for always having several young and beautiful ladies available for his pleasure. He was a large person, nearly six foot six, deeply tanned and very well-groomed. He was, in fact, a strikingly handsome man and considered by most to be a true gentleman.

He greeted Martin warmly, ushering him into his lush office overlooking Victoria Harbor. It was a grand view... Kowloon in the background with a variety of ships, sampans and ferries scuttling to and fro in the harbor. In the distance, a 747 was landing at Chek Lap Kok airport. Arthur buzzed his secretary and ordered the two of them coffee.

"Sit down, Martin. It's good to see you again." Arthur settled into his high back executive leather chair. "You've made a few jumps up the ladder since we last met."

"Just luck, Arthur," Martin smiled. "You know, right place... right time."

"That's bloody bullshit. Luck didn't have anything to do with it, if I can believe Richard Peterlie. How's the family?"

*Killing time,* Martin thought. *This old bastard doesn't give a damn about my family!* "Fine, Arthur. Thanks for asking."

Susanna entered with a tray containing the coffee. She was gorgeous, impeccably dressed and always so sweet to visitors from the States. She was a 100 percent Hong Kong Chinese classy lady. "Hi, Martin. So nice to see you again."

"Hi, Susanna. You too." A true statement, indeed.

"Shut the door, will you sweetheart?" Arthur purred, patting her on the rear. There was no such thing as sexual harassment in Hong Kong. Susanna's petite body disappeared and the door clicked shut. Arthur's face became very serious as he leaned forward in his chair. "Now, Martin... what the fuck are you doing in Hong Kong?"

The bluntness of the question surprised Martin. "What did Richard tell you?"

"He told me some cocky bullshit story about you wanting to look around... see some of your old buddies... do some shopping... like on holiday. I didn't buy that then and I don't buy that now. Peterlie is an asshole. He thinks we're all dummies over here. Now... you tell me the truth!" He pointed a manicured finger at Martin.

Martin smiled, and then decided to do just that. "Richard has offered me a job here in Hong Kong. I would still be working for him, but out of this office. I won't be under your command... just renting office space so to speak."

Arthur seemed to relax a bit. "I see. What kind of job? Doing what?"

"Working with the PRC... trying to establish manufacturing joint ventures."

He nodded. "Good. We need to do that. Been saying that for years." He paused. "Thanks for telling me. I won't let Richard know that you did." His attitude had turned friendly again. Martin was no threat to his dynasty. "Look the place over. Take any office that's empty. Your choice."

"Thank you, sir. I appreciate that. I don't know why he didn't tell you the truth."

"Because, like I said... he's an asshole! Anyway, have you made plans for dinner tonight?"

"No, not yet."

"Good. You're having dinner with me." He punched a button on the phone. "Susanna... get your sweet little derriere in here."

Less than three seconds later, she appeared, pad and pencil in hand. "Yes, sir?"

"Call Mikki... tell her to make reservations at the Windows of China in the American Club for... eight o'clock... four people. Tell her to bring Sabrina... we have a guest in town." He reached behind her and pinched her buttocks. She jumped.

"Yes, sir." And she was gone as quickly as she had entered.

"Do you like Chinese food?"

"Yes, I do," Martin responded.

"Good. I'll treat you to the best. Do you like Oriental women?

He wasn't falling into that trap. "I don't know, Arthur. I've never had one."

"Well, I'll introduce you to the best. The rest is up to you."

"That's not necessary."

Arthur dismissed the mild refusal with a wave of his hand.

"When in Rome..." he smiled. "Anyway, you need a dinner companion. If all you want to do is talk, then talk." He looked at his Rolex." I have a meeting at the Embassy in a few minutes. We have a guest office next to mine. Susanna will get you set up in there. Feel free to roam wherever. David will be in around nine-thirty. If you need anything, just ask him or Susanna. I'll send my car for you at the Conrad.... around seven-thirty. Dark green Jag. Wear a dark suit and a dark tie if you brought one." He stood, gathered his Saatchi briefcase and headed toward the door. He turned and peered over his glasses. "You'll be okay?"

"Sure. I'll be fine. See you tonight."

WCI leased the entire fifty-eighth floor of Pacific Place Tower II. There were over forty individual offices, five conference rooms and a small snack area. Martin walked around the area looking at empty offices, finally deciding on one that offered a similar, if not as perfect, view as Arthur's office. He posted a note on the door that the space was reserved by Martin McGuire. It was a very satisfying feeling.

The bottom three floors of Tower II consisted of high-end shops... expensive ladies' and gentlemen's fashions, big name jewelry stores and numerous electronics stores touting the latest in cameras, audio equipment and personal gadgets.

Martin walked around, looking in the windows at the vast variety of items and marveled at how busy the stores were. *Not a good place to turn your wife loose*, he laughed. He took the express escalator down three floors to the street entrance.

Keeping a close eye over his shoulder, he caught a taxi to the Star Ferry terminal and bought a ticket to cross the harbor into

Kowloon for seventy cents. He loved taking the ferry, always packed with interesting people going to and from the island. He had lunch at a restaurant called Dan Ryan's, after the famous expressway in Chicago, pleased to hear the actual voice of the first Mayor Daly giving a speech over the audio system. The restaurant had become a favorite place for the Americans to visit after a few weeks in mainland China. Sort of like a decompression chamber after a deep dive. The burgers and the homeland beers were great and made the trip back to normality not quite so drastic.

After lunch, he walked up Salisbury Road past the Peninsula Hotel, which had five Rolls sitting out front and turned up Nathan Road... taking his time as he passed several familiar shops and eateries. In four blocks he turned down five offers to buy a copy watch. He made a right turn on Moody Road and could see the sign he was looking for in the distance. Ronnie's Wellfit Tailors.

A face he recognized appeared in the doorway and the person belonging to it broke into a grin.

"Mr. Maguire! It's been a long time."

"Hi, Ronnie. How you been?"

"Just fine, Mr. Maguire. Come in! Would you like a beer?"

"A beer sounds great!"

The entire shop was no larger than the kitchen in his house. The walls were covered with shelves filled with bolts of cloth from floor to ceiling. In the rear was a small closet, three feet by three feet, where the customers tried on their basted together suits and dresses... efforts of the first fitting. Martin sat on one of the small stools as

Ronnie retrieved two cans of beer from the small fridge.

"I will join you… to celebrate the return of a loyal customer and friend."

"Thank you, Ronnie. How's business."

"It's good… but not like old times. In the eighties, I kept four tailor shops busy. Now, I have only two."

"Have your prices gone up?"

Ronnie laughed. "Prices always go up! You know that!"

After a short visit, Martin ordered two suits and three shirts… custom fit… all for less than $400 U.S. They were to be delivered to his hotel the next day.

Next he headed on down the street, enjoying the shop windows full of strange goods in the stores that catered to the locals. After a few blocks, he arrived at Wing On Plaza. He took the escalator to the second floor and walked into Jason's, a jewelry store where he had also shopped on previous trips.

"Martin! Hello, old friend! Welcome back to Hong Kong! You like champagne?" The stores in the U.S. could take a lesson in marketing.

"No thanks, Jason. Just had a beer at Ronnie's."

"Okay. You look well. What can I do for you this trip?"

"I need a nice string of pearls."

"You buy pearls for misses last trip," Jason reminded him.

"These are not for misses," Martin replied.

"Ieeeah! You are becoming civilized…like Chinese man. You have mistress?"

Martin smiled. "No, not yet." His thoughts went to Peggy.

The shop owner smiled… "But, you are thinking about it… I can tell. The pearls will do the trick."

"Perhaps…we'll see."

"Martin, my friend, before we look at pearls… watch my store. I have go pee very bad. I go down hall to the restroom." Before Martin could protest, the little man was gone, leaving him, a man he hadn't seen for two years, alone with five million dollars worth of jewelry. Only in Hong Kong!

A few minutes later, he was back.

"Thank you, Martin. I afraid my eyes turn more yellow than before!" he joked.

"I sold a three carat diamond while you were gone. Got nearly a thousand HK for it."

"You funny man. Let me find you nice pearls." Jason opened a drawer and started removing samples.

"How are things, my friend? How is Hong Kong doing these days?"

"Not too bad. Ten years ago much better."

"Yeah, Ronnie says the same thing. How do the locals feel about the handover?"

"I think no problem. As long as they will let us continue to make money and not fuck with our system."

"Will they do that?"

"They say yes. We will see, won't we?"

"I guess we will." Martin started to tell him that he was moving to Hong Kong when he suddenly realized that might not happen with the latest development involving Richard. "We'll see indeed."

By the time he got back to the hotel, it was nearly five P.M. He walked into the lobby and found David Choi waiting.

"Martin! Where the hell you been? I've been looking all over hell for you!"

"I had some shopping to do, David. Why were you looking for me?"

"Well," he stammered, not sure how to answer. "I just wanted to see if you needed anything. I can be your guide."

"David... I can get around Hong Kong just fine. I don't need you to help. Go home... I'm fine." *He wants an excuse to see what I'm up to,* Martin thought.

"Okay, if you're sure."

"I'm sure. By the way, where were you at six this morning?"

His face paled. "Home... in bed. Why?" Had Martin seen him?

"I thought so. Okay, go home."

David turned and left quickly.

He entered the lavishly furnished lounge and took a table where he could watch the interesting people come and go from the hotel. The attractive server was there in less than a minute, bringing a tray of exotic cheeses and tasty crunchies.

"Good afternoon, sir. What would be your pleasure?"

She was as cute as could be. *I'm not sure it would be a good thing to be single in this city,* he thought. He ordered his vodka rocks and sat back to relax. He couldn't help overhearing the conversation going on at a nearby table.

"Man. I'd love to try and split her open," the older man stated.

"Shit, she wouldn't give you the time of day."

"She a waitress, for God's sake. You think she's that particular?"

"She wouldn't touch you with a ten foot pole."

"She wouldn't touch you with a *twenty* foot pole!" Martin broke in. For some reason, he was upset at the two men. "The kind of woman you want is in Wanchai... at least the kind you can get. They hire out by the hour."

"I don't think any of this is your business," the younger man replied.

"Then keep your conversation down. That girl is the daughter of a friend of mine," he lied.

"Oh, sorry. Let's get out of here, Harry." Without another word the two men left a hefty tip and walked out. Martin felt great...as if he had just saved a person from harm. The cutie returned with his drink.

"Thank you so much!"

"My pleasure, sir. Please enjoy."

He did.

Martin walked toward the elevator when he was interrupted by the hotel manager from this morning.

"Mr. Maguire. I have taken care of the small problem that you encountered this morning. One of our security employees has decided to seek employment elsewhere. Before he left, he compensated you for your loss. You will find an envelope waiting for you in your room. I personally placed it there. I trust the rest of your stay will be without incident." He bowed, clicked his heals, and abruptly walked away.

The envelope was lying on his pillow. Inside was ten thousand Hong Kong dollars. Martin grinned. Two thousand to replace his supposed loss, and eight thousand to keep his mouth shut and not involve the police. The eight thousand was probably the amount of the bribe to the security guard.

Later he showered and dressed. Black suit, dark blue shirt and black tie. *That should be appropriate*, he thought, surveying himself in the mirror. At seven twenty-five, he took the money out of the envelope and put it in his shirt pocket.

He exited the elevator and approached the reception desk. Here, he had noticed earlier, was a glass container inviting hotel guests to deposit their loose Hong Kong change to help a local orphanage. One by one, he deposited the stack of reds, the common name for one hundred dollar Hong Kong bills, into the container. The receptionist from the night before was observing his actions, eyes wide with disbelief.

"Good evening, Mr. Maguire. How generous of you!"

"Not at all. I like to share my blessings with the less fortunate. Don't you?"

"Yes, of course... yes I do!"

*Yeah, right*, he thought, walking over to wait by the revolving doors.

# Chapter Sixteen

At exactly seven-thirty, the dark green Jaguar arrived under the hotel canopy.

The chauffeur, a middle aged Pilipino dressed in a black uniform, opened the rear door. "Mr. Maguire?" he inquired. Martin nodded and slipped into the plush interior of the car. *Man, is this nice or what!*

The immense power of the car could be felt as the driver pulled into the traffic and onto Hennessey Road heading toward Central. A few blocks later, he turned on to Cotton Tree Drive and started up the mountain.

Martin was confused. "I thought the American Club was in the Stock Exchange Building on the waterfront." He was becoming suspicious of every strange move.

"Oh, yes, sir. You are correct. I go pick up other dinner guests."

"Okay, thanks. No problem."

"Momen tai," the driver responded.

"Momen tai?"

"Yes… Cantonese for 'no problem." The driver smiled at Martin in the mirror.

The car wound its way up the narrow streets past the huge expensive apartment buildings. They sported names such as Tycoon Court, Harbor View, Queens View and Kings Allure. In two blocks, Martin counted four Rolls-Royces.

"Where are we?" he asked the driver.

"This called Mid-levels District. Very expensive flats. Only rich people live here."

"I believe that!"

The car pulled off the street and up a steep ramp, coming to a halt in front of a gray and pink marbled building. The sign in gold letters announced 'Hadden Court'.

"One moment, sir." The driver got out and entered the building. Wanting to see better, Martin got out as well, awed at the beautiful sight of the harbor below, lit up like a giant Christmas tree.

"Wow... what a sight," he said out loud.

"Sir? We should go quickly." The driver spoke, bringing Martin out of his trance.

Martin turned and, again, was stunned by the beauty of the sight. The driver was not alone.

They were Oriental, but not Chinese. They were impeccably and very sexily dressed, both well endowed in the chest area, another indication that they were not Chinese, and both were absolutely breathtaking.

The one with the reddish brown hair spoke first. "Mr. Maguire, hi... I am Mikki, Arthur's friend. This is Sabrina. She will be your dinner companion for this evening."

"Hello, Mr. Maguire," Sabrina spoke. Her voice was like tiny bells... so delicate... so musical. "You are 'Merican. I am so fortunate to meet you. Welcome Hong Kong."

Martin melted. She was perfection. The blackest hair he had ever seen, perfect breasts, clearly visible through the sheer bodice of the black dress she was wearing. Her skin was Asian dark, and flawless. She smelled faintly of carnations and her eyes were so black you could not see her pupils.

"Sabrina... how nice to meet you... and you as well, Mikki," Martin managed awkwardly, his eyes never leaving Sabrina's face.

Both girls laughed at his embarrassment.

"I think he likes you, Sabrina! He is so handsome... you will be lucky girl tonight!" Both girls broke into a fit of giggling and then jumped into the car, tugging at Martin to come with them. Seated inside, Sabrina turned to him.

"I see many questions in your eyes, Mr. Maguire. My mother was Royal Princess of Sabot, Malaysia. My father was a Chinese thief who had three wives, one in China, one in Hong Kong and one in Miri Malaysia. My grandfather, who was Malay, killed him when he found out about the three wives. I attend the university in Singapore for four years and I am tutored in the ways of the Kama Sutra. I come to Hong Kong one year ago to meet wealthy 'Merican. Someday, I would like to live in 'Merica."

Martin was almost speechless. He had heard of the Kama Sutra and could only think of one thing to say. "You are the most beautiful woman I have ever met!"

Mikki giggled and Sabrina lowered her eyes and smiled.

"She know that, Mr. Maguire," Mikki said. "She know that."

The view from atop the Hong Kong Stock Exchange building was almost as spectacular as from Victoria Peak. Like the one from his hotel, it is a view that is remembered for years. Martin only gave it a casual glance, his eyes returning to his dinner companion, where they would stay the rest of the evening. The three of them were seated at a secluded table next to a huge window, a table reserved for the affluent, Martin assumed. They ordered cocktails from the waiter, but before they arrived, Arthur appeared, making excuses for being late. Martin checked his watch. It was two minutes after eight o'clock.

"Bloody traffic can be hell sometimes. I see the girls have gotten you here safely." He smiled at Martin. "Harvey, bring me a double scotch on ice... my special brand," he told the waiter as he was sitting down. Then, he leaned over and kissed Mikki sensuously on the lips. She was a third his age, but here, it didn't seem to matter. There were several gentlemen in the dining room with much younger companions.

"Sabrina! You are looking simply smashing tonight! Don't you agree, Martin?" His eyes were riveted to her nearly bare breasts.

"Smashing... yes, that's the word," Martin managed.

"Oh, and Mikki... you are ravishing! As usual! By George, I am indeed a lucky man!"

The two girls giggled and replied in unison, "Thank you, gentlemen."

"I hope you don't mind Martin, but I have taken the liberty of ordering for us all. It's the custom around here. Dinner will be served Chinese style, one course at a time. I think you will like it." He kissed Mikki again. Their drinks had arrived.

Martin felt a warm hand on his thigh and looked quickly into Sabrina's face over the rim of his glass. He made no effort to remove her hand as she began scratching small designs on his leg.

"Tell me, Martin… what you like best about Hong Kong?" she asked.

He didn't answer right away, considering the question. "You," he said, finally.

The food was superb! It was the best dinner he had ever enjoyed… Chinese or otherwise. Thanks to his previous trips to China, Martin managed to work the chop sticks without putting out an eye. The first item served was a plate of English walnut halves, a small hot pot of boiling caramel, and a cup of orange juice. Following Sabrina's lead, one would pickup a walnut with the chop sticks, dip it in the boiling caramel, then quickly into the cold orange juice to cool and make the nuts crunchy. Martin loved them, eating quite a few more than his share. Next was a dish called Drunkin' Prawns. The live prawns were in a shallow dish and very active, jumping and flipping, splashing water on the table cloth. A pot of boiling rice wine was then poured directly into the dish. A cloud of steam surrounded the table. For approximately thirty seconds, the prawns went crazy, and then lay still as the wine cooked them to a bright pink. Talk about fresh seafood!

Each course seemed to have a procedure for how it was eaten. The Peking duck for example, was carved at the table. Only the crispy skin with the tiniest bit of meat attached was used. The hot slices were then placed on a soft Mandarin crepe, brushed with hoi sin plum sauce, garnished with a scallion floweret, rolled into a tube shape for eating. Magnificent! Next was a small bowl of broth soup with small squares of white meat floating on top. It was quite salty, but had a strangely familiar pleasant taste.

"Chicken?" Martin enquired.

"No." Sabrina giggled. "How you call...snake?"

"Really?" He should have known.

"Oh, yes!" Mikki joined in. "Shexing! Snake. Makes your pleasure shaft very hard and much long!" The two girls laughed again, covering their mouths with their hands.

"Well," Martin grinned. "Better bring me another bowl!"

Finally, the fruit was served... a signal that the meal was over.

Arthur and Mikki continued to kiss and fondle each other under the table during the entire meal, which took nearly an hour and a half. In between courses, Sabrina would caress his leg, each time a little closer to his groin. Their legs were touching and he could feel the heat of her flesh through the fabric of his trousers. By the time dessert was served, she was tracing the outline of his erection with a well-manicured nail. The soup was working.

"You are the most wonderful of dinner companions," he said softly.

"I much more than that, Martin," she replied, applying a little more pressure. "You will see."

He noticed her upper lip quiver ever so slightly. "Are you okay?"

She leaned and whispered in his ear." I want you so bad, I trembling inside."

Before Martin could respond, Arthur interrupted. "Well you two, Mikki and I have another engagement this evening. A private party... by invitation only." He winked. "Sabrina will see that you get back to your hotel, Martin. Right Sabrina?"

"Of course, Arthur."

"Good. I'll see you in the office tomorrow, Martin. Your money is no good here, so don't try to pay the bill. It's already taken care of. I hope you enjoyed your dinner... and your dessert." He winked. "Good night." In an instant, they were gone.

Martin felt a little awkward. "I... don't normally..." Sabrina put a finger to his lips.

"Shhhh. Don't speak... of normality. This is not normal situation. You not home. You in Hong Kong. To experience the true Hong Kong, one must not think of anything except the pleasure of moment. Come, I will show you."

They took the elevator down forty-three floors to the street level. The night air was still, heavy and warm with the humidity. She took his hand and led him through the thousands of people scurrying here and there, the street beggars and the night vendors, until they were walking along the waterfront. Here, there were only a few people present. She stopped once to kiss him tenderly on the side of the mouth, but pulled away when he tried to make more of it.

"Soon," she whispered.

They came to a small dock where a group of Chinese men were gathered. She spoke to them in Cantonese, bargaining. Then she gave one of the men some money and, as if by magic, a small sampan piloted by an old woman with a face full of wrinkles, pulled up to the dock. Martin was amused at the faded Mickey Mouse t-shirt she wore.

"Come." Sabrina took him by the hand and they boarded the small boat. It backed away from the dock and soon they were chugging out into the harbor. She spoke to the old woman in Cantonese.

"Where are you taking me?"

"You will see." Her eyes sparkled. The millions of city lights ricocheted off the water and bathed her face in a soft glow.

After a few minutes, the sampan slowed and pulled into a safe harbor behind a breakwater of huge stones. There were several large yachts anchored here, some softly lit, others dark and quiet. One of the larger yachts had a party going on the main deck. Martin could see the waiters scurrying around and people dancing to the music of a small band. *What a life*, he thought. *I could sure get used to this.*

The small sampan pulled up to a gleaming white and teak sixty-footer. The name on the side was "Mao Wenti". No Problem. Sabrina leapt on the small loading platform and he jumped on behind her. He followed her up the steep chrome stairway to the main deck. The ship was spotless...glass, chrome and teak polished to a high sheen.

Martin was impressed. "Wow! Who does this belong to?"

"It belong my family. We use to entertain business clients. My family in logging and paper business." She walked next to a sliding glass door and picked up the phone hanging on the wall. "Domi, it is Sabrina. Please bring champagne and such to the main deck and then prepare my stateroom. I have brought guest." She hung up and turned to Martin. "Do you like champagne?"

"Yes, sometimes." He knew this would be one of those times.

She touched a hidden switch and muted lights chased the darkness away from the deck, revealing a small glass-top table and four deck chairs. She sat and removed her shoes, pulling her legs up underneath her. A Barbara Streisand song of romance softly filled the air.

"Shoes are like brassieres... they most uncomfortable, always rubbing and pinching. I go without both as often as I can."

"I see." Martin replied, kicking off his own shoes. "I'm not wearing a bra either."

Sabrina giggled. "Come sit... listen to the harbor sounds and the music... think about how you will make love to me."

He sat next to her. "Sabrina... I am married. I don't think this is a good idea. I'm sure my wife would not understand."

Before she could respond, a door opened and a little girl approached with a tray of glasses, a bottle of champagne and food. As she came near, Martin could see she was not a little girl at all, but a very petite full-grown woman, barely five feet tall. She was bare-breasted, a colorful sarong tied loosely around the dark skin of her waist. Silently, she put down the tray, opened the champagne and retreated back inside.

"That is Domi," Sabrina said, pouring the wine. "She has been in my family's service since she was born. Her mother was my wet nurse." She handed a glass to him, they clinked and drank. The champagne was good... very good.

"She's beautiful," Martin commented.

"Yes. She's full blood Malay. She cannot speak."

"Really? Why?"

"I shouldn't tell you. Because of your culture, you will not understand. No, I will not tell you now. Perhaps, I will tell you later." She stood and walked to the railing, looking at the island. He rose and followed her, standing at her side.

"It is magnificent, the view." Waves were softly lapping against the side of the boat. A freighter loaded low in the water with large sea containers chugged its way through the busy harbor. Sabrina turned and wiped the beads of sweat from his brow.

"You are hot. I will cool you." She took the glass from his hand, removed his jacket, then his tie. As her hands went to unbutton his shirt, he stopped her.

"Sabrina... I don't think... I'm not sure..."

"Shhh. I am sure enough for both of us." She removed his shirt and threw it carelessly on the deck. Her hands caressed his chest. "Isn't that better?"

"Yes... that's better," he mumbled, enjoying the soft breeze as it cooled his skin.

"I will join you." Her hands went behind the back of her neck and the dress fell to her waist. Her breasts were shining with perspiration, glowing golden in the night lights. She tugged again and the dress fell to the deck. There was nothing else to remove. A wisp of curly black hair brushed the triangle of her lower belly.

"Oh, yes... this is much better."

"Sabrina... my God, you are so beautiful!" The magic of the night... the wine... the heat... it was all too much. His resistance faded as he fell to her powers. Soon he was as naked as she.

"I love 'Merican men," she murmured. "They are so hairy... and so much big here." Her hands found him in the darkness. "Do you want me 'Merican?"

"Yes," he whispered. "More than anything else in the world."

"Then have me. I am ready. The first time a man and woman

make love, it should be wherever the desire overcomes every-thing else. It is here... now." She lay back on the deck. "Come 'Merican. Take what I have to offer... and I will do the same."

Much later, they were inside her stateroom in a large circular bed, resting... having more champagne. He was drained... com-pletely satisfied.

"Tell me about Domi."

"Oh...yes. I should do that. Domi is a week older that I. When I was born, my mother was...without milk... so Domi's mother fed me. Growing up, I was a lot closer to her than my own mother. They were servants... so I always came first...before Domi. It was hard for her to understand. She became very jealous. When we were seven, she told her mother a lie about me... hoping to get her mother to love her more. When the truth was discovered, Domi's mother cut out her tongue. Then she gave Domi to me... to live out her life as my personal slave."

"That's incredible!" He should have been shocked... but he was not. In fact, he had no feelings at all. Suddenly, his mind went blank and he passed out. The jet lag and the alcohol had come calling.

## Chicago

"Martin will be home in a few days. Are you going to tell him?" Matt Halgren was seated at the kitchen table. Carole was making sandwiches. They had made love all morning and then went for a swim.

"Tell him what?" she asked, shutting the refrigerator door with her hip, her hands full of mustard and lunch meat.

"Well... about us!"

She stopped and looked at him sharply, then slowly set the things down on the table. "Matt... I hope... I hope I haven't given you the wrong idea. I love Martin. I have no intentions of changing anything. I find you very attractive and I wanted you. We had some fun... and I hope we can have some more... but, that's all it is. Fun."

For a minute he wasn't sure if he was angry or relieved. He decided he was more relieved. "I see. So, we just forget about what happened and go about our business?"

"Well, I hope you don't forget. I wasn't that bad, was I?" She smiled at him. "Besides, we might get a chance to do this again."

"I didn't mean that. Of course I won't forget. Ever."

"Good. Anyway, we still have a couple of more nights. You did say you would stay with me, didn't you?"

"You are something else!" was all he could manage.

## Hong Kong

Martin began to wake slowly, a bit at a time. His eyes opened to strange surroundings. Confused and disoriented in the dim light, he felt like he was being rocked back and forth. *Of course*, he suddenly realized. *I'm still on the boat! I am rocking!* He opened his eyes wide and could see bright daylight under the door. Naked, he went to the door and opened it, flooding the room with light. He turned to let his eyes adjust. The room was beautifully furnished... as grand as they come... couches and chairs of black leather, original oils on the walls and a bar at one end of the room. Then he noticed Domi. She was standing behind the bar wiping glasses, her bare breasts bouncing to and fro. She was smiling, her eyes staring at his groin. He realized he was still naked and made an attempt to cover himself with his hands. This didn't work very well so he grabbed a pillow from the couch.

"Where is Sabrina?"

Domi pointed to the door and then made a walking motion with her fingers.

"Gone?"

She nodded.

"What time is it?"

She pointed to a clock on the wall. It was 6:30.

"I need to get back to the hotel."

She nodded again and held up eight fingers, cupped her hands in the shape of a boat and pointed to him.

"A boat... coming for me... eight o'clock?"

Excited that he understood, she nodded again and giggled. He walked to the bed and sat down. "I need a shower."

Domi walked from behind the bar. There was no sarong this time. She was as naked as he. Shocked, he turned away. "Domi! What..."

She touched his shoulder and motioned for him to follow her. Still clutching the pillow, he did as she wanted. She was so tiny, her perfectly proportioned buttocks causing him to become somewhat aroused. She opened a small door and beckoned him inside. It was a huge bath with a walk-in shower. She entered the shower, turned on the water, and then reached for his hand to pull him inside. He dropped the pillow and did as she asked. *When in Rome...* Arthur had said.

The water was warm and soothing. He stood quietly, hands at his side as she washed every inch of his body. The sponge was soft and covered with suds. He was in a trance. When his erection was complete, she gently rinsed the suds from his body... then knelt ... and he was lost again in the pleasures of this strange culture.

# Chapter Seventeen

The boat came promptly at eight. His suit had been pressed and his shirt washed and ironed. Domi had disappeared. At eight fifteen, he stepped ashore at Queen's Pier, surprised to find a smiling David Choi waiting.

"Martin... jo-san! You are looking well."

"Good morning David. What are you doing here?"

"Arthur asked me to meet you. You want some breakfast?"

Martin realized he was starving. "Great idea. Where shall we go?"

"Peak Café. Car is waiting. They have the best Thai omelet in the world!"

That turned out not to be a lie. The omelet was superb.

Between bites, Martin thought again about his friend, Trevor, coming to Hong Kong soon to spy for the CIA. "Tell me, David, what do the people of Hong Kong think about the handover."

"Oh, I don't think they're too concerned as long as Mother will let them go ahead and make money, which Beijing has promised to do. I think they realize that Hong Kong is their business outlet to the world. I don't think they will fuck it up."

"Well, let's hope not."

"It will be one hell of a party, though. Even though it's a few years away, the city fathers are already planning the celebration."

"Already?"

"It will be the largest display of fireworks ever in the world... so they promise."

"I hope I'm here to see it," Martin said, wishfully.

Back in his temporary office, he answered his e-mails and then sent one to Richard, informing him that he had picked out his office space and was going to go look at apartments today. Actually, he had no intentions of looking at apartments until all of this was over. Just as he finished the e-mail, Susanna entered the guest office.

"Martin, you have a message from United Air. Something about your flight on Friday." She handed him a memo. "Here's the number and the name of the agent to talk to."

"Thanks, Susanna."

He dialed the number and asked for Marla. "Mr. Maguire, thank you for calling. I'm afraid we have a problem with your flight on Friday. Because of mechanical reasons, we have had to change the plane type from a 747 to a DC10, which has a different seating plan. The problem is we no longer have a seat for you in Business Class."

"Oh, no. I don't want to make that trip in coach!" Martin was perplexed. "What are my options?"

"Well, sir, I'm afraid we don't have anything else available on Friday... but if your plans will allow you to leave on Thursday, we'll upgrade you to First Class at no additional cost."

Martin thought about that for a second. No reason he couldn't leave a day early... at least none he could think of. "Is today Tuesday?" He had lost track of time.

"Yes, sir...today is Tuesday."

"Okay, fine. Let's do that. I'll leave on Thursday. Same time?"

"Yes, sir. Same time and same flight number."

"Okay, great. Thanks."

"Thanks for flying United, sir."

*Won't hurt to get home a day early,* he thought. Carole's image came into his mind.... followed by the image of Sabrina and then Domi. *I'll have to tell her. No way will she understand. Maybe I won't tell her. Maybe. Should I call and tell her I'm coming home early? No, I'll surprise her. She'll like that. First class, huh. Twist my arm!*

When he returned to the hotel, he was pleased to find that his new suits and shirts had been delivered. Quickly, he undressed to try them on and was just pulling up his pants when there was a knock on the door. "Just a moment," he said loudly, zipping up his pants. He opened the door fully expecting to find housekeeping. He was not prepared for a smiling Sabrina.

"Hi, 'Merican! Remember me?"

"Sabrina! Hi... yes, of course...come in."

She was even more beautiful than he had remembered; dressed in designer jeans so tight, she must have put them on at an early age and grew into them. Her blouse was thin silk and held together by a single button, showing both the upper and lower portions of her unbridled breasts.

"I come to show you Hong Kong. I am your personal guide! For all day and all night!"

"Sabrina... you don't have to do that."

"Yes... how else can I make love to you and make you want to bring me to 'Merica?"

Martin was mortified. "Sabrina... I told you... I am married. I can't bring you to America!"

"Oh, I know that! I just make joke! I can go to 'Merica any time I want." She laughed. "Let's just have some fun today." She reached and unbuttoned the single button, letting the silk float to the floor.

"This time... we do it in your bed!"

"You want to go shopping?" It was two hours later and they were sharing a glass of wine on the lanai.

"Shopping?"

"Yes! I take you to Stanley Market! You want go?"

"If you would like." He had been there before on a previous trip and had enjoyed it. In fact, he had bought several gifts for the people back home there... a good place to practice your bargaining skills.

They dressed and took the elevator down to the lobby where Sabrina arranged for a car the rest of the day.

"My family will pay!" She notified him gleefully. "I do this all the time!"

The drive to Stanley took nearly thirty minutes, but because of the interesting sights, the time went by quickly. Soon they were walking among the many stalls and shops in the market. The noise from hundreds of people crowding into the small area was like that of a turkey farm. Martin was having fun. He bought Sabrina a colorful silk scarf, skillfully arguing with the shop keeper until he reduced the price from eight U.S. all the way down to three.

Sabrina giggled and jumped up and down when the battle was finally over. She would have been no happier if he had bought her a ten carat diamond. The shop keeper smiled and said something in Chinese which caused Sabrina to become angry. She answered with venom in her voice and spat at the shop keeper's feet before turning quickly away.

Martin caught up with her and grabbed her arm. "What was all that about?"

"He called you a stupid gweilo and he called me your whore! The Chinese think they are so superior! They smile at you and take your money and, at the same time, they curse you!"

Martin laughed. "Yes, I know. I'm used to it. Gweilo is not so bad."

"You know what it means?"

"Not exactly."

"It means *foreign devil*."

"See, not so bad. Let's get a drink."

Immediately, her mood changed back to one of happiness. "Oh, yes... come. We go to Stanley Bistro. It only a few blocks."

They shared a glass of beer and some fish and chips, seated where they could watch the tide rise in the bay, thoroughly enjoying the moment.

"This is good day, Martin. I remember it forever."

"Yes... it has been a very good day," he agreed.

"I must stop on way back at Wong Sin Temple to burn joss sticks for thanks. The gods have been good to me."

"Can I burn some as well?"

Martin awoke to the sound of clinking ice as the flight attendant prepared the First Class cabin for dinner. He glanced at his watch and realized he had been sleeping for six hours while his body was trying to recover from the previous twenty four hours of sexual frenzy. He raised the seat back and stretched his aching back. Even in First Class, it was a grueling flight. Four more hours and he would be home. *I hope Carole is not in the mood for sex. I need to rest up first.*

## Chicago

Carole rolled over and looked at the luminous dial on the clock. Three A.M. She slipped out of bed and into the bathroom quietly, not wanting to wake Matt. *I'll let him make love to me one more time before he leaves this morning. Martin will be home tomorrow. I have missed him. Sweet Martin.*

The plane touched down at O'Hare at 5:15 A.M., one day early. One of the advantages of flying First Class was that you were first off the plane and in the Customs line quickly. By the time he got to the luggage carousel, his bags were waiting. Ten minutes later, he stepped off the tram into the remote parking lot. Ten minutes after that, he turned onto the interstate. He was twenty five minutes from home.

Matt's breathing had nearly returned to normal after their early morning session. He kissed Carole on each breast and swung his legs over the side of the bed.

"I'm starved. You hungry?"

"Kind of. You put the coffee on. I'll be there in a minute and fix us some breakfast." She headed toward the bathroom.

Matt pulled on his baggy under shorts and went into the kitchen. He was bent over the lower cabinet retrieving the coffee when the back door opened and Martin stepped into the room.

"What the hell... Halgren? What the fuck...?" Martin was in shock.

Slowly, Matt straightened up and turned to face him.

"Where – is – my - wife?" Martin asked slowly.

"I...I think she's in the shower." Matt swallowed hard.

Martin set his suitcase down. "I see. Don't leave. I'll deal with you in a minute." He headed into the master bedroom. The door to the bath was ajar and he could hear the water running. He stepped into the room and softly called her name.

"Just a minute, Matt... unless you want to join me. You wanna?" She opened the shower door and froze. Her face turned ash white. She shook her head as if trying to make him go away. She could not speak. A clump of soap suds slowly worked it's way down between her breasts.

"I guess I caught you at a bad time, huh babe? Well, maybe I'll come back later... and then again... maybe I won't." He turned and walked back into the bedroom, vaguely aware of the messed up bed, the condom wrappers on the night stand and various articles of clothing strewn about the room. He went back into the kitchen. Matt was sitting at the table, his head in his hands. He started to say something. Martin held up his hand and stopped him.

"Don't say anything. There's no need." He picked up his bags and went out the door. *Well, I guess I don't have to worry about telling her about my Hong Kong fling, now do I?*

Alone in his office, he was busying himself with the stack of mail in the in- basket, trying to make sense of it all. The phone rang. It was Matt Halgren.

"I don't want to talk to you."

"Listen… I know I've fucked up big time. I know you can have my job for this if you want… and I won't blame you if you do. But, before you do… please, let's go ahead and complete the plan to nail Peterlie. I know I don't deserve it, but I'm asking you for that much."

"I don't know. I'll think about it." Martin hung up the phone. *Let the sonofabitch worry about it for awhile.* For a long time, he just sat and stared at the wall. Then he picked up the phone and dialed.

"Clark residence."

"Peggy? It's Martin. I'm home."

"You're back? So soon?"

"Yes. I came home a day early and surprised Carole in bed with our friendly FBI agent. I'm still in shock."

"Oh, Martin! I'm sorry!" She was stunned…but she wasn't sorry.

"Yeah… bummer. That's one reason I'm calling. I need somewhere to stay for a few days. Is your place available?"

"Of course it is! You know where the key is?"

"Thanks, Peggy. Yes, I know where the key is. Listen, I'm planning on bringing Richard down next week."

"Okay. I want to be there for that." She was already mentally packing and planning to leave. It was a six hour drive from St. Louis. She could be there by three o'clock.

"Good. It will be nice to see you. You can come home sooner if you want." He wasn't sure why, but he had a strong desire to see her. He remembered their embrace when he left.

"I'll be there this afternoon. What are you going to do... about Carole?"

"I don't know yet, Peggy. I'm not sure."

"Okay... I'll see you in a few hours."

He told his secretary he was going home to rest and left the office. The key was easy to find and soon he was in Peggy's shower, trying to overcome his exhaustion and the jet lag. He opened his suitcase and donned the soft robe, compliments of the Conrad Hotel, and went to the liquor cabinet. Here he found a full bottle of Grey Goose and fixed himself a stiff drink. Even though it was only eleven o'clock in the morning... his body was still on Hong Kong time. Jerry Springer was on TV and two girls were arguing over which man was the father of their baby. *Who cares*, he thought, and finished half the drink in one gulp. He set the glass down and promptly fell asleep in the recliner.

Peggy could hear the TV when she opened the door. It was a little after three in the afternoon. In the living room, she found Martin sound asleep, spread out in the chair. She smiled. His robe was not completely covering up his business, a fact that would have caused him much embarrassment if he had been aware of it. She picked up a coverlet from the couch and carefully spread it across his lap. He never moved.

She took her things into the master bed room and unpacked. Although she had been living with Richard for awhile, she still had plenty of clothes left in her closets. After fixing a light snack, she returned to the living room, turned the TV off and waited for him to awake.

## Hong Kong

David Choi turned the lock on his office door, opened the well-worn address book and dialed a number. In a small, dark office, deep in the Hall of the People, a telephone rang.

"Wei!"

"Chang Siew Pang."

"Speaking."

"This is David Choi. I have a report on Martin Maguire."

The mention of Martin's name brought him to attention, his failed attempts to have Martin killed always on his mind.

"Yes, Oily Mouth Choi! Tell me he has choked on a rotten dog bone and I will be filled with glee! Or perhaps you have arranged for him to fall from the ferry and drown! Please... tell me he is dead!"

Only a month ago, he had managed to work his way back from the demotion this barbarian had caused him to receive and was now the assistant to the Minister of Foreign Trade. And, he was part of the plan involving the take over of the joint ventures. David Choi, who he called Oily Mouth because of his ability to speak American English, had been his paid informant at the WCI Hong Kong office since they had sat next to each other on the trip home from the US.

"No, Mr. Chang... he is still alive. I'm afraid our attempt here failed. He has become suspicious and watches everything carefully... fully alert to possible dangers."

"Curse the gods. I must wait even longer for my revenge."

"His visit here in Hong Kong was only to look at housing. He is being promoted to be in charge of the joint ventures project and is moving to Hong Kong."

"Aieee! Yes, I have been informed. So, when we kick the barbarians out of our country and take over the factories... perhaps he will be held responsible! A little humiliation for him will ease my pain somewhat. Are you sure he suspects his life is in danger?"

"Yes... I am sure. It will be difficult to catch him sleeping. I have confirmation that Peterlie received your last package. He was upset at your threat to harm Maguire, but everything else is still on schedule."

"Good. I guess there is no need to try and harm Maguire at this time. Perhaps, if he comes to China... I will have the pleasure of killing him myself! That would be a blessing of the gods! Keep me informed of any other developments."

"Yes, of course. About my... payment?"

"It will be in your account tomorrow."

## Chicago

Martin stirred and opened one eye. The darkness of the evening had filled the room. He looked at his watch. It was a little before seven. Then he realized he had a cover over his legs... and he felt the presence of another. He was not alone.

"Peggy? You here?"

"Yes... I'm here."

He opened his eyes wide and sat upright in the chair. She was sitting a few feet away on the couch.

"Hi. When did you get here?"

"Three hours ago."

"What have you been doing?"

"Watching you sleep."

"Really? I bet that was interesting." He stretched. "Thanks for the blanket."

"It was a necessity. You were trying to show me your... you know."

"Oh, God! I'm surprised you didn't run."

She laughed. "I kind of liked it, really. Are you hungry?"

"Yeah... I'm hungry."

"Okay. I'll fix dinner. We have a lot to talk about, don't we?"

"Yes, we do. Let me get some pants on and I'll help."


## Saturday morning:

"Mr. Drubbens, please." Martin was squinting at the swimming pool through the patio doors, watching Peggy swim as he waited for the CEO of the company to answer. *She's quite a lady*, he thought. *Make somebody a great wife... like me, maybe.*

"Hello, this is Charlie."

"Mr. Drummens... you probably don't know me. My name is Martin Maguire. I work for Richard Peterlie."

"Martin... yes... I have heard a lot of good things about you from Richard. Didn't you just get a promotion?"

"Yes, sir, I did. I'm sorry to bother you at home, but there's a matter I need to discuss with you and it won't wait. It's very important... for the company."

"I see. Why don't you discuss this with Richard and he can tell me about it on Monday?"

"Sir... believe me, if I could, I would do just that. But it... it involves Richard... and the CIA and the FBI and the Chinese." There was silence... no response. "Sir, I would like to meet with you... along with an FBI agent to discuss this. You must not call Richard. It's very important!"

"You are scaring me, Mr. Maguire. I hope this is not some type of prank."

"I assure you, sir... it is not. You need to get our company attorneys and the head of security together.... and meet with us... today... this morning!"

Peggy had come in from the pool, drying her hair with a towel.

"Did he take your call?" Earlier, they had discussed the possibility that the CEO of a large company such as WCI may not take a personal call.

"Yes. He wasn't sure I was on the up and up at first, but I convinced him. We meet in three hours."

She looked very nice in a bathing suit...very nice. "So, what do we do now? You and me, I mean?"

"I don't know, Peggy. Whatever we do, I want it to be a clear decision... not muddled by the fact I just caught my wife screwing another guy, and not because you just caught your guy doing criminal things. If there is going to be an 'us', I want both of us to be sure."

"You're the only... one I have, Martin. I'm already sure of that."

He took her in his arms and held her wet body close. "You are a fine woman, Peggy Clark. I would never want to hurt you."

"Help me get out of this wet suit... then I want a better look at what I saw briefly under that white robe you had on yesterday."

Martin smiled. She was exactly what he needed at the moment.

Three hours later, the two men left the office of the CEO and stood in silence as they waited for the elevator to take them to the lobby. Once inside, Matt Halgren spoke. "Thanks… for letting me go ahead with this."

"I didn't do it for you. You are a rotten bastard! I did it for the company."

"You're right. I am a rotten bastard!"

Martin had presented the group made up of Charles Drummens, two company attorneys and the Vice President of Security with the papers Peggy had given him. Needless to say, they were quite shocked. He and Halgren had been questioned at length as to the validity of the documents and how somebody such as Richard Peterlie could have been persuaded to participate in this blatant corporate espionage.

"He was probably threatened… and offered a lot of money. That combination will cause a lot of decent people to become… not so decent," Halgren had offered.

"Well, Martin, you did the right thing in calling me," Drummens remarked. "I rarely take personal calls at home unless I know who it is. I'm glad I did this time. Thank you both for explaining this most unfortunate situation. Rest assured… we will take the appropriate action. I'm sure my colleagues here will counsel me as to what that should be."

# Chapter Eighteen

The original plan had been changed. There was no need to try and trap Richard into revealing his role in the corporate espionage. The copy of the CFD report was enough. At seven-thirty on Monday morning, Richard Peterlie received a phone call.

"Peterlie, here."

"Richard... this is Charlie. My office... five minutes." End of conversation.

When he walked into the large impressive office of his boss, Richard's normal confident demeanor vanished immediately. Charles Drummens was not smiling. Nor were the VP of Security and the three attorneys seated in the chairs at the small conference table.

"Sit down, Richard," Drummens ordered, pointing at a particular chair. "We would all like for you to explain the meaning of this document." He slid over the copy of the correspondence Martin had given to the group on Saturday.

"I...uh... I've never seen this before," he stammered. "Where did you get this?"

"Where we got it is not important. What's important is that it is addressed to you and you are mentioned in it in several places. This document threatens the life of one of my employees!"

"Peggy... Peggy Clark gave it to you, didn't she?" He was red-faced, but his lips were void of all color. A tiny slobber had formed at the corner of his mouth.

Drummens shook his head. "Not good having a traitor in your camp, is it Richard? You <u>will</u> have a letter of resignation on my desk by the end of the day. We will most likely press charges with the FBI and who ever. Now get out of this office and get out of my building."


## Beijing

It was a little before three A.M. when the dark limousine drove past the Beijing Hotel and approached Tiananmen Square. A lone worker was climbing up a bamboo scaffold; a paint can in hand, preparing to touch up the large portrait of Mao on the wall next to the entrance to the Forbidden City. Even at this hour, there were several people milling about the Square.

The car turned left at the next street and pulled behind the darkened Great Hall of the People, stopping next to a door marked "DANGER- ELECTRICAL" in Chinese characters. The two armed soldiers standing guard opened the door and admitted the occupant of the car. Inside was the secret elevator that went directly to the top floor. Only a few people knew about this elevator.

The door opened and the man stepped into the personal accommodations of the leader of the People's Republic of China, Chairman Rung Ru Seng. The two most powerful men in all of China were now in the same room.

"Thank you for coming at this late hour." The man was sitting in near darkness at a small table that held two candles and a wicker-covered teapot with two cups. There was a haze circling his head from the cigarette dangling from his lips. The visitor took a seat.

"Not a bother, Great One. Sleep seems to avoid me more and more these days. I am lucky if I can fall asleep for a few minutes in the chair after my evening meal."

"Yes... I am the same. There is so much to do. Would you like tea?"

"Tea would be perfect, Great One." Rung poured the cups full, put out his cigarette, and promptly lit another.

"We have some difficult tasks to take care of. The Americans have found out about our plan to take over the joint ventures. They have threatened to stop all progress unless we can assure them that their investments will be secure."

General Chin Lin Hua, the top-ranking military officer and the head of the Secret Police, removed the lid from his cup and sipped the tea. "That is not good news." He removed a pack of Xing Tu cigarettes and joined the *Great One* in a smoke. He would have preferred the American Winstons he had in another pocket, but knew that would not be wise. "Do you have a plan?"

"Yes." He paused. "But, it will be unpleasant for you. We must replace the Minister of Foreign Trade... and his deputy immediately. I want them convicted of corruption and crimes against the Central Commission... and then publicly executed."

"I will see to it."

"It is unfortunate that the Deputy of Foreign Trade is your cousin. I am sorry."

"Yes. We grew up together in a small village not far from here. He always wanted to grow up and be a Party member." There was a moment of silence.

"And you... what did you want to grow up to be?"

"A bus driver." Both men laughed.

"I wanted to be an actor in the opera," Rung said, then laughed again which ended in a fit of coughing. He extinguished his cigarette.

"What are the thoughts of the Committee... about this incident?"

"As usual, they think what I tell them to think... that this is only a temporary situation... a rock in the middle of the path... that needs to be removed. It has taken us thousands of years to come this far. What is another twenty? Eventually, we shall have everything the Americans have."

"I was hoping we would see it in our lifetime. Then, your portrait would be on the wall beside the greatest of the great."

Rung smiled. "We are the same, you and I. Amah... bring fresh tea," he ordered.

The old woman emerged from the darkness and took the tea pot away. In a few minutes she brought it back, hot and steaming, but not before removing the tape from the small recorder hidden in the bottom of the wicker basket and inserting a fresh one.

"Then... the matter is settled?"

"Of course, great one. Tomorrow... or later today."

"Good. That is done." He took a long pull on the rancid cigarette and then a sip of tea. "I have another issue. I would like you to share your opinion on Hong Kong, 1997."

Chen's face softened. "Finally... our daughter will return. It will be a great day."

"Yes. I am undecided how to... manage the control of this lost child that has been poisoned by the foreign devils for so long. What are your thoughts?"

General Chen Lim Hua also took a long sip of tea as he thought about how to answer this delicate question. "When I was a boy, my grandfather cut off the thumbs of a man who had stolen food from our village. He explained that the man would not be able to use the chopsticks and, therefore, not be able to eat without encountering great difficulty. I see Hong Kong as our most important outlet for goods to the rest of the world. I don't think it would be wise to cut off her thumbs. Let her stay a free trade society... no taxes... no tariffs. Of course, you would have the final say... but where you can, let her govern herself."

The Chairman lit another cigarette. "I agree. I can step in and change things anytime if necessary. Yes, I agree." The Chairman stretched his small frame. "Thank you. You may go now. I think I will try to sleep."

Later that morning, Deputy Chang Siew Pang was on his way to the office of his superior, the Minister of Foreign Trade. He had been summoned and was feeling good these days, causing him to step lively. The joint venture project appeared to be progressing faster than anticipated. He was sure to get a bonus. It was with bitter thanks that it was due to the efforts of his nemesis... Martin Maguire.

As soon as he stepped into the room, he knew there was something drastically wrong. There were several uniformed soldiers waiting on each side of the door. Then he noticed his leader, standing in front of his desk... in handcuffs. He turned to leave, when he was stopped by a soldier holding a pistol to his chest. Quickly, a set of handcuffs found their way to his wrists as well.

The two men were taken to the Fungai Punishment Center on the edge of the city. That afternoon a magistrate found them guilty of crimes against the Central Commission and sentenced them both to death.

A few hours later, Chang Siew Pang was huddled on the dirty cot in his cell, trying to accept his fate. His thoughts were interrupted by a visitor. He looked up to see his cousin standing just on the other side of the bars. He rose, walked over to the bars and spat on the floor at his visitors feet.

"This is all your doing? I'm to die... your closest of cousins, your closest friend... you have ordered me to die? You will have my blood on your feet!"

"Yes. Unfortunate joss. But you must remember... you are dying for Mother China... The Middle Kingdom...so we can complete the plan. You will die a hero... a secret hero, but a hero nonetheless. Grandfather would be proud of you. Goodbye my cousin."

"I will not say goodbye to you. You were the lowly bus driver. I was the loyal Party man. The gods have made a terrible mistake. We should be in each other's place."

"Perhaps you are right. But even if you are... you will still be dead soon. The gods will make no trade."

Three days later, the two government officials were kneeling with a group of common criminals as, one by one, a pistol was put to the back of their heads and they were shot. Martin Maguire was no longer in any danger.

## Chicago

After his brief meeting in Drummen's office, Richard Peterlie went to his office and hastily wrote a letter of resignation and dropped it into the company mail. Next, he drove to his home, packed a small bag, retrieved certain items from his safe along with ten thousand dollars in cash and drove straight to O'Hare Airport. In the parking garage, he pulled into a handicapped space, knowing they would find the car quicker when security noticed there was no handicapped card on the mirror. He locked the doors and took the elevator down to Ticketing. He bought a one-way ticket to Montreal. Next, he took the escalator down to the arrival level and got in the line to wait for a taxi.

"LaSalle Street bus station," he ordered. Richard Peterlie was no dummy. He knew the authorities would be trying to arrest him before the day was over. At the bus station, he threw the airline boarding pass in a trash can, bought a ticket to Indianapolis and in thirty minutes, he was heading out of the city on a Greyhound. Three hours later, he bought a bus ticket to Cincinnati. Three hours after that, he took a cab to the airport, which was actually located in Kentucky. He bought a ticket to Tampa. At 8:24 P.M. he boarded a flight to Rio de Janeiro.

The meeting took place at the Chinese Embassy in Chicago. All those who attended were among the highest ranking officials of the different entities represented: World Construction Industries' CEO, the Chicago heads of the CIA and the FBI, the Chinese Ambassador from Washington and the newly appointed Chinese Minister of Foreign Trade, Madam Sing Fu, who had been rushed to the United States for the sole purpose of this meeting. Madam Sing assured all present that the Chairman and the Central Commission were appalled at the discovery of the corruption that had infected the progress of the joint ventures and technology transfer programs between the two great countries. The parties involved had been dealt with severely and there was no longer a threat of the Americans losing control of joint ventures or other investments in China. She was very convincing.

## Hong Kong

David Choi was getting dressed for his date with Missy Wu at Rachel's Dance Emporium in Wanchai. He had paid five hundred U.S. dollars for the pleasure of being the first to bed this delicious flower from Sichuan Province, recently sold to the establishment by her parents for one thousand yuan. She had just turned fourteen years old.

He had brushed his carefully styled hair and applied cologne to his neck when there was a knock on the door.

"Who is it?" he yelled, through the wood.

"I have an important message for David Choi... from a Chang Siew Pang."

"One moment, please." A message from Chang! This was exciting!

## Three days later.

Arthur Stephens pushed the intercom button on his desk. "Yes?"

"Susanna... ask David Choi to come to my office.

"I'm sorry, sir, but nobody has heard from David for three days now. He has not been at home and he hasn't called in.

"Really! That's bloody strange. No idea where he is?"

"No, sir. It's as if he has disappeared from the earth!"

Four days later, David's chopped up and smelly remains were found in the trunk of an abandon vehicle in the New Territories district of Kowloon. It was strange, but there was no investigation ordered by the local police. The WCI office people would never know why he was killed. Just a terrible turn of joss.

## Rio

Richard Peterlie walked into the Bank of America on Miguel Street and approached the young man at the desk marked NEW ACCOUNTS.

"May I help you?"

"Yes, I want to open an account. I have $7,000 U.S. to deposit."

"Of course, senor. That will only take a few minutes." After the paper work was completed and Richard was handed a receipt for the $7,000, the young man smiled and asked, "Will there be anything else, senor?"

"Can you arrange a transfer to my new account from my bank in Switzerland?"

"Of course, as long as you have the account number and the proper identification."

"Yes. I have that information."

"Good." He retrieved a form from a desk drawer. "How much will be the amount of the transfer?"

"Two point three million U.S. dollars."

The young man swallowed. "Two point three million dollars?" He actually squeaked on the word dollars.

"Yes, two point three... million."

"I will require the assistance of my supervisor. Please give me a moment."

"Of course."

The man left his desk and returned in a few minutes with a much older and obviously higher ranking bank official.

"Mr. Goodale?" The older man took the seat of the younger man.

"Yes. Richard Goodale."

"So pleased to meet you. My name is Raul Costus. I will handle the transfer of your funds. Does the name on the account in Switzerland match the name on your passport?"

"There is no name on the account in Switzerland. Only an account number and a PIN number. The name on my passport is not important. I will be doing business as Richard Goodale."

"I see. Forgive me if I may seem to be so bold, but are you a fugitive?"

"Only from an ex-wife," he lied.

The older man smiled. "Oh, yes. I understand. Very good, sir. The transfer will take an hour or so. Would you like to wait, or is there somewhere we can call you when the transaction is completed."

"I'll wait."

## Three Months Later:

Martin checked the calendar on his desk, and then looked in his rolodex and wrote down an address. He walked to his office window and stared at the USS California as she unloaded sailors onto the skiffs which would take them to the Hong Kong Fleet Store, intrigued that most of them would end up in a Wanchai whorehouse before the night was over. At least the girls there were controlled by the Hong Kong Health Department and were disease free.

The harbor was busy as usual... like so many little water bugs scurrying here and there. He would never tire of the beauty of this vista. A China Air 747 from Beijing was landing at Kai Tak, a sight that would soon be gone forever with the completion of the new airport. His thoughts strayed to the events of the past few months. His unexpected divorce... his relationship with Peggy... his unexpected promotion.

When he had finally calmed down enough to talk to Carole, she had admitted having an affair with Matt Halgren for over a year before Martin had caught them in the act. She also admitted to being unfaithful with another man during his first trip to China, but she would not tell Martin who it was. For some reason, he never told her about the night with Sabrina. He could not see where it would serve any purpose. They separated and divorced peacefully.

He and Peggy were together for awhile and the sex was great, however, they decided that was probably all it would ever be. So, they chose to remain dating friends, enjoying an occasional dinner and a romp in bed afterwards.

Then, the big surprise. The really big surprise.

He returned to his desk and pushed a button.

"Yes, sir?"

"Susanna, could you come in please."

She was in the room in less than a minute.

"Yes, sir?"

"Have you talked to Arthur recently?"

"Yes, yesterday. He was still packing up Peterlie's personal stuff so he could move in to his new office. He said the view was not nearly as good as here!"

Martin laughed. "No, I'm well aware of that. He'll do fine in Richards's old job, though, once he gets used to Chicago."

"He is worried about the winter time and he said he hasn't found one decent restaurant yet! And, there is no American Club at all!"

"Poor Arthur."

"Yes... poor Arthur," Susanna giggled. "The problem with the English is... they are just too damn British! My bottom always had bruises all over it!"

"That's more than I need to know!" Martin replied, smiling. "Listen, would you order two dozen roses to be delivered to a Ms. Peggy Clark in St. Louis. It's her birthday. Here's her address." He handed the slip of paper to her.

"An old girlfriend?"

"Perhaps... maybe. Someone to visit when I'm back in the States."

"You men! One in every port, heh?"

"Yeah... something like that."

"Are you going to bring her over here?"

He inhaled through his teeth. "Oh, I don't know. It's pretty nice just the way it is."

"I see." She laughed. "So, you like living in Hong Kong." It was said as a statement.

"I love living in Hong Kong."

"You make a great subsidiary President! I'm so lucky to work for you."

"I can be mean, you know!"

"Sure... big tough American." She laughed. "I am so scared!"

He smiled. "Will you please not tell the people that it is you that really runs the place?"

"Okay... I won't tell. Now, I'll get the flowers ordered right away."

"Good. Then call Sabrina and tell her we are having dinner at the American Club tonight, eight o'clock. Have her invite Mikki... our logistics manager from the L.A. office is coming in this afternoon for that meeting tomorrow. He'll need a dinner companion."

Susanna smiled. "Now you are a full-blooded Hong Kongese. You want to pinch my bottom?"

"Maybe... later," he teased. "Oh, and call Trevor Chan at the Embassy. Tell him I'll meet him for lunch at Jimmie's Kitchen... at 1:30. Okay?"

"Yes, sir. Oh, by the way, are you going to Sha Tin to the horse races Saturday? I must send an RSVP."

"Should I?" He had been invited to attend the season finale as a guest of the U.S. Ambassador and sit in the governor's box.

"Oh, yes! Everybody who is anybody will be there."

"Well, in that case, I guess I'd better go!"

# CHAPTER NINETEEN

## Two years later.

"**I**s everything ready, Susanna?"

"Yes, sir. I have reserved a suite at the Peninsula and arranged a ful-time car and driver from A.I.T. I thought about getting a Rolls from the hotel, but then decided not to. They are providing a new Mercedes."

Martin was excited. The CEO of World Construction Industries was coming to Hong Kong. "Okay. I must admit I'm a little nervous."

"It will go fine, Martin, even though we don't know for sure why he is coming."

"He said he wanted to go over our year-end results and look at the budget for next year."

"Yes, but he has done that every year since I started working for Arthur, and this is the first time he has come here to do it. Always before, Arthur went to Chicago."

"So you said. Well, we'll find out tomorrow, won't we?"

"You will. It may take me a little longer."

Martin smiled. "Maybe I won't tell you," he teased.

"Oh, yes, you will, Martin Maguire! Don't forget who really runs this place!"

She smiled sweetly and went back to her desk.

Martin closed his eyes and reclined back in his leather chair. He was so lucky to have her. Susanna Ling had been the Executive Secretary for the top man at the Hong Kong facility for nearly twelve years now. There was little she didn't know about what was happening in the company, having established and cultivated contacts all over the world with people in similar positions. More than once, she had given Martin a heads up on things coming down the road that he would not have been aware of otherwise. This allowed him to make decisions that later made him look like a genius to the Board and to his boss, Charles Drummond. Yes, he was indeed lucky to have her. In part, he had Arthur to thank as well. It was he who encouraged Susanna to develop these relationships with the other executive secretaries in the company. The fact that she was beautiful and sexy as all get out didn't hurt either.

He snapped back to reality, checked his *authentic* Rolex, grabbed his suit jacket and headed out the door.

"I'm going to get my hair cut. I'll be back in plenty of time to go with the car to the airport at 5:00. You did make reservations for dinner at the American Club?"

"Of course, dear bossy. Eight o'clock for four people. Sabrina and Mikki are looking forward to meeting our CEO."

Martin's face registered shock. "You didn't! No, of course you didn't. One of these days, young lady!"

"Have a nice hair cut, Mr. Maguire. I'll see you later."

He took the elevator down sixty-four floors to the street level and got into the taxi queue. It was just after two and the line was not long. A few minutes later, he climbed in the red cab. "Fleet

Store, Central." The driver held up a hand to signal he understood and pulled out into the heavy traffic. Most cab drivers understood English, but they rarely spoke to their passengers. This one was the exception.

"You American?"

"Yes, I'm an American."

The driver grinned. "What you think of your President... Cleenton?"

Martin was surprised. "Why do you ask?"

The driver chuckled. "You know... the Lewinski girl... under the desk."

Martin was amused. "Well, I'm pretty sure he wishes he hadn't been so foolish."

"Yes. Foolish. He make one big mistake... always pay the girl... then they no talk. Always pay the girl!"

"Thanks, I'll remember that!"

"Yes, always pay the girl," he repeated for the third time. He continued to chuckle all the way to the Fleet Store.

The U.S. Navy Fleet Store was located on the harbor and was the disembarking station for all Navy personnel going to and from the ships anchored in the harbor. It contained a McDonald's, a U.S. Post Office, and several small stores selling Chinese goods and oriental rugs to be sent back to the States. It had the only barber shop with an American barber in all of Hong Kong.

George Parker had been cutting hair, mostly for sailors, twenty-three years in the same little cubbyhole located in the rear of the building. Born in Dothan, Alabama, he was a breath of fresh air with his drawn out Southern accent, always telling homespun stories that never failed to entertain. His clients included several American high muckety mucks, as he called them, including the American Ambassador and most of his staff.

"Hey, Martin. Thought y'all might be coming in today."

"Oh yeah? And why is that, George?"

"Well, I figured ya'd want to look your best for your boss, now wouldn't ya?" He rolled the unlit, ever present cigar from one side to the other, obviously proud to be privileged with such knowledge.

"How did you know about that?" Martin asked, climbing into the chair.

"Trevor was here this morning."

"Oh, I see. Did he tell you where we are having dinner?"

"No, he sure didn't. Where're y'all having dinner?"

"I'll bet you five Hong Kong reds you can't find out before eight o'clock tonight."

"You're on, brother. You're on!"

Back in the office, Martin told Susanna that if anybody asked, she was not to disclose the location where he and Charles were having dinner tonight.

"Is there a reason?"

"Yes... five hundred reasons," he had answered.

At five o'clock, the limo came and they headed for the airport. The plane was twenty minutes late, not bad considering it was a non-stop flight all the way from O'Hare. As president of the subsidiary, he had a pass for the VIP room where certain government officials and elite business men were able to enter Hong Kong without enduring the shouting and shoving of the people in the regular airport arrival hall.

Charles Drummond looked fit; tanned and trim in his six hundred dollar suit that looked as fresh as if he had just put it on. Martin marveled at this, convinced that he himself always looked like a wrinkled prune when he had to make the flight.

"Martin, good to see you!" His hand shake was as firm as they come.

"Welcome to Hong Kong, sir."

"Good to be here! That's a darned long flight!"

"Yes, sir, it is. Are you tired, sir?"

"Oh, not too bad. And, let's get rid of the sir crap, okay? Makes me feel old. Charlie will do just fine."

"Of course. Your first time to Hong Kong?"

"Actually, no. I was here in 1960. USS Virginia. A twenty-year old sailor in Hong Kong. I'm afraid I didn't do much sightseeing. We had been at sea for eleven weeks. Wanchai still there?"

"Oh, yeah, although I expect it's changed some."

"I'm sure." He smiled. "You have a car waiting?"

"What are our plans for tonight, Martin?" The car was making good time towards Kowloon and the Peninsula hotel.

"Well, let's get you checked in at the Grand Dame of the Far East, perhaps have a drink there, and then I've made reservations for dinner at the American Club. They have the best view of the harbor and Kowloon, plus one of the best Chinese restaurants in the world."

"That sounds great. I've heard a lot of good things about the American Club and, of course, the Peninsula. Several of my friends have stayed there. Have you, Martin... stayed there?"

"No, sir, I mean Charlie. Before moving here, I don't think I could have gotten you to approve of the Peninsula on my expense account."

The older man chuckled. "No, I suppose not. A lot has changed for you, hasn't it?"

They were interrupted by Martin's cell phone.

"Maguire."

"Hey, Bubba! American Club... Windows of China... eight o'clock... 500 red in my pocket. See ya soon!"

"I'll be damned!" Martin muttered.

"What?"

"Nothing important, sir."

"I'll have your best scotch, on the rocks, with a couple drops of bitters. Martin, what about you?"

"Grey Goose vodka on the rocks."

"Good drink. I have that a lot as well." He paused. "How are you doing, Martin? I'm not talking about the job... I'm talking about you, personally. How are you doing?"

"Really good, Charlie. It couldn't get any better... for me."

"I'm pleased, Martin. You deserve it. Our factory in Liuchou is spitting out tractors like crazy. We have enough orders for the next two years' production already. Once these Chinese get going, they really get going."

"Yes. If we can just keep them from taking quality shortcuts, we'll be okay."

"That's what I understand. Well, we'll keep the pressure on. I have some good men in place over there."

Martin had met all the "expats" stationed in China when they came through Hong Kong. "Yes, they're all good men," he agreed.

Their drinks arrived, along with an array of fine crackers and black caviar. "Compliments of the Peninsula, gentlemen," so stated their waiter.

"If the hors d'oeuvres are free, what do the drinks cost?" Charlie asked.

"I think if you have to ask, Charlie, you're in the wrong place." Both men shared a good laugh. They sipped the drinks and tasted the offerings with great satisfaction.

"Martin," Charlie became serious, "Have you ever heard anything of Richard?"

"Peterlie?" Martin was not prepared for that question. "Well, no sir. Not since... not since the shit hit the fan, if you will. Why?"

"Well, you know the FBI has never found him. Looked all over Canada for two months. Obviously, he didn't go there. The Chinese swear they have not had any further contact with him, although they have admitted that he was on their payroll. They claim they paid him over two million dollars for his part in that fiasco."

"Wow, that's a lot of money. He could be anywhere with that!" Martin helped himself to another caviar covered cracker. "Why are we talking about Peterlie?"

"I have reason to believe he is working for our number one competitor. He had access to all our long-range plans... the five, ten and twenty year marketing strategies. Suddenly, Koronato seems to be beating us to market on all our new products."

"Yeah, I know they've been kicking our ass in a lot of areas."

"Exactly! I have racked my brain and the only answer I can come up with is Richard."

"Yes, I could see where you would think that. Have you checked for the possibility of other leaks?"

"Oh, yes. Security has checked every possibility…every man or woman with that particular knowledge, and they have come up with nothing, so far. They have assured me it is no one currently within the company."

"Charlie, you would be amazed at how easy it is to find out secrets. I just lost five hundred dollars to a guy who had no way to find out where we were having dinner tonight. But he did."

"I'm not talking about losing five hundred… maybe five hundred million. I think it is Richard."

"Why are you telling me this?"

"I want you to find him."

"Richard."

"Once a fucking spy, always a fucking spy. Find him."

The next evening at 7:20, Martin said goodbye to his boss as he boarded the plane back to Chicago. They had pretended to spend the day going over the budget and other areas of interest. In reality, they were putting together a plan… a plan for Martin.

"Have you thought about hiring a professional… a private detective or somebody like that?"

"Yes, I've thought about that. I want you to do it. I trust you."

"Well, of course, I'll do my best, sir."

They shook hands and Charles Drummond went through the door marked Departures.

The next morning, Martin told Susanna to hold down the fort and, for the second time in three days, took a taxi to the Fleet Store. He found George sitting in his own barber chair reading the racing form from Happy Valley.

"Ah, my pigeon has showed up," he said, looking up as Martin came through the door. He was smiling from ear to ear. "You didn't have to make a special trip to pay me."

"Yes I did. We need to talk. Buy you a beer?"

"Sure! Five reds and a beer? This is a good day, indeed."

The two men walked to the Fleet Store MacDonald's and Martin ordered two bottles of Budweiser. This MacDonald's was the only one in the world, that he knew of, that sold beer... due to most of its clients being young Navy personnel. Outside on the large lanai, they took a seat next to the harbor and away from others. Martin took a sip of his beer and then counted out five, crisp, 100-dollar bills, laying them on the table.

"George," he decided to be blunt, "are you a Shu-side?"

George was not prepared for that question. He looked at Martin's face with surprise. "What do you know about *Old Friends*?" His eyes were squinted, the gaiety from the moment before gone in an instant.

"Not much. A slip of the tongue here and there... cocktail party... overheard conversations. Rumors."

"I see. Why are you asking?"

It was Martin's turn to smile. "Come on, George. No one knew where my boss and I were having dinner except me and my secretary... and I know she didn't tell you. Yet, you found out. It's real, isn't it... this organization that calls each other *Old Friends*?"

George looked away, studying the ships in the harbor... thinking. He liked Martin Maguire, and for some reason, he trusted him. "Martin, if I tell you about Shuside, you must never admit you know anything about it. To a non-member, we don't exist... and membership is by invitation only."

"I see. Who does the inviting?"

"I'm not sure. Do you want to be a member?"

"I don't know, George. Do I want that?"

"Yes... you probably do."

"How does it work?"

George was silent for a minute, gathering his thoughts. He shook his head, not sure he should be telling his friend about this secret organization.

"Well?" Martin urged.

"Okay. Today, somewhere here in Kowloon is a room full of computers and a couple dozen hackers. I Don't know where... I don't want to know where. They're constantly gathering information... financial, medical, business deals... anything they can find by hacking into other peoples files. This is the modern way, although some of it is still done by word of mouth. Before the computer, it was all done that way. A person who had some valuable information might share it with another... if they were good friends and trusted each other. That's where the name comes from. The recipient always pays a fair price for the info... depending on what it is worth to him. The seller never set the price."

"Really! What if the recipient doesn't pay?"

"Well, I guess he wouldn't be a friend very long, would he? There have been a few cases over the years where somebody didn't pay. They ended paying with their lives."

"So, you found out where I was having dinner from a computer geek?"

George laughed. "No, of course not. I just made a phone call and offered a hundred dollars to find out. Every major restaurant maitre'd, hotel concierge, limo dispatcher, travel agency, hospital... they all have members. Someone made a call... someone knew the answer. It was a quick hundred for them."

"Why you? Why did they invite you?"

"You mean, why a lowly barber? You would be surprised the things people tell me. I don't know why, but they do. And, I have several interesting clients... such as the American Ambassador, a couple of admirals and even a subsidiary president or two."

"Okay, I get your point."

"Oh, I don't give away any military secrets or anything, but say one of the skin joints in Wanchai is worried about making his payroll. I might just know when the next ship was coming in. Stuff like that."

Martin smiled. "Only in Hong Kong."

"Yeah, somebody tried it in New York but it didn't work. Too much greed. The sellers couldn't stand not setting the price. So, it never got off the ground."

Now, he knew. Shu-side did indeed exist.

When he was back in a cab, Martin dialed Trevor Chan's cell phone.

"Where are you?" he asked, as soon as heard his friend's voice.

"Dan Ryan's. What's up?"

"Stay there. I'll be there in twenty minutes." He disconnected. "Drop me at the Star Ferry," he instructed the driver. He found Trevor with a very attractive local girl who worked in the snack bar at the Embassy. "Hi, Sherri, how's it going?" he asked, sliding into the booth next to Trevor.

"You are very brave cowboy to interfere with my hot date!"

Trevor informed him, finishing the last of his cheeseburger.

"I know. You two will survive. I suggest you both go home and take a cold shower."

"I take shower with you, big shot president!" Sheri offered. "Any time!"

"Sorry kid. Better stick with Trevor. He's got a lot more to offer than I... at least three more inches."

"Shit... you mean you only have one inch?" she laughed.

"Thanks a lot! Curse the gods... can a man have no respect?"

Martin became serious. "We need to talk. When you are finished with your evening, come to my flat. It doesn't matter how late it is. It's very important."

"You can go now, Trevor," Sheri responded. "I'm not in the mood for... you know. I'm too tired tonight. Go now. I will find my way home. Thanks for the burger."

"You sure?" Trevor asked, secretly thankful, anxious to hear what his friend had to tell him.

"Yes, I'm sure. Go now."


The two were alone on Martin's lanai, drinking a beer.

"The FBI couldn't find him? How can I help?"

"The FBI is not the CIA. The CIA can follow the money trail. Two million dollars moving about the world is enough to attract some attention. We find where the money went, we find Richard Peterlie. The Chinese said it was originally deposited in a Swiss bank. It was probably transferred some place around two years ago."

"Two million is not a lot of money to transfer from a Swiss bank."

"Not for a corporation or a business. But for an individual, that's a lot."

"Perhaps. Okay, I will see what can be done. What are you going to do next?"

"I'm going to take a few days off... stay with Sabrina on the boat. I need to rest up for this next adventure."

Trevor smiled. "Some rest."

"Yeah, well. At least I can keep my mind off the Chinese projects for awhile. This assignment will probably take me far away from the Middle Kingdom."

"Yes, it may. I think it is safe to say you have the dragon under control for the time being. I'll be in touch. Travel with care, my friend."

# THE END

**The following article appeared in the September 24, 1997, edition of USA Today.**

CHINA CORRUPTION: The Communist Party expelled 121,500 members for corruption and punished 37,492 members for criminal acts between October 1992 and June 1997, the Xinhua news agency said, The Central Commission for Discipline and Inspection released the figures in a report trumpeting the success of its battle against corruption. The figures showed that the Party expelled an average of more than 2,000 and punished over 650 members each month over the 57 month period.